AQUA DOMINATION

So they entered that bathroom once more, where too much had already happened. Mary was afraid, but she was suddenly, almost sickeningly, aroused. My own body, she thought, is a traitor.

'Strip,' David ordered.

He and Mary undressed in silence. The bathroom was warm and bright, with sunlight gleaming on tiles and taps and stainless steel rings. When the man and woman both stood naked, David tossed and kicked their clothes and shoes out of the bathroom and closed the door. It was all too obvious that he was terribly angry, and Mary felt a tingle of fear that shuddered along every nerve of her body in a way that was intensely voluptuous. David's cock was fearful in its massiveness and quivering rigidity. Never had it looked so much like a dreadful weapon.

By the same author:

PLEASING THEM
CRUEL TRIUMPH

AQUA DOMINATION

William Doughty

This book is a work of fiction.
In real life, make sure you practise safe, sane and consensual sex.

First published in 2006 by
Nexus
Thames Wharf Studios
Rainville Road
London W6 9HA

www.nexus-books.co.uk

Typeset by TW Typesetting, Plymouth, Devon

Printed and bound by
Clays Ltd, St Ives PLC

ISBN 0 352 34020 7
ISBN 9 780352 340207

You'll notice that we have introduced a set of symbols onto our book jackets, so that you can tell at a glance what fetishes each of our brand new novels contains. Here's the key – enjoy!

cp (traditional)

cp (modern)

spanking

restraint/bondage

rope bondage/hojojutsu

latex/rubber/leather/enclosure

fem dom

willing captivity

medical

period setting

uniforms

sex rituals

One

Stretched out on the bed, Mary tried to concentrate on Jack's cock and her physical sensations as Jack screwed her on and on. Too on.

She would not think of David. But how can you not think about something?

David and his damn bathroom. David and his insanely peculiar fetish for combining watery soapy sex with extreme domination. She would not think of him. Or his bathroom. And all the strange equipment he kept there. At all costs she must instead concentrate on Jack's penis. Straight sex. Nothing kinky.

'Hold my wrists!' she blurted out. 'Hold me down! Fuck me without being so damn polite.'

'Oh, Mary, you know I'm not like that,' Jack replied, the calm voice of reason. 'But I'll do it for you.'

'You'll do it for me,' Mary muttered in disgust. 'If only you could do it for yourself, we might get somewhere.'

Having her wrists held down above her head helped Mary a little. Surely she could come now, and stop thinking about David.

But then she had a horrible suspicion that Jack was too polite to truly hold her down and fuck her brains out, so if she struggled she would win. That was sickening.

David was a nasty little sadist, a creep, but at least he made a woman know for sure that it was useless to struggle, so then she could struggle if she wanted to, without the fear that she might win.

Mary knew she should not struggle against Jack, and yet she simply had to know if he was man enough to hold her down. So she tried, and instantly flipped him over. She was a big, strong and fit young woman. She freed her hands, gripped his wrists and rode his body, grinding her hips down on him, devouring his cock.

'Oh, ah,' he moaned as he started to come.

Mary could not let Jack shoot inside her, he was too weak to deserve the honour. She slid her pussy away, still holding his wrists tightly, raised her hips high, and watched his silly penis spray lots of juice over his belly. Served him right, damn him. David would never have let her get away with anything like that. Jack could only groan like a dying dog as his cock jerked and shot, all untouched. Unwanted.

'Why did you do that, Mary?' Jack moaned.

'Because I could. Because you let me.'

All at once, not knowing herself what she was doing, Mary turned and sucked up Jack's juice. She spat it all over Jack's face, and then she lowered her unsatisfied pussy on his wet features, engulfing and submerging him in her slobbery hot femaleness. Holding his wrists, she rubbed her gaping wet lips on Jack's face, and came powerfully while he struggled and protested. His cries turned to meaningless gurgles and splutters under her arse.

'You're crazy,' Jack gasped a few minutes later, after she had satisfied herself. 'You should go back to that crazy bastard David. You complain about what he did to you, but really you're just as crazy as he is. Or even more. I bet you encouraged him.'

'Even I wouldn't be crazy enough to go back to David.' Mary laughed. The very idea struck her as ridiculously funny.

Go back to David, with his insane bathroom, designed and equipped for nasty kinds of watery domination.

2

Aquatic restraint. Severe bathing. Bondage bathroom. Shackles in the bath and whips for a soaped female. The water bed with straps. Good clean fun! Slippery sadism. Costumed cleansing, with bizarre equipment.

Nasty David, oh so cunning, so quiet and polite and funny, so good to be with. So cruel. She would not even waste time thinking for one instant about him, that was for sure.

Forget the wonderful lubrication inside and out, forget the heat, slipperiness and pressure. The breathless yearnings. The shocking orgasms of breathlessness.

Mary refused even to think of David. For the millionth time she refused.

Instead she looked at Jack, and thought of her victory over him, her triumph. Which filled her with loathing, disgust and contempt.

Three days later, Mary got out of her car in front of David's house.

So there it was again, the place where she had suffered, leaving her with nothing left to do unless she could make it all happen again, only even more so. And she told herself she would never be that stupid. And she rang the doorbell, she rang the doorbell of such an ordinary-looking, yellow-grey brick, early 60s house in Leighton Buzzard that she could hardly believe her own memories. Leighton Buzzard, for God's sake.

She rang the doorbell though the bottom had fallen out of her stomach and there was suddenly sweat all over her hands. People were mowing their lawns, that was how Sunday it was. Either he was there or he was not there, she told herself, and it did not matter either way, and yet she knew the fear that he was not there and she knew the fear that he was there, he and all himself.

And David opened the door.

'Oh. Mary.'

3

'Hi,' she said. She waited for him to say something, but the silence went on too long. 'Christ. You could try to be a little bit glad to see me. You could even try to pretend, it'd be better than nothing.'

'Well. It's a surprise.'

'I tried to phone you, but I couldn't get through.'

'I got rid of my phones and computer.'

'So now you have to expect surprises like me turning up,' said Mary. 'That's an interesting contradiction, having to expect surprises.' She paused, but nothing happened in the pause. 'You're not even going to ask me in, are you? You selfish bastard. Always were and still are.'

'It's not a good time,' said David.

'There are no good times with you, David.'

'Ha.'

'You don't want me to come in, do you? I'm coming in anyway,' she told him angrily, and pushed past him into the house. It gave her a little frisson of delight. He had been her master, yet now she was not afraid of him. But even at that moment of pleasure, there was a little disappointment. She was so tall, and so strong from working out, while he was really quite small. Had he always been so small? 'Don't worry if you have a new victim here. I'll tell her you and I finished a long time ago.'

'I've finished too. With all that. There's nobody here,' said David. He seemed so empty and down that the word 'nobody' might have included himself. 'I'm sorry, but I really want to be alone right now.'

'Do you think I care about that?' Mary stated. 'Do you seriously think I give a fuck?'

'No, I guess you don't,' David murmured, averting his grey eyes from her gaze. 'Come in, if you must.'

'I must,' Mary insisted. She stepped into the house and David shut his front door with a heavy sigh.

'Are you moving?' Mary asked, seeing boxes of stuff packed and apparently ready to go.

4

'I hope so. I don't know where I'll go, and if I did I wouldn't tell you. I won't tell anyone from the old days.'

'What old days? We're too young to have any old days.'

'Those bad old SM days.' He led the way into the kitchen and turned on the kettle. 'That's all over. I'll sell the house and take off.'

'Why did you quit work? I phoned your office. Pete said you were burned out.'

'Oh, he said that, did he? Fuck him. Well, he's probably right. But fuck him anyway. That boring arsehole. Not that I give a toss what that slimy little shit said. I'll kick his fucking head in.'

Mary felt oddly pleased to see David wake up and show some healthy nastiness. Then the state of the kitchen sank in: it could have been a set for a post-apocalypse movie, in which the last remnants of mankind hid out in the ruins of their destroyed civilisation, while outside roamed mutant insectoids intent on eating human brains or having sex with big-breasted young women. There were half-empty cartons and dirty dishes on every surface, and the smell was not good. In the midst of it all, David leaned against a wall, stared at nothing, and blended into the scene of defeat as effortlessly as if he had died there last year.

It was not easy for Mary to find clean cups or anything else, but David did not look capable of helping, so she did her best, reflecting that in this house nothing had ever been easy. She made two coffees and found some biscuits that had not gone soft or mouldy.

'You're taking a rest between jobs?' Mary said brightly. 'That's a good idea.'

'What's the use of talking?'

'How many points do I get if I know the answer?'

'You talk too much.'

'Not at all,' Mary snapped. 'You used to gag me so I could only moan and whimper, but now I'm going to

5

talk for once. You don't have to listen, I know you're not interested, so I'll just talk to myself. I suppose that's all people ever do anyway, talk to themselves even if they imagine they're talking to someone else. Nobody's listening. You're lucky in this world if someone even pretends to listen. Nobody cares about anyone else – and maybe that's a good thing. At least it's a kind of freedom. So I'll talk to myself. I'll tell myself about myself, what else can anyone do? I lost my job and I thought I'd drop in and see you on the way to visiting my parents. I was just curious to see how badly you were getting on. And it does look bad. Anyway, I've proved something to myself, so I'll soon be on my way.'

'OK.'

'I'm going to the bathroom,' Mary announced.

'Why?' he asked in surprise, looking at her more sharply.

'Because the joy and excitement of our conversation is making me piss. No, I just have to say goodbye to it. Is it locked?'

'No.'

David's house had two bathrooms. The one upstairs was ordinary. Mary went to the one downstairs. How simple it was to just walk in. And yet how terrifying and complex. A bathroom. The bathroom. The place that haunted her dreams and nightmares. Or she haunted it. Surely she had died here, and came back now as a ghost. To this very same bathroom. As she opened the door her stomach churned, and she farted. She had come back to that bathroom.

We all like to say that we can recover from the mistakes of the past, that we can deal with the suffering that has been forced on us by the world's evil. We tell ourselves that we will never make the same mistakes again, for we are better people now, stronger and more intelligent, armoured by all our bitterly won experience. We not only claim that the shocks, agonies and horrors

6

of our former selves had some value, but also we expect that there will be no suffering in our futures, for now we can succeed where previously we failed and failed and failed.

We lie. Mary knew that for sure as soon as she took her first step into that bathroom. Her eyes darted around, she tried to see everything at once. Then she sat down and took a piss. Terrible. It was terrible how dirty the bathroom had become, almost as bad as the kitchen. What had happened to David? Once he had kept everything so clean, and it was a sick disappointment now to see the grime and stains and dust and mould, this disgusting deterioration.

No, she could not accept this filthy bathroom's judgement on her past. She had to clean it all until it looked sparkling and new, to put right her memories. Make the past serve the present and all that crap.

Empty was the large black cupboard in one corner, which had once held a wealth of perverse, bizarre equipment and costumes, a truly shocking mass of frightening, cruel items. The sight of the empty cupboard gave her the strangest pang of sadness. He must have thrown it all away. That part of her life had gone. It is scary to think that anything has finished, even something bad.

She returned to the kitchen where David sat, apparently lifeless, though the level of coffee in his cup had certainly dropped, proving he was still alive.

'I have to do something here,' she told him firmly. 'It'll only take an hour or so.'

'An hour or so?' David exclaimed.

'The bathroom is filthy. I can't leave it like that. This is the last time I'll ever see it, so it has to be bright and clean and cheerful, not dirty.'

'It sounds like one of those girly things.'

'Yes. And the other thing is, what did you do with the garments and equipment? Did you just throw it all away?'

7

'I will do, but I haven't yet,' said David with sudden defensiveness. 'It's in the shed. I'll throw it all out tomorrow.'

'Huh! I bet it's been there for months,' Mary exclaimed. 'And you tell yourself every day that of course you'll throw it all out tomorrow.'

'I don't give a damn what you think,' David insisted, but he looked annoyed.

Mary was pleased to have annoyed him. Anything was better than being ignored. 'I want a few things from your collection, if you're really going to throw it all out.'

'Take anything you like. I don't care.'

'Thanks. Those things were around my body, David. And inside. I can't just leave them all to be thrown out. It's not ordinary rubbish, not after what happened to me. Think how the binmen would laugh.'

'Let it go, Mary. Forget the bathroom. Just leave. Yes, go now. I won't let you stay here any longer. I just want to be left alone.'

'I'm staying an hour or two, David. Let's talk frankly: if you try to throw me out, I'll beat the shit out of you.'

'Let's not talk quite so frankly,' said David, the ghost of his old good humour showing in his eyes. Fuck, Mary thought. She would have to punch and kick the little rat if he started to regain his charm.

'I've been working out a lot, and I've taken courses in karate and self-assertion.'

'All right, do what you like for one hour,' David cried, raising his hands in mock surrender. 'Karate and self-assertion! One or the other might be OK, but both is overkill. You've become an American.'

Mary went to the garden shed and found five big black plastic bags containing David's collection of fetish garments and domination equipment. She took them into the bathroom, then went back into the kitchen and gathered all the cleaning materials she could find and deposited them beside the bags. It struck her that she

8

might want to hold out for a long time, so she got a bottle of mineral water and a stock of muesli bars from the kitchen. It pleased her to think she had provisions for a siege.

She locked the bathroom door and looked around. What a mess. The only good things were the sunlight streaming in through the big windows at the far end of the room, and the view of David's overgrown, untended back garden, a line of trees fine in the sunlight, and a high white fence. The nearest house was some way off behind the trees and fence, and it did not give anyone there a view into the bathroom.

The bathroom was hopelessly sordid compared to this sunny view. Mary shuddered at the memories it awoke in her, a host of images and sensations and shocks and the absolute perfection of exquisite, tormented delight. She hoped she could find, by cleaning the bathroom, some kind of closure.

Everybody uses that word now, because in our hearts we know there is no such thing.

She took a deep breath, and started. Working quickly but methodically, she cleaned the walls, the three showers, without cubicles, along one wall, the windows, and the huge mirror. There were stainless-steel rings fitted to the walls. Mary polished these rings very carefully. She washed the tiles that covered most parts of the walls.

Contentment grew in her. Next she cleaned the sink and toilet, and after that she washed the empty water bed that lay folded in one corner. She polished the big black cupboard, now so empty, and she cleaned the blue, sand and white tiles on the floor that sloped very slightly, so that water would flow into the three drains. She cleaned the drain covers. Lastly, and most carefully of all, she cleaned the taps and rails and metal rings of the bath and then the bath itself: a scarlet metal rectangle with rounded corners. Some seven feet long,

9

four feet wide, and nearly two feet deep, this was the bath that had been the setting for the supreme raptures and terrors.

Two years had passed since she had fled that house. The victim returns to the scene of the crime, thought Mary. No, she told herself. It was not that simple. If only it could be. She was more than a victim.

How much better the bathroom looked now! She felt a real pride and joy in her accomplishment. Everything sparkled and gleamed. Delightful. She took off her rubber work gloves and tossed them towards the locked door. Then she wondered what to do next. Even as she began to wonder, the answer came to her so clearly that she knew it had been in the back of her mind all along: she had to take a bath. She had an excuse, if she wanted an excuse, in the fact that she was hot and sweaty after all her determined exertions. She had to take a bath. It would be another step in overcoming her past.

Shivers of strangeness shuddered through her flesh as she put the plug in and turned on the water. Too much had happened here. It was impossible that she had returned to the scene of so many nightmares. Nobody could be so crazy.

Slowly she undressed, feeling a disturbing sense of unreality. Knowledge of her own extreme arousal and excitement flooded her all at once, so strong as to be almost unbearable. Naked, she faced herself in the big mirror, and saw defiance in her face as though she expected her own reflection to confront her with terrible accusations.

There she was, that was her all right. She could not help but admire herself in the mirror, and indeed to do anything else would have been a kind of dishonesty. Mary had a great body, tall and powerful, with long legs and full but firm breasts with large nipples that David had once loved to tease and torment. As she recalled this, they tingled and grew even bigger and harder. All her muscles were in good tone from the various kinds of exercise she pursued with such enthusiasm or, as some said, fanaticism, and this love of working out, together with her broad hips, gave her buttocks a gorgeously rounded and strong magnificence.

Her face was good too. Mary knew these truths about her body and face no matter what other doubts she had about herself. She played with her straight, shoulder-length dark-chestnut hair, veiling her face, peeking out between its strands, surprising herself with the look of a madwoman. Then she adopted her serious and composed look, and was the image of a confident and successful young businesswoman. Mary could look like all kinds of people, and often played this game with the mirror. She pretended to be an empress, and impressed herself with her look of imperious arrogance.

Who, she wondered, are all these people, and just what are they up to inside me? Which was her real face anyway?

Magic was in that glass, for David had often ordered her to stare at her own absolute humiliation. Now Mary posed before it, all alone. One after another she adopted the positions of restraint, suffering and worship. She could feel the exquisite constriction of her bonds squeezing her towards orgasm, feel David's hands, mouth and cock on her helplessly immobilised flesh, and she could smell her own excitement and fear.

David, she thought. Now she realised that she had come to this house hoping to defy him. He would beg her to submit to him like in the old days, and she would refuse, assert her independence, and leave. Instead, he had insisted on telling her quickly that he had given up domination, and had told her to get out. Reality had failed to live up to Mary's fantasy scenario. David was always ahead of her, just out of reach.

Slowly she moved her hand to her pussy, which felt swollen, tingly and possessed by a hunger that was hard to bear. Impossible.

'Shit!' Mary said to herself. Turning away from the mirror, she grabbed a black plastic bag containing part of David's collection, and tipped it out on the floor.

Straps and ropes and cords, harnesses, helmets, suction devices, belts and gags, vibrators and probes and tubing, clamps and clips and dildos, syringes, brushes, whips and cuffs tumbled out along with three big black beetles. How dirty it all was. How hopeless and sad. Mould, slime, dirt and dust, rust and nastiness. It was sickening that all her orgasms and ordeals, those odysseys of the flesh and spirit, had come to this dismal end.

Diligently she set to work cleaning some items from David's collection, and she experienced a series of stirrings and flashbacks as she handled each piece and recalled incidents of suffering and ecstasy. How expert David had once been! He had mesmerised her with his dynamism and skill, she had been his slave – and now he was nothing, nothing at all, and she too was clearly nothing to him. Not, of course, that she cared about him, or about what he thought. Now she was free and strong, she told herself. And there it was again: loneliness.

Mary cleaned just the items that caught her fancy, and laid them out in a neat row. Then she recalled seeing a bottle of bath foam liquid at the bottom of the cupboard, and she fetched this and poured what was left of it into the slowly filling bath. It was an old bottle that had not been touched for a long time, she observed. David had clearly given up his love of bizarre sex in a foamy bath, his own peculiar combination of fetishes. How could anyone abandon their deepest fantasies and longings so rich and strange? If you give up your own strangeness, what do you have left?

Serve him right that she had come to disturb him a little. After she left, taking with her some of these items from his collection, he would surely have to think about her sometimes. Yes, one night when he could not sleep and the full moon burned bright against the curtains, he would feel regret that he had lost her beauty and courage.

Mary sat down on the tiles near the big window in a slanting rectangle of sunlight that felt warm on her naked skin. There she drank her bottle of mineral water and ate two muesli bars, and she watched how intricately the leaves of the trees danced and wavered dark against the blue sky in the passing zephyrs, and she stared at a big glossy blackbird that sat on the fence and looked right back at her, and she thought about how she had just lost her job and her boyfriend Jack both, and so what, and she thought about David and all the insane things he and she had done, and she felt she ought to be very sad and unhappy right then, but instead she saw leaves and sunlight and the blackbird and she knew some kind of happiness, the kind that sneaks up on you without reason after a long period of miserable slow-motion suffering, the kind of unexpected contentment that hits you as the truth. Despite everything. Screw everything. Turn up the defiance.

Mary felt the time had come to go over to the offensive. She made her selection from the items she had cleaned, and then she put on a strong and broad black plastic belt, fastening its three buckles as tightly as she could, constricting her waist. Next she fitted a beautifully made torment bra of narrow, encircling, interconnected scarlet plastic straps, both strong and intricate, with shiny plastic rings for her nipples. Revelling in her excitement and anxiety, Mary fastened the twelve buckles of the cruel bra as tightly as she could, after pulling her taut nipples with some pleasing difficulty through the rings. How tautly the flesh of her tits bulged between the myriad straps of the bra! Breathing heavily, a sheen of sweat gleaming on her lovely young body,

Mary admired herself in the mirror for two minutes, and her long fingers teased her breasts and pussy.

Fingers fumbling and clumsy with fear and anxious excitement, Mary took a long, thin red cotton cord, and tied the two ends of it to metal rings at the front of her belt so that a loop hung down.

She took a hot shower and then she knelt in front of the mirror and soaped every part of her exposed flesh, working up a good lather but refraining from granting herself orgasm. She was afraid of herself once more, but she no longer cared. After wetting a flannel in the bath, she lay it over her pussy. Wet heat, lovely.

Heart beating faster and faster, she pulled the loop of cord between her legs to her back, and then she put her wrists in the loop and twisted the cord around them so she not only had, after all this time, the exquisite thrill of feeling bound and helpless, but also the delight of feeling the cord press against her pussy, cushioned deliciously by the flannel. She lay face down on the tiled floor, and slid back and forth pretending to try to escape from three men who mocked her futile efforts and prepared to take turns in her cunt. Never had she tied herself up like this, and she had not planned to do it, but it had been an irresistible impulse. How exciting it was! Her body hummed with power and lust as she slid around the floor, lubricated with soap. Nothing was as sensual as this weird combination of bondage and soap in the bathroom where David had taught her strange lusts.

Gazing into the mirror she saw herself so helpless and vulnerable, a shiny female worm. She twisted the cord around her wrists to loosen it, and then she brought her legs up and back, finally managing to put her ankles inside the safe embrace of the cord. Now she felt even more helpless, and she could pretend to struggle even more, tensing her legs as well as her arms as though straining to escape, doing wonderful, cruel things to her

14

pussy even as her nipples pressed against the cool tiles. She arched and tensed in exquisite constriction.

How impatient David must be getting! He wanted her out of his house, he must be wondering what the hell she was doing. Surely he suspected the truth. Soon he would bang on the locked bathroom door and, when she refused to open it, he must kick the door and shatter the flimsy lock. Then she would panic, and be unable to free herself before he bound her for real. How could he resist the temptation to punish her and use her beautiful, helpless body? Desperate to come, Mary writhed and wriggled about, rubbing her flesh on the soapy, slippery tiles. It was going to be difficult to come like this, and perhaps it would prove impossible, but Mary imagined that a cruel master – not David, but a better man – had given her exactly five minutes to try to have an orgasm, after which he would bind her spreadeagled to rings in the floor, and chastise her, not letting her come for many hours while he fucked a lovely young girl in the bath, gaining pleasure from Mary's humiliation.

And this ideal master who was definitely not David had an assistant, a young male sadist learning the ropes, literally as well as figuratively. Now the assistant had to punish Mary.

She crawled slowly over the floor towards a scrubbing brush beside the bath, and got her left breast over its stiff plastic bristles, then ground down on it, punishing her teat that protruded so taut and provocative through the plastic ring of her harshly compressing bra. Slowly she writhed, and the cord pressured her pussy cruelly. She tried to plead for mercy through her gag, but all she could do was mumble and drool.

No, they would not have pity on her. Helplessness and suffering only excited these two strong men she had imagined, and their cocks got harder as they enjoyed her nude writhings in restraint. They would punish her in strange ways, and their huge stiff cocks would use her body uncaringly, doing anything they could imagine that would give them pleasure.

And Mary came with sickening force, squirming in her bonds like a tormented worm, her body and soul exploding in a rapture that was utterly overwhelming, an atrocity of ecstasy. Slowly, she freed herself from the cord and removed her gag, belt, and bra. Standing naked, she looked down at herself, and touched her belly and breasts, feeling the skin she lived inside.

So now she knew. The orgasm that had just thrilled her to the core had been more satisfying than any she had shared with Jack. In future she would just masturbate. No need to be bored by ordinary men like Jack, or frightened and hurt by strange men like David – not that there were other men like David. If what she needed was to be humiliated, restrained and chastised, she could do that little job herself. Think of all the trouble and disappointment she could avoid by being her own tormentor!

Masturbation was logical after all. Everybody was alone inside their own bodies and minds, and the idea of any kind of communication between human beings was only a comforting lie. It was time she learned how to live as very few people ever did live: without the facile, unreal support of illusions. Coming back to this damned bathroom of crazy David had been a good idea after all. The shock of seeing this chamber of horrors once more, after two years, had cleared her mind and helped her to understand herself, which meant she could understand everything.

True, the bath itself was formidable, even without David, its creator. It was huge. It was as red as fresh-spilled blood. Worst of all, it had shiny steel rings at its ends, sides and bottom, attachment points for restraint, and Mary knew how strong they were, how impossible to budge. David had told her with some kind

16

of crazy pride that each of those rings had a metal root set deep into a metal frame that surrounded the bath. Yes, of course David was insane.

Mary did not step into the bath. She took a deep breath, lying on the cool tiles face down at one end, and then she slid forwards into the warm water with her arms stretched out in front of her, and she looked down at the scarlet bottom of the bath, and she felt the shiny steel rail at the end of the bath stroke her whole long body, and then all of her was inside the hot, sensuous caress of the water, it enveloped her body like a warm wet giant's mouth, and all she could hear was the murmur of the water from the tap falling into the bath, a sound that was an interference to stop her thinking too much, a womblike reassurance like the sound of her mother's blood from a time before Mary had been born, a time when she did not have to live in the world with all its complexity of choices.

Laughing, she rolled over and floated on her back. How good it was just to float!

Obviously she had to come again. She put on long black plastic gloves and admired herself in the mirror. How strange she looked! Yet that was the real her, her in David's bath, more real than she could ever be in any office or anywhere else. Now she was stronger. Now she could do anything she liked, because she made the most difficult decision any human being can make: she granted herself absolute and unconditional freedom.

Embracing and caressing and supportive, the sensuality of the warm water flooded her body and soul as she lay back in the bath with her feet toward its glittering taps. Mary stroked her body all over, loving the feel of the plastic gloves sliding over her skin, so well-lubricated by the bath foam liquid that turned the hot water so deliciously slippery. What was sex in a dry bed compared to this exotic, scented, luxury of heated, wet slipperiness?

How long and wide that scarlet bath was! So long and wide that even a tall woman like Mary could float there without any part of her body touching the sides or ends.

Fantasies of being tied up and helpless danced in Mary's mind as she rolled around in the deepening water and thrust out her tits and arse, just as if David were there and she was striving to distract him from punishing her by presenting her body like a sex slave. She masturbated with crazed vigour, splashing and jerking about like a fish trapped in a too-shallow pond.

Pain and pleasure in alternation: that was what Mary granted her flesh now, like an empress graciously bestowing favours on her wretched, quivering subjects. This was what David had revealed to her as her soul's greatest delight, it was what he had given her with a patience and skill that might have been insane, but was also thorough and convincing. He had rarely given her quite enough pleasure to make her come, so that in the end she was taken over the brink by pain.

Pleasure and pain until Mary was torn apart by orgasms of sickening force, orgasms that were not so much a delight as a psychic devastation. David had given her this addiction. After that, what use could simple fucking and sucking be to Mary? Now, in David's bathroom again after so much time had passed, what else could she do but strive in solitude to recreate past pains, pleasures, and horrifyingly exquisite humiliations?

'Do you know what your trouble is, you stupid cunt?' she said to herself quietly, her other self there in the mirror. 'You've always been afraid that you're different from other people. And you are! But stop being afraid of it.'

She glanced at the ceiling, seeing the two small mirrored panels and thinking of the cameras that David had sometimes put there to film secretly through the two-way mirrors. Was he filming her now? Mary doubted it, but she wondered if, despite his manner, he could still show some interest, some redeeming remnants of voyeurism and sadism.

Lust renewed itself in her strong and healthy young body, as she looked at all the great stuff in David's collection. So many strange items for her to play with!

Looking up from the leather, rubber, plastic and metal items designed for the sexual subjugation of human beings, she saw through the window how the vivid green trees moved tremulously in the light wind, their branches shivering, as if chilled, as birds came and went with their hungers and disputes, while overhead sailed huge fluffy white clouds like mountains in flight to an unknown paradise.

How beautiful all the world was if seen in the right light, thought Mary, her body and soul still suffused by her own inner light of ecstasy. Why was it that nearly everybody was bad, stupid or confused, even though they were living in a world where every tree, bird and cloud could show its own radiance that sang of beauty and goodness?

After thinking about it for a minute, Mary decided she did not know, so she might just as well masturbate.

Two

By the time she was satisfied, the sun was setting, and the tops of trees burned golden green, such a delicious light that she felt she could taste it on her tongue, a warm sweet and sour. She emptied and cleaned the bath, then carefully dried all the gear she had used with such pleasure. She got dressed and she left that haunted bathroom where she had both exorcised and exercised her personal demons.

Mary carried three bags of domination gear back to the living room where David was still watching TV, or at least was sitting in front of it. Even the half-eaten sandwich at his side had an air of apathy and defeat. As for the fourth bag of gear, Mary carried it outside and put it in the boot of her car. From her bag she took a hairdryer, and then she went back into David's kitchen and dried her hair. After that she knew she had to leave even though she would rather have stayed until David lost his temper, if he still had one to lose.

'I'm going now,' she told him, making herself sound casual and bright. 'I'm sorry if I disturbed you. Though you don't look very disturbed. Unfortunately. I was in a bad mood, but I feel much better now after masturbating in your bath and playing with some of your gear. We could go out to dinner now if you like.'

David shook his head slowly.

'OK,' Mary continued. 'I can see you want me to just go away now. But despite that, I'll just go away now anyway.'

David stared at her, and the faintest hint of a weary, sad smile appeared in his eyes and mouth. It was nothing really, hardly even the ghost or the memory of the radiant, childlike smile she had once been warmed by, but all the same it made his face less of a barrier, and it made Mary remember. She did not want to remember, but she was weakened by the feeling that had haunted her for months, that human souls were separated by vast distances and locked inside the cells of their bodies in solitary confinement.

She remembered, despite herself, what good company David could be. Used to be. How funny and nice he had often been even though he was a fetishist and sadist.

'You've got guts, Mary,' David said slowly, and quietly. It was as if he were not only trying to remember how to talk, but also feeling far from sure that he should even be trying. Mary was certain that for a long time he had been living, if living was the word, buried deep in silence and solitude. 'You're honest. That's everything.'

'Don't start praising me.' Mary laughed. 'If you're going to start being nice, that's not fair. I can stand anything except you being nice.'

'Always do the unexpected. First rule of a cruel master: keep them guessing, keep them off balance. What crap, really! Thank goodness I've given all that up.'

'You've given it up, but you don't exactly seem to have found peace of mind.'

'Oh, I'm OK,' David insisted wearily. 'So, why did you come back anyway? Looking for some kind of closure?'

'I suppose so. Whatever closure means. I don't really know, it was some sort of impulse thing. I've been very angry lately. Maybe I hoped you'd annoy me, and then I could've beat up on you and felt better. But you haven't insulted me. Yet.'

'Life is full of disappointments, Mary.'

'You're a difficult man to hate now that you're so down. Look, can I cook something? You don't look like you're even eating properly. I could cook dinner and I promise I'll leave after that.'

'Thanks, but no thanks,' said David, clearly worried by Mary's friendly offer.

'You want me to go quickly. I see.'

'Don't be offended.'

'Don't worry. I've lost the urge to hit you.'

'Can you keep it lost? No, the thing is, I just want to be alone. There's nothing personal in my wanting you to go.'

'I believe you. Well, I might as well be off.'

David saw Mary to his front door and they said polite goodbyes. She got into her car and told herself not to feel sorry for him. It served him right to be depressed.

As soon as she arrived at her parents' home, two hours later, Mary wondered why she had bothered to come. She told herself that they were able to fully understand and appreciate her. In theory. Besides, she was feeling confused and surprised after losing both her job and her boyfriend Jack in the last ten days – why not try to stabilise herself by checking out her roots? She wondered if she had decided to visit her parents to give herself an excuse to drop in on David, whose home was on the route from her small apartment to her parents' place – well, it was more or less on the route, if you decided, very sensibly, to take a scenic, unhurried, roundabout route instead of a straight line. Mary told herself that it was only natural to have some slight curiosity about David. What other feeling could she have? She refused to listen to her inner voice of unreason.

'How's work?' Mary's mother, Jill, asked at once.

'I quit,' Mary replied. It was not quite a lie.

'You're so wilful! What will you do now? Why did you quit?'

'Why not quit?' Mary shrugged. 'It was just a boring routine office job.'

'It was paid work! You always want to take it easy, have fun. Most of life is boring and routine, but that's life and you have to accept it.'

'No I don't,' Mary insisted, with a cold calm certainty. 'I want something better. I'm never going to have a boring routine job ever again.'

'You're so stubborn. If only you could be more like your sisters.'

'Everybody should be themselves, not try to be like other people,' Mary snapped. She could hardly believe that she had only just got here and already her mother was criticising her. Literally, she felt breathless and suffocated, as if she could not get enough air into her lungs.

Mary had been born when her mother was forty. It had been an accident, she guessed. Always she had felt unwanted, and always seemed to be the victim of unfavourable comparisons made between her and her two elder sisters, who her mother seemed to think were perfect.

'Now, now, let's not start arguing,' said her father, a weary man in poor health since an accident had made him retire from the factory where he had worked for so many years. Now the factory's site was a car park.

Next morning, Mary awoke in her old bedroom. It certainly had been a mistake to come here. David should have stopped her. Not that it was any of his damn business, but all the same, he should have stopped her. So that was one more item to add to the list of David's mistakes and crimes.

Suddenly she heard Jack's voice, and thought that she had finally begun to hallucinate. The way her life was going, it was only to be expected that she would go crazy. She went downstairs and there he was. Jack. He and Mary had argued and broken up after Mary had humiliated him with her bum.

23

'I had to see you again, Mary,' said Jack. He looked impressed by his own impulsive action. 'Your friend Alice told me where you were going.'

'Did she really?' Mary sighed, writing off another friend. No more Alice.

'Jack said he just had to come and see you right now,' Mary's mother gushed. 'Even though he has so much important work, he dropped everything and came here. That's so romantic! It's like something in a film.'

'Yes,' said Mary. 'Unfortunately.'

'Let's go and sit down like civilised people instead of standing around here like antelopes,' Mary's father insisted. He was obviously a lot less impressed by Jack's romantic action than his wife and Jack were. Part of Mary was a little impressed and flattered, but mostly she was annoyed.

The four of them sat down and had coffee in the perfectly clean and tasteful house that Mary's parents had worked so hard for over the decades, driving themselves to exhaustion, enduring boredom, surrendering their freedom and embracing routine so that they could have this house to decorate and furnish and clean and clean and clean and then decorate again, acting as servants to the house while it devoured their money and their years. Mary could not see the point. It was like listening to a joke and not understanding the punchline.

She devoted a few per cent of her attention to Jack's conversation with her father. Jack was taller, more handsome, much more communicative and currently more successful than David, Mary thought, and he had never scared the living daylights out of her. He would be a good partner for any woman, a fine father, and an all-round good human being. Jack was virtually perfect. It was obvious he was David's superior in every way, especially now that David had burned out in depression, despair, apathy or laziness or whatever the hell it was.

David was finished, he was history, a wreck. By God, Jack was boring.

How Mary wished David had come chasing after her instead of Jack! Then she could have had the satisfaction of saying no to David, no matter how he begged. It would have been a sweet victory.

No doubt David had wrecked himself attacking the barriers around the human mind and human sexuality. The odds had been too great for him, it had always been hopeless, all his exertions had been futile, he himself was doomed. His strength had given out, the barriers were too strong. He had tried to escape from the prison that most human beings spent their lives building and maintaining and strengthening around their souls, everybody a prisoner and at the same time a guard. David had tried to live, so, of course, he must die.

'Why did Mary quit her job?' Mary's mother asked Jack.

'So she can get a better one,' Jack replied. His eyes met Mary's and she knew he was proud of the way he was covering up the appalling truth about the day that Mary had gone mad, as everybody put it, in the office, in the sacred workplace.

'We invited Jack to stay the night,' Mary's mother told her quietly when the two women were in the kitchen. 'You'll share a room with him, won't you? Even your father says it's OK.'

'I am not spending the night with Jack. We broke up. It's over.'

'Why not? He's a good man. At least think twice about him. Look at how good he is compared to that crazy David. Jack would never make you so upset you got ill.'

'No he wouldn't,' Mary conceded gloomily. But she still slept alone that night.

Next day, Jack and Mary drove to the shops with her parents. Mary pretended to be good. That night, Mary's parents went to bed early, leaving her and Jack in front of the TV. Jack soon started trying to persuade Mary that they should get back together, but when he put his arm around her, she thrust it away angrily.

'Don't touch me. You and I are finished, and the sooner you accept that, the better.'

'I know what the problem is. David taught you to like kinky sex, domination or whatever you call it, and you're angry with me because I'm not even willing to try it.'

'Yes. It's like saying you don't like oranges when you've never even seen one.'

'I admit I was wrong, OK? Let's give it a try. Tomorrow we'll go to a hotel. After a great meal, we'll experiment with domination. You teach me. I'm willing to learn.'

Mary was shocked, not so much by Jack's idea as by the surge of lust that filled her, rushing through her like a cooling wind on a terribly hot day.

'All right,' she agreed. 'Let's try that. But nothing now.' She already had the feeling that Jack's idea would not work out, that in fact it would be some kind of fiasco. But she was strong enough not to be afraid of fiascos, which at least had energy and life. Besides, she was curious. Nobody had ever dominated her except David. What would it be like to be tied and teased by another man?

Next day, after lunch, she said goodbye to her parents with relief on both sides, and then Jack drove his Rover and she followed him in her Golf. Since they both lived and worked in Leeds, it was convenient to stop at a hotel near Nottingham, where they had stayed before, in the days before Mary suddenly realised that Jack was the world centre of boredom.

When they arrived at the hotel, Mary carried the black plastic bag of items she had taken from David's collection to their room, and she refused to be embarrassed by the curious glances it attracted. Certainly it was an unusual item of luggage for that expensive hotel where everything was so carefully designed to create a subdued atmosphere of lifeless good taste. She also refused to tell Jack what was in the bag, which excited his curiosity, and instead hurried him outside again. They did some shopping, then went to a Chinese restaurant and enjoyed a good meal. Back in their hotel room, Mary felt aroused, more by the situation than by Jack.

'Now will you tell me what's in that bag?' he asked.

'Domination gear,' Mary replied, and emptied it out onto the bed.

'Oh, my God. That's frightening. This is obviously stuff you and David used. It looks so cruel. It's terrible.'

'Yes, but we don't have to use all of it,' said Mary. Jack's reaction made her a little ashamed of having used these items, and it was natural for her to transform her shame into irritation. 'We can just use these cords to tie me to the bed.'

'Tie you to the bed. It's so strange.'

'You suggested this,' Mary snapped.

'Yes, but I was so afraid of losing you. Now that it comes to the crunch, I'm shocked all over again. It's awesome. I've always been shocked by perversity.'

'For fuck's sake,' Mary sighed, and opened a bottle of strong cider. She poured a glass and drank it quickly, desperate for alcohol to numb her sense of sickening disappointment and cruel betrayal. 'You've tricked me, Jack. That's horrible.'

'I didn't mean to trick you. It's just that I hate to take advantage of you. An obsession with sado-masochism is surely a symptom of childhood trauma and deprivation. Wouldn't it be better to consult a good psychologist?'

'You can't imagine how bloody awful you are. Couldn't you just tie me up and spank me?'

'I could never hurt and humiliate a woman like that.'

27

'Well, how can you hurt and humiliate a woman? I'll take whatever I can get.'

'The very idea is disgusting.'

'You can't dominate me? All right then, I'll just have to dominate you.' Mary did not feel she was making a serious suggestion. Rather, she spoke out of her exasperation with Jack's disapproval of her deepest desires.

'You'll dominate me?' said Jack. 'Really? That would at least be easier. You're the expert, so it'd be more logical too.'

Jack's tone of suppressed excitement made Mary realise just how much he was aroused by the idea of being dominated. Suddenly she understood him much better. 'Maybe we should try it at least once to find out if it helps our relationship,' Jack said. It was pathetic how hard he was trying to sound cool.

'Yes, let's try it,' Mary said with a slight shrug. 'It's no big deal.' She felt a surge of curiosity. Revenge was also a motive, though she could hardly have said why. It was as if everything had gone wrong, and so she would take her revenge for that fact against Jack simply because he was making himself available as a victim. Most of the relationships in the world, she reflected, were formed like that: here is a victim.

'Let's start,' said Mary. 'Strip off.'

Jack obeyed instantly, a fact that Mary found curiously pleasing. So, she thought, this is what it feels like to have power. Soon Jack was naked. His fully erect cock pulsed, rising and falling with every beat of his heart. Usually he took longer to get it up.

From the goodies on the bed she chose a tawse, a gag, some cords and a box of clips. Suddenly she had an inspiration: she would dominate Jack in the bathroom rather than the bedroom. Why not? That was what David had done to her, so she was used to it. She could do a better job on Jack in there, and she would surely come more.

'Go and take a shower,' she ordered.

She gave him two minutes, then followed him into the coldly sterile hotel bathroom. Jack looked alarmed as he read in her face and superb bearing a new depth of motivation and resolution. She put her pieces of domination equipment in the sink.

'Lie down on the floor,' she ordered sharply. 'Other way round, you fool. Your head here, your feet there.' Quickly, Mary tied his hands together behind the toilet bowl, and then she fastened his ankles together, using red cotton cords that David had used on her. So many times. So many ways.

'I feel so helpless,' Jack murmured, gazing up at Mary in awe.

'Yes, it's easy and exciting to be helpless, isn't it?' she replied with real bitterness. 'Any damn fool can be a victim, and so every damn fool is. The hard thing is to take the responsibility of refusing to be helpless and passive and weak. The acceptance of the dominant role is the beginning of courage.'

'You're thinking of David. As usual.'

'No, I'm not! Oh, now you've made me angry. Shut your mouth. You'll regret what you just said, you bastard, you'll regret it the rest of your stupid, lousy life.'

Contempt for Jack filled Mary as she saw how frightened he was. As if I were as dangerous and crazy as David, she thought. How could Jack think that? He must be a coward. She hated cowards.

Slowly and with great pleasure, the pleasure of anticipation, Mary began to strip. Nudity seemed to pad stealthily towards her like an animal she secretly loved, a deadly carnivore that visited her in blackness and silence. Pride warmed her as she revealed the magnificence of her body, and she thrilled to the imminence of ecstasy. Pleasure stalked. She haunted Jack with an unhurried revelation of her height and strength, her curves and her femaleness, all her perfections suddenly untouchable, and so transformed into the ultimate desire of unattainability.

29

Hunger and fear ran across his face as she taunted him by her very existence. By her own experience she knew that not only was he afraid of her, but also of his own dark desires, his own personal and solitary abyss.

How good it felt to have him helpless! So this was how David had felt when he dominated her. No wonder that used to be his consuming passion. Mary knew now why she had to dominate Jack: it would help her to understand David.

'You're so gorgeous,' Jack gasped.

'Of course. What, you only just noticed?'

'I never saw you clearly until now.'

'Oh, shut up. Who cares about anything you think or feel or say?' Mary snapped. 'You're nothing. Now there's only one real person in this room. You have ceased to exist.'

What would David say if he could see her now? She seemed to actually hear his voice, and what he told her was that she had not fully secured Jack's legs. It was odd to virtually hear David like that. She put the ends of the cord around Jack's ankles under the bathroom door and closed it firmly. There, now he was secure. Thanks for the advice, David, she thought.

'I'm going to sit on your face,' Mary stated. 'You will use your tongue to worship my bum.'

'I can't do that,' Jack replied in a tone of disgust. 'It's dirty.'

'You've just made the greatest mistake of your life,' Mary snarled. 'You've made me angry.' Suddenly, she squeezed his balls and, when Jack opened his mouth to cry out, she slid a pear-shaped red rubber gag between his teeth and fastened its leather straps around his head to hold it in place with a swift certainty.

Shocked, Jack tried to cry out, but the bloated, bitter gag reduced his efforts to unimpressive bleatings through his nose.

'You refused to lick me when I ordered you to. And now you insult me by having an erection. That's the final straw. I order you to make your cock go soft right now. If you disobey me again you'll regret it the rest of your life.' Mary lightly brushed Jack's cock with the very tips of her fingernails, and it pulsed with blood, straining taut with lust. 'So, you're determined to defy me. You demand the most extreme punishment.'

Lightly, teasingly, Mary caressed her full, taut breasts.

'You think you know what's going to happen now,' she told Jack quietly. 'You've read it in books, seen it in magazines and movies.' She leaned over Jack and touched the tip of his cock, then whispered her next words so quietly that they were next to silence. 'You know nothing about what is going to happen. Nothing at all. This is the end of your old life.'

Standing next to Jack, whose terrified eyes were staring fixedly at her, Mary began to masturbate.

'You've made me so angry, Jack! You've always refused to dominate me. You thought I was weird. Yet you came crawling to my parents' house because you couldn't get me out of your mind, you knew I was special. Well, you're not special, Jack. You're ordinary and I'm bored with you. I hope I never see you again after tonight. Do you realise what that means? It means I can do anything I like to you now, because I don't have to worry about your reaction, your feelings, the future of our relationship. But even that isn't enough. I need to suffer too. It excites me. It helps me come more often and more strongly. If men are too cowardly to punish me, I must do it myself. So what I do to you, I'll also do to myself.

'And,' Mary whispered, 'the amount of pain I can enjoy is simply shocking. And the level of pain I can endure is even higher.'

She knelt beside Jack and leaned forwards so that her breasts' perfection overhung his face; so cool and untouchable, such a beautiful danger.

31

'We think we need all sorts of things,' Mary murmured. 'We're wrong. We have exactly what we need here and now: our bodies, our fears.'

Mary took her right breast in her left hand and squeezed it with a dreamlike slowness, compressing and raising its yielding flesh with such a gradual tightening that there seemed to be no movement, but rather a growth of tension like the growth of a tree that finally shatters concrete with its unstoppable tenacity.

And Mary struck. The sharp fingernails of her right hand attacked her rigid teat, sinking in with sublime cruelty.

'No more compromises,' Mary gasped.

Jack rolled his head in disbelief and terror, bleating through his nose, struggling uselessly to escape his bonds. As Mary was crazy enough to hurt herself so much, was there any act so extreme that she would not perform it on his helpless flesh? Surely not. All at once, from every inch of his skin, sweat swam forth in a tingling eruption. He tried to free his wrists, but could not.

Mary knew, there was no going back. She would punish herself and this fool, this Jack, so severely that it had to be the start of a new life. She would be a Viking, and burn her boats on the beach of a new land so that there would be no temptation to go back to the past.

Hands shaking with lust and slimy with sweat, she picked up a set of small black plastic and shiny metal clips in a box. She stood so tall and proud, straddling her prisoner. He gazed up at what had become the centre of the universe: her engorged and streaming cunt.

'How hard your cock is,' Mary hissed mockingly, breathing hard as she rode her own discomfort like a masterful rider on a superb and spirited mount, a stallion that pawed the ground and snorted in the energy of its fine fettle. 'Obviously you get a big kick out of seeing me in pain. And yet you haven't the guts to embrace your own excitement honestly and dominate me yourself. You're a hypocrite. You're a coward and a weakling. I hate you.'

Mary squatted over Jack's chest, leaning back to thrust her bulging vulva at his face. Magnificent with obsession, her superb young body gleamed with highlights that accentuated every sleek, firm curve. For fifteen minutes she tormented her own pussy and breasts in majestic and alarming silence. Sweat dropped onto Jack again and again. Drip, drop. Each like a burning kiss on his skin. He thought he must go mad. His cock thrashed. It jumped left to right, up and down, jerking about like a wild rat in a small cage. He would have sold his soul to be allowed an orgasm. To jet! To spurt! Mary gazed and gazed into his eyes. Surely she was a witch, and could see all the way to the back of his head.

Smiling dreamily to herself, Mary stepped into the bath and turned on the water. Sighing with delight, she stroked every inch of her flesh with her soapy hands.

Happiness filled her like a hot drink on a bitterly cold day, and she caressed her breasts. Jerking and quivering like a desperate fish out of water, Jack's stiff cock looked merely silly and annoying, a nasty thing that needed to be squashed.

How good it is to cut loose and dominate another human being, Mary thought. Now she could certainly understand David much better, and perhaps even begin to forgive him for all he had done to her. How could he, after all, have resisted the temptation to treat her with such ecstatic cruelty?

'I'm going to fuck you,' she told Jack. 'Listen carefully now. If you can manage not to come for twenty minutes, I'll release you and you can do anything you like with me. To me. I'll obey your every command, no matter how disgusting. But if you come before the twenty minutes is up, then I'll punish you until dawn. It

33

will be a truly terrifying ordeal. Just twenty minutes! Surely you can do it? But you can't. I'll make you come. Perhaps I won't even move. I'll still make you come. I'll milk you. I'll suck you in and spit you out.'

Mary straddled Jack and lowered herself on him like a beautiful spider settling down to devour a neatly wrapped, paralysed fly. She held his cock and swallowed it up in her slippery vagina as if it were nothing at all.

And then she did nothing for five minutes except play with her breasts and clitoris. She refused to move her hips or use her formidable internal muscles. Jack believed what she had said about releasing him if only he could refrain from orgasm. He believed what she had said about punishing him for hours if he came too soon. All he had to do was to hold out for what was, after all, a very short time. Then she would release him and he could tie her up, whip her and fuck her brains out. Then whip her again. All he had to do was to refuse to unleash the pent-up lust burning in his twitching cock. That was all. Very simple. Easy.

And of course he could not. Against all logic and sanity he had to thrust upwards at the triumphant slut straddling him and playing with herself.

'What a fool you are.' Mary laughed. And she came. She came and she came and she came. For nearly a minute she was possessed by an unbearable ecstasy that made her cry out, weep, cough, and finally laugh. Muscles locked rigid, she arched and writhed, impaled on a captive penis. Her internal muscles clamped and pulsed, writhed and swirled, like a mass of intertwined snakes bathed in hot oil and striving to crush their prey.

'That was good,' Mary stated when the last spasms had passed. 'That was very good. Now I'll make you come.'

Terror gripped Jack, and he tried to relax his every muscle to avoid orgasm. As soon as Mary began to methodically milk his cock with her highly trained internal muscles, he knew that his efforts were useless. He was doomed. Smiling slightly, Mary clenched and relaxed her cunt, gripping the captive penis around its head, then around its base. Jack was sucked up into her hot, oily succulence. As he started to come, Mary lithely scrambled off her prisoner, lay beside him and gripped his cock so that his mighty spurts deluged and spattered her face. She could not help being a little impressed by the huge amount of fluid he spurted, with such force that she actually heard a spattering sound as it sprayed so violently against her skin. Jack screamed again and again through his nose as if he would never stop.

'Now see what you've done!' Mary exclaimed. 'How dare you come over my face like that, you disgusting pig? I already had some severe punishments in mind for you, but now I know that they aren't severe enough.' As Mary spoke, cream kept dribbling down into her mouth, so she spat it out. 'I'll have to make new plans now that you've insulted me with your filth,' she complained, looking down at her breasts as little rivulets flowed over their curves. 'What I'll do to you will be so bad that you can't even imagine it now. And when I do it to you, you won't be able to believe it.'

Mary turned on the tap to begin filling the bath. She poured in a large amount of bath foam liquid. How she would enjoy herself! Soon she would transfer Jack into the deepening water. She was strong enough to do that even if he resisted.

Then he would learn the true meaning of domination with heat and slipperiness, wetness and humiliation. There is nothing that cannot be done in a bath.

Three

Early the next morning, Mary drove away from the hotel without Jack. She felt proud of herself, for doing what all the self-help books and articles said she should: being proactive instead of passive.

Happy singing filled the car, and it was Mary's singing. She would defy the world by being herself – but, no, she was no longer interested in the world, so there was no need for defiance. But if her free soul demanded the absolute and unconditional surrender of her flesh, so be it. Let her own flesh fear her! There would be no more compromises.

'This is all well and good and true,' said Mary to herself. 'But what shall I actually do next?' It seemed dull simply to go back to her flat and look for a new job and a new relationship.

A sign came into view, pointing the way to some place she had never been before, not at all on the way to Leeds, logic and normality. So she followed that sign. She felt it showed the road to freedom even though it actually said Melton Mowbray. Around noon she stopped to have lunch, and an hour after that she was feeling so sleepy that she stopped at a small hotel and slept the rest of the afternoon like an overfed cat.

Waking up hungry, she drove to a pizza place and devoured a jumbo all by herself, then went back to the hotel and slept without the dreams and nightmares that usually annoyed her so much. Next morning she had breakfast in Peter borough, then walked into a charity shop because she sensed there was something for her in there, though she knew not what. And there it was: a cardboard box full of science-fiction paperbacks from the 1950s and 1960s, all of them in excellent condition. David loved science-fiction books, especially old ones. Or at least he had. Now it seemed he was too depressed to be interested in anything, including Mary. Especially Mary.

She got the box of books at an absurdly low price, and one old man thought she was so good-looking that he even insisted on carrying them out to her car. Mary had that kind of effect on men. So, she thought, now she had to take these books to David, because he loved to collect them so much. She had not known what she was going to do that day, but now she did. This was obviously fate. Not her decision.

A brief look at her map told Mary the route to David's, so she set off, in such a good mood that she sang to herself rather than turning on the radio. Beside the road, huge machines were getting in the harvest. Probably David would just tell her to go away and stop bothering him, but so what? She would give him the books anyway, because she wanted to. It was not a way of saying thank you, as she had no reason to thank him. It was not even an attempt to ingratiate herself with him, she was beyond that. He was nothing to her, in fact it looked as though he was, these days, nothing even to himself.

It was just a bunch of old books, that was all.

After lunch at a Tesco's, she drove back to David's house in a leafy, sleepy street drenched in hot sunshine and rang the doorbell. On David's face when he opened the door was a look of annoyance and suspicion.

'Don't look so serious,' Mary said with a laugh. 'I'm not going to force my way in this time. Here are some books I rescued from a charity shop. If you don't want them, just throw them away. Goodbye and good luck.'

Mary turned away and walked back to her car. She was certain that David would maintain his lack of enthusiasm and would not call her back, and she told herself again that she did not care anyway, but of course she hoped he would call her back. He did not call her back.

As she was opening her car door, two young women jogged around the corner.

'It's Mary!' one of them exclaimed, and they both came to a halt.

'Hi, Faye! Hi, Carol!' Mary said, surprised and pleased to meet these two nice girls again. During the confusing period when she had more or less lived with David in an on-again, off-again fashion she had enjoyed some good conversations with Faye and Carol, who lived nearby. Both girls' parents had consulted David about their investments.

'I can't believe you're here,' said Carol. 'We haven't seen you in ages.'

'It's so nice to see you again,' Faye said with real pleasure and warmth.

'What are you doing these days?' Mary asked. 'Going to university?'

'Yeah,' Carol replied. 'We've finished the first year. Now it's the summer break, but we've got a lot of projects and stuff.'

'Our parents are away on holiday, so we've got two houses all to ourselves,' said Faye with innocent pride.

'We have fun,' said Carol, and giggled.

Faye blushed and gave her friend a nudge. Mary wondered what they were getting up to. Then she heard David's voice. She was amazed how her heart leapt.

'Oh, Mary,' he said. 'Don't go yet, OK? Hi, Faye. Hi, Carol. When you're through talking here, come back inside, OK, Mary?'

'OK,' she replied.

David turned away and went back into his house. Faye and Carol looked at Mary and could see she was thinking hard.

'We won't keep you,' said Carol. 'But look, we really want to talk with you. You're one of the few people we can trust. We want to tell you something and maybe ask your advice. So you must see us really soon. Visit us today or tomorrow. Please. I mean it.'

'I will,' said Mary. 'I want to, I'm intrigued.'

The girls expressed their pleasure, said their good-byes, and went off jogging together, though they kept looking back at Mary as though to make sure she did not intend driving off.

Things, thought Mary, are getting interesting. She took a deep breath and walked back into David's house, joining him in the kitchen where he was making coffee.

'Carol and Faye look great,' said Mary.

'They really do look great,' David agreed, not sound-ing enthusiastic, but rather speaking as an expert on women.

Mary sat down at the table and tried to be very quiet. A voice at the back of her mind told her that if only she could be very quiet, she might be allowed to stay a little while.

'These books are very good,' David said with some reluctance.

He doesn't want to be nice to me, he thinks it might be dangerous, Mary realised. She decided to pretend to be a quiet, calm woman.

'Look, a very early Jack Vance paperback novel in near-mint condition,' David murmured, almost speak-ing to himself as he laid the books out on the table. For all his depression and apathy, there was now a spark of interest glowing in his eyes. 'Jack Vance is a genius. America's least-known genius. Would it sound crazy if I said he's the best writer of the twentieth century?'

'I believe you.'

'Yes, but you're notoriously gullible,' David muttered.

He poured two cups of coffee and gave one to Mary, then sat down with her and looked at the books, marvelling at cover art, titles and authors.

'Well, now I know,' he said. 'The last thing to go in a man is the collecting habit. I'd thought I could never take an interest in anything again. Just look at this early Phillip K. Dick. Wonderful spaceships.'

'What happened,' asked Mary, 'to make you lose interest in everything?'

'I don't really know,' David said with the slightest of shrugs, as though he could hardly be bothered even to shrug. 'I got sick of my work. I mean, derivatives are hardly even real. I got sick of my sex life. I'm a sadist, an extreme sadist, as you know better than anyone. I'm a sadist with a bathroom fetish. That's just silly. I got sick of everything, Mary. Work, sex, people. So I quit everything. I can live on my investments.'

'Sounds like clinical depression. Did you see a doctor? You should. Get some treatment. Depression is terrible. You can't simply accept it.'

'I just don't care,' David replied. 'So, what are you up to these days? Did you say you'd quit your job?'

'Huh!' Mary laughed. 'You don't want to know about me. You just don't want to talk about yourself.'

'You're clever,' David admitted ruefully.

'I'll tell you about myself anyway. I quit my job and got fired at exactly the same time, after I mashed a big cream cake into the face of a bitch who really annoyed me in the office. She was lucky I didn't punch her. And since I saw you last, I've dominated my ex-boyfriend Jack. Very severely. He came running after me but he wouldn't dominate me, so I tied him up in a hotel bathroom and gave him the works. It was hell. For him, I mean. For me it was pretty good.'

40

David looked up from the early Ace Double paper-back he was perusing to stare at Mary. She felt it was the first time he had truly looked at her, the first time he had seen her, the first time he had shown any interest in her, for two years. Perhaps it was the first time ever. It was a pure delight in her heart.

'So,' David said after a long pause. 'You mashed a cake into the face of a colleague, and you dominated your boyfriend.'

'No, my ex-boyfriend. He was already ex at that time, and now he is so much more ex. I convinced him of his status with my bum.'

'And you masturbated in my bathroom, I recall you saying.'

'Yes, using restraint and equipment.'

'Obviously,' sighed David, 'I really screwed you up with our unfortunate relationship.'

'Oh, no!' Mary laughed. 'Dream on! You're not that good, David. Sorry to disappoint you, but you didn't screw me up. I was born screwed up. Shit, anyway, I'm no more screwed up than anybody else. I'm just more honest, and I express more. I do more.'

'You do more,' David echoed, and laughed a small, tentative laugh that sounded rusty from long disuse.

'Fuck, now I feel ten times better because of all the crazy stuff I've done lately,' Mary said with her habitual sincerity and truthfulness that hardly anybody had ever liked. 'You know, David, the thing is this,' she added, leaning towards him and touching his arm briefly. She spoke in an urgent whisper. 'I am so fucking sick and tired of trying to pretend to be fucking normal. Or even halfway normal. I'm never going to try like that again, David.'

'I agree,' David replied. 'Fuck being normal.'

For a few minutes the man and woman sat in absolute silence. They drank coffee, had a biscuit each, and said not a word. David sorted his books into little piles, one for each publisher. Then he sorted them again, by writer. Then he arranged them in the order they were published. There are many ways in which a man and woman can sit together and say nothing. To her surprise, Mary realised that this particular silence was companionable. Despite all the terrible events and the shouting matches of the past, here they were sitting like the oldest of friends who say nothing because they no longer fear silence. Mary felt warm and cosy.

Lust came into her mind and body, taking her by surprise once more. She decided to ignore it and to leave quickly. Obviously it would be insane to even think of having sex with David even if he had begged her to, and there was no chance of that happening. He was certainly determined never to get involved with her again.

So what.

'Let's have a bath together,' she said.

David started as though he had had an electric shock. He had trouble getting any words out. 'We can't begin it again, Mary,' he said at last. 'We mustn't. We have to be determined. For both our sakes. It's too dangerous. For both of us. We were lucky that you ran away two years ago.'

Mary leaned over the table and touched the huge bulge in David's jeans.

'You got a full erection,' she pointed out quietly, 'as soon as I spoke.'

'My cock is not intelligent. My cock is very stupid and very cruel. I'm an absolute sadist. There is nothing else, that's all there is. You must leave now, Mary. I beg you to leave.'

Mary knew that he was right. Of course she ought to leave now.

'Don't be afraid,' she said gently. 'We'll have a bath together and it will be good, I promise.' She held his hand and looked into his eyes. 'I'll have a bath with you and we'll have a great time, because I insist on certain conditions.'

David's erection inside his jeans was hurting him. He grimaced, and handled his penis so that it was at a better, less painful, angle.

'What conditions?' he whispered hoarsely.

And Mary knew she had him. Her mouth filled with strangely bitter saliva. She knew triumph.

And she knew fear.

'You can dominate me,' Mary stated. 'But no restraint and no gags. You can whip me and punish me and order me around and you can humiliate me and you can insult me verbally. But I may well insult you back, verbally I mean. You can fuck me and order me to suck you. You can dress me up. It won't be a perfect scene for you because I won't be helpless, but it'll be interesting for us both to see just how much punishment I can take without being restrained. Bound helpless. It'll be more interesting for you than sitting around watching TV or however the hell you spend your time now that you don't work and you're so depressed.'

Mary said all this with as much outward calm as if she were talking about the weather. Inwardly, however, she was profoundly fascinated and exquisitely terrified. Mounting in her body, mind and soul was an excitement of an order she had hardly thought possible for any human being.

David was hooked, she knew that for sure. He had taken her bait despite all his very real determination not to have anything to do with her ever again. But what could she do with him now that she had him hooked? Was he nowadays a small enough fish for her to reel in safely? Or was he a deadly shark, as in the old days, who could drag her down into deep waters and devour her utterly?

'I make furniture,' David announced.

'What?'

'I make furniture, especially tables. Individual, one-of-a-kind, handcrafted tables. Using fine woods. I don't just watch TV.'

'Fine! You're a craftsman.'

'I can't make them as well as I want to make them,' David sighed. 'But I know you don't want to hear about my carpentry now. Look, Mary, I'm sorry I asked to hear your conditions. Actually we can't have a bath or do anything else together. It's too dangerous. What I want to do now is read this great book of Robert Sheckley short stories, then reread this underrated Katherine Maclean.'

'I'll be back in a minute,' said Mary as she stood up. She went to her car, got her black plastic garbage bag full of David's equipment, and took it into the bathroom. There she turned on the taps of the huge red bath, and she poured in the rest of the old bottle of foam bath liquid. She returned to David in the kitchen.

'After we have a bath I'll clean this place up a bit,' she told him. 'It needs it.'

'You're pretty scary nowadays, Mary.'

Mary gazed into David's eyes and shivered. Within this man, an evil power was awakening. He wanted to dominate her, to use her body. David had tried to be good, and now she had turned up and tempted him back to his old evil. How bad she was! Naturally, Mary could not help but feel proud.

'What the fuck.' She laughed. 'We'll have a few orgasms, you can treat me like shit, and then I'll go away again and you can glue the spine of this William Tenn and then make a better table because you'll feel better. Come on, let's go into the bathroom.'

'You really will have to go away again. You can't stay here, or even come regularly. We'll do this once and then you'll go, right?'

'I promise,' Mary lied cheerfully. Bored with telling the truth all the time, she felt rejuvenated by the lie. It was fresh and bright. In fact, she decided then and there, she would go when she was good and ready. She might leave tomorrow, or she might leave in a month's time.

If she could make David beg her to stay, that would be the perfect time to go.

By force of old habit they went into the living room to undress, after closing the curtains. David had never liked to see clothes lying around in the bathroom where he indulged his dark urges. I thought I had thrown away all those old habits, Mary said to herself, but now they all come back, the same old nightmare, a descent down black stone steps into the heart of David's ritual. His dangerous obsessions. But an old nightmare was so much better than nothing.

Naked, standing apart, they stared at one another like boxers meeting for the third time in a big fight, like animals wondering which can devour the other, like followers of some unholy nameless religion, like a lonely man and a lonely woman afraid and longing.

David's unusually large cock seemed even bigger than Mary remembered. His body was small, but his erect cock would have looked big even if he had been the tallest of men. This combination of small body and huge cock made him seem all cock. It was, for Mary, hypnotic.

'You have a fantastic body,' said David, his voice roughened by a terrible lust. As he stared at her, his cock pulsed up and down with the rapid beats of his heart, so ferocious was the tension of its trapped blood.

Mary could not say anything. Two years ago she had run away from this crazy man. She felt she had been running for her life. Now she was back. Now resumed the course of time.

She wanted to hug and praise him, to show some tenderness. But she knew he would despise her for that weakness, her need for a little show of normal affection, so she hung back. For a moment she felt he might come forwards and take her in his arms, but then he abruptly turned away. And she followed him into that bathroom, that room of watery, bubbling pain and slipperiness and

45

absolute tension. Breathless she followed that man of final confusion.

When they closed the bathroom door behind them, the sound had the air of finality in Mary's ears, as though she and David had been sealed in here together for eternity. Sunlight streamed in through the tall windows at the far end of the room, double-glazed windows which were soundproof. Mary was glad that she could scream as much as she liked in this room of all rooms, and only she and David would hear. There was a fine freedom in being able to scream for once, instead of trying to pretend that there was nothing to scream about, that the way people lived was good, that the world made sense. In reality there was plenty to scream about even before David began her chastisement. Yes, and the sunlight shone in. How beautiful it made everything look, how lovely. So there would be pain and beauty.

All hesitation gone, David opened the cupboard, selected pieces from his collection, and lay them beside the bath. Mary shivered. Time had circled.

They laughed as they got into the water, they laughed awkwardly to relieve their tension. Suddenly they stopped laughing and gasped with the shock of joy. Kissing and groping and stroking they lay down in the foaming warm water, and they revelled in the feel of one another's exquisitely desirable bodies all wet and slippery. Mary loved that slipperiness that made her so aware of every part of her own body, and every detail of her terrible lust. Water was a map of the skin, a map on the skin, showing all that was in the skin.

Writhing like snakes, they pressed and rubbed their hot flesh together, four clever hands everywhere. Mary knew again the purity of desperation. For two years she had told herself that she did not need that bastard David and his disgusting, freakish bathroom designed for sex of extreme strangeness. For two years she had

46

lied to herself. Now all that had gone. There was only slippery wet flesh.

'Suck my cock,' David ordered, standing up.

Slavishly, Mary suckled on his bloated tool, kneeling in the bath, holding his shaft in one hand while she used the other for fervent masturbation. David held her head in both hands and fucked her mouth with short sharp strokes.

'You filthy whore,' he gasped. 'Stop jerking off. Just pay attention to me, you silly slut.'

'I need to come,' Mary cried. She stopped masturbating and sucked David's cock with wonderful skill and passion, worshipping it. Her teeth grazed the taut surface of the giant glans, and her tongue lashed around the rim, making David pant and groan.

'You'll go down on all fours and I'll whip your arse,' David stated. 'If you can stay in position and take your punishment, I'll fuck you. If you don't, I won't. I don't need to fuck you, Mary. I can jerk off and hose you down, that's just as good for me.'

Pissed by his arrogance, frightened by her own desire to surrender to David absolutely, Mary all at once stood up and at the same time hooked her right leg behind David's legs and pushed his body. She had judged it perfectly, and he fell down flat in the water without hitting his head, not that Mary would have cared much if he had. Before he could recover from the shock of being dropped, Mary had grabbed his torso and arms between her long, stunningly powerful legs, and held his wriggling body helpless.

'On the other hand, we could do this,' she said, and began to masturbate with both hands, rubbing all around her clitoris. Very quickly she came with a series of groans and choking gurgles that sounded strange even in her own ears. She was impressed. The real thing!

'You fucking bitch, Mary. Next time I'll tie you down and whip you,' David yelled, red-faced with fury.

'There won't be a next time, remember?' Abruptly, Mary let David free from the deadly scissors of her legs. 'That was just to show you I don't have to do anything. Whatever I do is up to me. Now you can whip my bum.'

And to David's further astonishment she went on all fours in the bath, submissively presenting her strong and luxuriantly curved buttocks and pussy.

'Thwack!' sang the leather whip, making music with the instrument of her flesh. The blow landed on Mary's left buttock. She made no sound. Neither did she move. Her steely will made of her own lovely body a victim. David lashed out at her back three times more, higher up. The ends of the tails curled under her body to kiss the sides of her breasts. His next two blows, vicious and cutting, were more deliberate attacks on her vulnerable flanks and, with each of his strikes, he insulted her with crude words hissing between his teeth. Mary remained silent and unmoving, except for a turn of her head so that she could cast a beseeching look on him with her big, dark, liquid eyes so wide with longing and fear. Then she stuck her tongue out in extremely provoking mockery.

'Why don't you scream, you stupid bitch?' David complained. When he dominated Mary he often insulted her verbally, but it never bothered her, as she knew it was a part of their special kind of sex. He never insulted her when his cock was not hard. Well, not much. 'I'll make you scream, Mary. I'll make you roll up into a ball to protect yourself, or run away again. Coward! Hold your position and take every blow I give you, or I won't fuck you again, you understand?'

'Yes, sir,' Mary whispered huskily, feeling the most exquisitely perverse sensations tingling through her body, shocking her soul into full being. David waited a full minute, making Mary wait and sweat. He held the cat in his right hand, high, poised ready to strike and, with his left hand, he stroked his cock. He cracked the heavy whip twice without touching her flesh, to add to her anxiety. Each time his sudden movement and the hiss of the leather thongs made her jump.

Suddenly, when she least expected it, he laid a splendid cracking blow across her provocative, utterly female, gleaming wet buttocks. She let out an animal howl of pain and shock, and her muscles convulsed so that her jerking limbs splashed water from the bath. Then she resumed her posture and turned her head away from him as if striving to prove her devotion and submission by refusing to annoy him with the gaze of her big, dark, eyes, so beseeching and compelling.

Such absolute surrender and proof of strong will-power filled David with rage. It was as if she let him whip her arse because it was the perfect way for her to show him her strength.

'You think you're better than me.'

'No, no, I never think that.'

Grunting with effort, David struck her across the buttocks twice more. Now Mary did cry out, and she sank down in the water, holding her arse. David prayed that he had ended her defiant insanity, her delusions of masochism. Surely now she would run away again, leaving him the freedom and pleasant irresponsibility of solitude. But no! The crazy bitch reared up on all fours again, whimpering with pain yet resonant in every superb long curve of her body with a frightening stubborness. Mary's teats, impossibly, swelled to a huger size as if to show her audacious defiance by a decadent engorgement.

Sickened by his need for her, delighted by his cruelty and power, frightened by her willpower and endurance, David resolved to destroy her will once and for all, and gave her a blow of absolute male strength and ferocity against and between her buttocks. Mary screamed and collapsed. She had broken. Now where was her pride in submission, her defiant stubborness? She rolled around curled up in a ball, clutching at her arse, sobbing bitterly, panting for breath. Trembling like a wounded ant, she flinched and squirmed.

'No more, no more, I can't stand it,' she pleaded in a high-pitched childish voice, so unlike her usual tone of calm confidence. She was lying.

David trembled with lust as he gazed down like a god on this lovely young female creature, this yearning animal. He cast his cat-o'-nine away, and it fell with a heavy thud on sand-yellow tiles. Mary saw the look on his face. Sobbing and shuddering, she managed to tear away her hands from her stinging buttocks and uncurled her long body in the foaming waters of the scarlet bath, displaying her femaleness and desperately proffering it to her conqueror. She stretched out her arms, torso and legs, she grasped the shiny steel rail set beyond the end of the bath, she parted her legs and raised her arse in absolute surrender. Engorged, the mouth of her cunt was exquisitely swollen and protuberant, dark pink, flecked with foam, gleaming in blatant and final invitation.

David pounced on Mary's superb nudity and sank his cock into her slippery vagina. He was astonished by the power of her internal contractions, which squeezed his cock long and hard at both the entrance and the core. He thrust at her savagely in a hard and fast rhythm, and her floating, quivering body was all pulsations and shuddery pants. It undulated and writhed under his thrusts so that he seemed to be flying.

What a cunt she had! He remembered that when Mary was at an extreme of excitation her vaginal muscles went into involuntary spasms, and she also had exceptional voluntary control whenever she chose, but surely her internal muscles had never in the past had such strength? She must have gone into training. It was a cunt in a million – it sucked, it massaged, it gripped and it writhed, all oily heat. He could hardly bear to admit that its power was frightening.

Amazement filled Mary also. It was not only that David's huge cock was fucking her to pieces and it felt great, but also it was just so damned right that he was in her, it gave her such an absolute lust and delight. The pain of the blows from the cat still burned all over Mary's body, but it mingled and blended with the thrusts of David and the tight grip of his hands on her breasts, so that the pain was transformed into extreme stimulation that amplified delight.

For an eternity David blasted out his soul into the core of her magnificent, tensed and shuddering body, which jerked in spasms under him like a fish impaled on a spear and, as his seed burst out to spatter and spray her womb, that cunt of hers clutched and sucked on and on and on until burning yellow blackness and deafening silence swallowed them up, and it seemed that their bodies, minds, souls, even time and the universe, had all been irrevocably shattered.

Finally, David heard himself laughing the choking laugh that possessed him rarely, at the height of his most powerful orgasms, when nothing could exist any longer except for the deepest reality of a mindless hilarity.

Then they lay side by side in the big bath, gasping for breath and unable to speak. Even when Mary was able to speak she could not say a word, for her mind was alive with all kinds of strange things that she wanted to say, or even to sing, and she felt sure that if she spoke, her ideas and feelings would alarm David. Surely this sadist of hers had great fears.

'That was pretty good fun,' he said at last, with the air of a man trying hard to keep it casual, without conviction.

'I enjoyed it,' Mary agreed. She wanted to give words to the song in her heart, but instead she told her heart to shut the fuck up. What use was it anyway to have a heart?

'Just don't forget that you're leaving after this.'

'I won't forget,' Mary replied demurely. Which is not the same as saying I will actually go, she said to herself.

'At least you're sincere.'

'Don't try to look on the bright side. There is no bright side.'

'That's too sincere for sure. I bet when you were a kid –'

'You talk too much, Mary. I'm going to get some ice cream.'

Good, thought Mary. They would eat ice cream together, and she would surely be able to trick him into having a real conversation for once.

David returned from the kitchen with a quart tub of chocolate ice cream, and another of apricot.

'You forgot spoons,' Mary pointed out.

'This is to humiliate you with, not to eat,' David explained, shaking his head in disgust at Mary's naivety. 'Though we'll eat some as well.'

'Give me your orders.'

'Get out of the bath. Kneel down on the tiles like a good slave and smear your whole body with ice cream.'

'Yes, sir,' Mary agreed with a provoking kind of meekness, and crawled out of the bath onto the tiles, into a framing rectangle of sunlight. She took two handfuls of ice cream from the tub and slowly massaged her breasts, shivering with a fresh lust that surprised her, that made her gasp and bite her lip. It amazed and alarmed her how quickly and strongly she was aroused not only by caressing herself with the slippery, cold ice cream, but also by obeying David's orders. Hot from the bath, hot from whipping and fucking, her flesh welcomed the chill slithery kiss of the ice cream, and her clitoris seemed to hum like a bumble bee. Kneeling, she gazed at David with blazing brown eyes, a look in which mingled anger, arousal, the excitement of humiliation and a peculiar defiance, as though she were challenging him to abuse her, to put her through her paces, while she was gathering her inner resources to embrace and surpass even his most extreme and bizarre demands for her surrender in degradation, and so win a strange and alarming victory.

'You fucking bitch,' David gasped. He stood over her and stared into her flashing eyes so clear with intelligence, character and light of compelling purity. 'Next time I whip you I'll do it ten times harder.'

'What next time would that be, sir? You've ordered me to leave, and I must obey my master.'

'Whore!' David snarled. His penis throbbed in renewed and startling erection, huge and rigid, growing so quickly that it made him gasp.

Mary turned around and bent down, parting her legs and arching her back to thrust out her swollen pussy. She smeared great dollops of chocolate ice cream over the taut twin spheres of her arse, and sighed with delight as the chill ooze soothed her whipped flesh. The combination of stinging and cool comfort was marvellously arousing. Slowly, she bent down to lick drops of melted ice cream from the sand-coloured tiles with her tongue at full extension.

'Humiliation suits you,' David gasped huskily. 'You dirty bitch, you slimy whore!'

Mary lay on her back and smeared handfuls of ice cream over her arms and legs, breasts and belly. Finally, she went to work on her pussy.

'Push it inside,' David ordered.

Sighing with pleasure, Mary took handfuls of creamy coldness, rolled them into cylinders, one large and one small. The large one she squashed into her vagina, and the smaller one was addressed between her buttocks.

'Oh, you whore,' David groaned. He took apricot ice cream in his hands and made shiny stripes all over

53

Mary, turning her into a zebra woman, a fantasy animal figure of lust. He mashed ooze into her hair, then pressed and rubbed handfuls into her mouth and all over her face, coating her features as he pressed his penis against her cool, firm tits' delightful greasiness. He sucked creamy slime from her breasts and pussy, then spat it out over her face.

'You silly slut,' he gasped. 'You don't even know how disgusting you are, how perverted and humiliated.' He held the shaft of his cock and thrust its head into Mary's mouth, while smearing a handful of ice cream over her eyes so she could not look at him with her aggravating pride.

Alternating between her mouth and vagina, he used her in every position.

And he felt afraid of her terrible and powerful submissiveness.

Four

And it was another three hours before they left the bathroom. By then they had worked up a fine appetite, so they drove to an Italian restaurant. Mary thought how nice it was to have a meal with David. She could not help feeling happy and hopeful even though she told herself she must not. Hope was always the first step on the road to disappointment. What was there to hope for from David anyway? He was nuts.

'I suppose you might just as well stay the night,' David said grudgingly, looking at his watch as they left the restaurant. 'And leave tomorrow morning,' he added meaningfully. 'We might just as well go the whole hog and see a movie. Almost like a real couple, eh, Mary? Except we're not.'

'I know, I know. Don't state the obvious.' Mary laughed. 'I hurt all over.'

Both Mary and David had a great love of films, especially seen in cinemas. Mary reflected on all the good ones she had seen in the past with David. Just seeing movies with him seemed to be, when she looked back, a major part of her whole life.

They enjoyed a comedy and went back to David's house. Mary felt very sleepy, and had a good night's rest in the spare bedroom, alone. She awoke early the next morning, so early that she tried to go back to sleep at first, but her mind became so active that she got up instead. Very quietly so as not to disturb David, she went into the kitchen and had a light breakfast. She was so careful that she managed not to even clink a spoon on her coffee cup, or make a tiny clunk when she put a plate on the table. It was such a lovely morning that she decided to go jogging, feeling the fresh air and exercise would help her to reach the right decision.

For she had to make a plan. It was vital that she either be determined to leave David immediately or to stay on for a few days. If she was not determined either way, David would gain the upper hand and she would end up feeling lousy. It was OK that he whipped her and fucked her ruthlessly, but she did not want him to get one over on her.

If she left immediately – even before David woke up – she would surprise him and perhaps tempt him into phoning her. Suppose he did not. Well, that would only prove how stupid and cowardly and depressed he was, so again she would be the winner. Obviously she should leave. She could always return unexpectedly.

Unfortunately, she did not feel like leaving right now. So how could she stay for a few days and yet be sure of winning? Somehow she had to get David addicted again to punishing her and having strange sex in that bathroom of his, and when he was hooked she could suddenly leave him, so that he missed her and realised how much he needed her. How great it would be if she could make him beg her to stay! That would be a win.

Jogging reminded many parts of her body how sore they were, but Mary enjoyed the feeling, as it informed her what a wonderful time she and David had enjoyed yesterday. Pain was good if you chose it, for any chosen pain reminded you that you were alive. And sexual pain was not truly, or simply pain. For Mary it made sex into an occasion. Better to have a ritual feast of bittersweet sensuality and worship than just plain old sex.

She went around a corner and there were Carol and Faye. They waved to her and she waved back. The three of them jogged towards a meeting in the middle of the street. How good-looking they were, thought Mary. Charming and confident young women of true loveliness. Carol was stunningly tall and strong, with a shapely body on endless powerful legs. She was a Valkyrie out of Viking legends, an imposing beauty with pale-blonde hair so long that, unconfined, it fell all the way straight as rulers to her broad hips, though now it swayed in a ponytail. Faye was a real contrast, shorter and slighter, with a tiny waist and amazing breasts that seemed far too big for her body. Her eyes were large dark pools, and her light-brown hair was cut very short. How proud of them their boyfriends must be, thought Mary, and they surely did have boyfriends, for they looked so happy they must be in love.

'Good to see you!' cried Faye, as the three of them met and came to a halt.

'We have a lot we want to talk about with you,' Carol told Mary.

'It's personal stuff,' said Faye. 'The thing is, you're one of the very few people we can trust.'

'And respect,' Carol added.

'Don't say "respect", it makes me feel old,' Mary joked, and they all laughed.

'Can you come with us and have breakfast?' Faye asked, and gave Mary a smile of genuine good-natured sweetness.

'I'd love to.'

'Let's go that way,' said Carol. 'It's prettier.'

Onwards jogged the three of them, with golden sunlight, sky of light-blue crystal, and vivid green so bright all around, the light of their own personal dawn that most people were too lazy to see.

Soon they reached Carol's home, which was big and impressive. Her parents were both genetic scientists, but, they used to jokingly tell Carol, her remarkable tallness was not the result of genetic engineering. They were away on holiday, as were Faye's parents, with Faye's younger brother. This left Carol and Faye with two houses to live in without any family supervision, a situation they clearly enjoyed. Mary had breakfast with the two girls.

'Do you have boyfriends?' she asked.

'No,' replied Faye and Carol at the same moment, shaking their heads.

'Actually we're sort of involved with each other,' said Carol.

'We decided you wouldn't be shocked or offended,' said Faye.

'And you were right,' Mary assured the girls.

'That's what we wanted your advice about,' said Carol. 'Do you think we should tell our parents?'

'Don't bother. The less parents know about their children, the better it is for everybody.'

'So in our place, you'd try to keep it a secret from your parents?' Faye inquired.

'If I were in your place I'd blurt out the truth all the time and offend everyone and have fights with everyone, because I'm me.'

'That's good,' laughed Faye.

'You're one of the few people we trust,' Carol told Mary.

'Don't trust me. I'm a disaster area. Work, family, relationships: disasters.'

'Who cares?' said Carol. 'You look confident and happy, what else matters?'

'Yes, I became confident and happy when I gave up,' laughed Mary. 'Abandon all hope, care about nothing, and then life starts.'

What nice innocent girls they were – innocent of suffering that is, which to Mary was real innocence, far more important than being sexually innocent. Their basic seriousness was part of their innocence. Both were working hard at college she felt sure, and now that it was the summer break they were doubtless doing a sincere job on their projects. Carol wanted to work in forestry, while Faye was fascinated by geology. Both of them were all friendliness, sincerity and gentle warmth. What problems, thought Mary, they would face in later life! It was safer to understand evil from the inside rather than being good. She would be doing them a favour, toughening them up, if she could somehow bring them to understand even a little of her and David's peculiar evil.

'I'm sure you're right, Mary,' said Faye. 'Our parents are old-fashioned. Especially mine. Why tell them anything? Anyway, Carol and I have both been with men and it wasn't so bad. Maybe we're just going through a phase.'

'It's always good to experiment,' said Mary, without spelling out David's kind of experiments. Even if she had wanted to, it was not so easy to explain the allure of SM in the bathroom. Wet domination. It was such a speciality.

'Human sexuality is a mess,' said Faye.

'Don't worry about it,' Mary advised cheerfully. 'It doesn't matter what you do. If you're straight you'll have problems, if you're lesbian you'll have problems, and if you're celibate you'll have problems. So, obviously, the only thing to do is learn how to ignore the damn problems.'

It was nearly ten when Mary got back to David's house, but he was still asleep. Mary set about tidying up and cleaning the kitchen as quietly as she could. Truly the whole house was in a mess. It must help David feel a little less depressed if his place did not so closely resemble the end of the world on a rainy Monday afternoon. Then she prepared a nutritious lunch, as David was so thin, and consuming such unhealthy food. Not that she gave a damn what he did, but if she fed him well, then he would miss her all the more when she left.

Grumpy as a bear trying to give up heroin, David made his appearance around eleven. Mary ignored his bad temper and got him to eat a good combined breakfast and lunch, which seemed to take the edge off his irritability.

'I went jogging with Carol and Faye this morning, then had breakfast with them,' she told David at the strategic moment when he was enjoying dessert. She went on to paint a bright and colorful picture in words, showing these lovely young women isolated from their parents and their peers, living as though they were castaways on an island, in a mood of sexual discovery and experimentation. Mary's words and facial expression practically oozed implications of bizarre sensuality.

'What the hell are you suggesting?' David demanded, glaring at her in suspicion.

'Nothing. What could I suggest?' Mary replied innocently, trying not to overdo the innocence. 'I mean, I'm leaving anyway, and you're not interested in them or me.'

'Good! Just so long as you realise that,' said David. For a full minute he managed to stay silent. 'Come on, you might as well tell me what plan you had in mind,' he exclaimed, and then he laughed a little. His laugh sounded weak and rusty from lack of use. 'You know I'm dying of curiosity. Faye and Carol are lovely girls and you have some crazy plan about them, don't you? You're so cunning. But you're nuts too. Carol and Faye would run a mile if we tried to get them into the bathroom.'

'Oh, you guessed my idea. Ten points. So they'd run. That's why we'll let them introduce themselves to it,' Mary said with complete calm, giving David a warm smile and a sweet look from her bright brown eyes. I spoil him, she thought. 'We'll ask them to house-sit for a couple of days while we go away. They'll discover the bathroom and your collection, and you can set your hidden video cameras to record the results, if any.'

'You really are crazy! That's an evil idea,' said David. Mary thought that his attempt at moral outrage was not nearly so convincing as when she herself pretended to be innocent and harmless.

'Oh, you're interested in them.'

'All right, I am. You can always see through me.'

'You're so depressed that you're underground, David. You're burrowing towards the Earth's core. Introducing two innocent girls to the insanity of your bathroom is just the sort of thing that could help you feel better. It'll be a good project.'

'A project!' David exclaimed, and had a fit of coughing. 'Forget it,' he told her when he had recovered. 'It's hopeless. It's immoral and insane.' He pretended to read an Alfred Bester anthology for thirty seconds. 'Your plan doesn't even make any sense,' he burst out, putting his paperback down carefully, as it was a mint 1968 edition. 'Why should we need a house-sitter if we're only going away for a couple of days?'

'We need them to look after our cat.'

'There is no "we" so there is no "our", don't forget that, Mary. Most of all, there is no bloody cat. We are extremely catless.'

'Ha! You said "we" too! Gotcha.'

'Oh, shut up,' David snarled, but he could not help feeling intrigued by Mary's plan. She could hear it in the tone of his snarls. 'You're the most annoying woman I've ever met.'

'Good. That means you'll remember me when you've forgotten the others. We can easily get a cat for Carol and Faye to take care of. I love cats. I'll take good care of the cat all its life.'

'You're nuts. You've really lost it,' said David. He finished his ice cream and peaches in an angry way that made Mary smile. 'Shit,' he said. 'You're right, Mary. It's an interesting idea. Will they or won't they do anything in the bathroom? I have to know.'

'Well done,' Mary told him. 'You haven't completely lost your guts and your balls after all. You just mislaid them for a while.'

'Oh, shut up.'

'Well, I'll be going home now. I don't have to worry about you now that you have a project.' Mary was bluffing. If David called her bluff, she would fall back on plan B, which was to vomit, weep and throw herself at his feet.

'No, now you have to stay a couple of days,' David said with reluctant firmness. 'I can't lie to those poor girls like you can. Anyway, it's not fun unless you see it through with me. But after we watch the tapes together you'll leave.'

Mary did the washing-up, and David went into the shed to work on a piece of furniture, or perhaps to try and reanimate a dead body like Frankenstein, for all Mary knew. She decided to tackle the house seriously. First she finished cleaning up the kitchen, then she set the living room to rights. After that she went into the bathroom and divided David's collection into two piles. She cleaned and polished all the items in one pile, but the other pile she placed in garbage bags for disposal, feeling these pieces were too far gone, with perished rubber, tarnished metal and discoloured or warped plastic. Handling these familiar items made her wet. Lastly she cleaned the water bed thoroughly and refilled it. Now the bathroom truly was as she remembered it, as it should be.

Feeling good, she made dinner, then told David he could come and eat if he liked.

'You spoil me, Mary,' David said as they ate the meal together. 'I don't deserve it.'

'I know you don't,' Mary agreed sincerely. 'I've sorted out some of the stuff from the bathroom to throw away, stuff in bad condition. So Carol and Faye will only see things that look nice.'

'Good idea,' David agreed. He hesitated, then asked, a little sheepishly: 'Is there still plenty of stuff left?'

'Yes, don't worry,' said Mary. 'Anyway, we – I mean "you", as there is no "we" – you can always replace it.'

'I'm like a cocaine addict, trying to give it up, then trying to find some cocaine I imagine I might have dropped on the carpet last year.'

'Yes, you are like that. It's deeply pathetic. And funny.'

'I don't know which is more annoying, Mary: you agreeing with me or you arguing.'

'They're equally annoying,' Mary stated. 'And it serves you right.'

After dinner she went to her room and stayed there reading a book on relationships. There was nothing in it about bathroom domination. As usual. Really she wanted to have another bath with David, or even straight sex on a bed, but she decided it would be better to leave him alone so he could learn how much he missed her. She had to keep him off-balance, like in karate. She was good at karate.

Next morning they went shopping, had lunch in a vegetarian restaurant with too many plants in pots, then got a cat from the RSPCA so they would have a plausible story to tell Carol and Faye. It was a black and white cat, a sterilised female with a gentle, trusting expression. Her name was Ellie. When they got home, they gave Ellie food and milk, and they stroked her and showed her around the place. She settled in immediately, relaxing in the way that cats do when they trust the people they are with. Mary was glad to see that David was so nice to a cat, as it seemed to suggest that one day he might just possibly learn how to be nice to a woman. She tried to sneer at her own optimism.

That evening, Mary visited Carol and Faye. She asked them if they could take care of her and David's cat and stay in their house, and they said of course they would. The three women watched TV and ate together, and when Mary went back to David's house she repeated the previous evening's performance and avoided him, in order to give him a false sense of security.

Faye and Carol came round at 1 p.m. the next day, a time Mary had chosen so that David would be out of bed. He was on his best behaviour, and the girls found him the same charming, unusual and funny man they remembered from the past.

Ellie the cat got on fine with Carol and Faye, so David and Mary made a fairly quick getaway, not wanting to be around when the girls had their first ever sight of the bathroom. Faye and Carol had the run of David's house save for David's bedroom, which was locked, due to the fact that here were mounted two video cameras looking down through the one-way mirrors in the bathroom ceiling. A motion detector would turn the cameras on and roll tape whenever someone was in the bathroom while electric heaters prevented condensation forming on the ceiling mirrors. Mary enjoyed sharing with David the feeling of conspiracy.

He and I are not really bad, she thought. We just like doing bad things.

After driving to Aylesbury, Mary and David did a lot of shopping, had dinner, then took separate rooms at a hotel. Mary did not approve of the separate rooms part, but she made no protest, on the grounds that it was good strategy to grant David such small wins so that he would become overconfident, thus enabling her the final triumph. Whatever form that might take. Next day they saw a bad movie and visited a museum at the site of a minor Civil War battle, then drove back to David's home, reaching it in the evening, as a brief shower lay the dust of summer. They thanked Carol and Faye, who soon departed. Both girls seemed a little nervous and excited.

'They obviously had a good look at your crazy bathroom,' Mary commented.

'Look is probably all they did.'

'Let's watch the tapes.'

'No,' David insisted. 'Let's eat first. We can at least postpone the disappointment of finding nothing on the tapes.'

So Mary cooked another fine meal and they ate it.

After dinner, Mary went into the living room while David fetched the tapes from the cameras upstairs.

'We got something,' he said. He turned on the TV, and rolled the tape from the camera that looked down through a one-way mirror on the big red bath.

Mary felt guilty about spying on Faye and Carol in this way. It was truly a rotten way to treat those nice girls. All the same, she could not work up more than slight, enjoyable feelings of guilt.

On the TV, Carol entered the bathroom. She stared around her in amazement, taking in the huge red bath, the water bed, the shiny steel rings set into the tiled floor and walls.

'Faye! Come and see this,' Carol called.

The sound picked up by a microphone in the bathroom ceiling was not very clear, but Mary and David could understand what the girls said.

'Wow! Some bathroom!' Faye exclaimed as she joined Carol. 'They must have sex in here, don't you think?'

'Sure. Why not? Looks like fun.'

'I wonder what they keep in here?' mused Faye, as she went to look at the big cupboard in the corner near the window. 'Let's have a look.'

'We shouldn't,' said Carol. 'Let's do it.'

They opened the cupboard and stared in awe.

'Wow!' Carol exclaimed. 'Weird stuff.'

'This is bizarre,' Faye said quietly. 'It's all stuff for sex, right?' She sounded frightened.

'I guess so. Weird sex. Shit. Look, it's stuff for

65

bondage and domination and like that. Mary and David must be into strange sex.'

'I can believe it of him, but she seems so nice and normal,' said Faye, which pleased Mary.

'Nice people are into strange sex nowadays,' Carol mused. 'Even bondage and domination and sado-masochism. I read about it in *Cosmo*.'

'I guess I'm old-fashioned. But I never heard of people doing all that in the bathroom.'

'That is unusual,' Carol agreed. 'God, that's why there are steel rings set in the floor and walls!' she exclaimed, waving her hands. 'Wow! And in the bath! Oh God.'

'Oh, that's really crazy. I'm scared. So one of them ties the other up and does weird things to him. Or her. I guess Mary ties David up, don't you think? She's big and strong and he's kind of small.'

'You never know. He might want to compensate for his stature by dominating a strong woman.'

'Huh,' David snorted. 'Smart girl.'

Subdued and fascinated, Carol and Faye took out many items from the cupboard and discussed how they might be used. Both talked in small voices and grew afraid.

'We shouldn't be doing this,' Faye said nervously. 'Come on, let's go. I'm scared. This stuff is terrible.'

'It's an evil room,' Carol agreed.

They put everything back in the cupboard with great care, trying to make it look like they had never touched a thing, and left the bathroom.

The first period of recording ended, then the second began, as Faye and Carol returned to the bathroom.

'Over two hours later,' said David, pointing to the time display at the bottom left-hand corner of the screen. 'Maybe they have a plan. I bet they just spent two hours talking about the bathroom.'

'They have a plan! Great!' Mary exclaimed as Carol and Faye began running a bath. Mary had restocked the bathroom with bottles of foam bath liquid, baby oil and all kinds of soaps and lotions. Faye and Carol chose a bottle and poured a generous amount into the red bath. The waters began to foam.

'I feel nervous,' said Faye.

'It'll be fun,' Carol insisted. 'Anyway, it's always good to try something new. Expand our horizons.'

Swiftly the two girls undressed, displaying to Mary and David the perfection of their nudity. Faye's remarkable breasts were fascinating: huge and rounded like melons, yet firm and high above her tiny waist. It seemed almost impossible that her petite body could support such giants. Faye's red-brown hair glowed in the sunlight slanting down into the bathroom and reflecting off the polished tiles and shiny rings. Carol's remarkably tall and strong body was a striking contrast. Her legs were impossibly long, and her arse was wonderfully large and rounded, jutting out like a pair of soccer balls. Hair of pale spun gold fell down her long torso to her broad hips as Carol tossed her head in excitment like a magnificent mare eager to win the big race. The naked young beauties embraced and kissed, with four hands exploring warm flesh. Carol stooped to suckle on Faye's teats in turn. From the girls' warmth and tenderness, it was plain that they were truly in love.

Mary was deeply aroused and moved. How sweet they were, and how innocent! How brave they were to face the dangers of David's collection and that bizarre bathroom! Mary had once enjoyed a teenage affair with another girl, a brief and secret fling which had shown her she could enjoy sex with another woman.

Now the girls went to the big cupboard. God, thought Mary, they are going to try some equipment. It was a delicious shock. Sure enough, they took out a strap-on dildo and bodysuit of black plastic straps joined together by shiny steel rings.

'Good choice,' said David. 'Shit! This is amazing.'

'Way to go, girls,' Mary cried happily. What fun it was to be a voyeur with David!

Serious and quiet, as if they were performing some strange religious ritual, the girls worked together. First they washed the plastic dildo which was flexible, and lifelike in colour. In the cupboard was a tube of lubricant, and they smeared some of this on a knobbly stem at its base, and pushed this into Faye's vagina. Soft ridges around the base of the dildo engaged her labia and clitoris. Then they set about fastening the numerous black plastic straps of the intricate body harness attached to the base of the dildo by four stainless steel rings set into the plastic.

'Oh, this feels so strange,' murmured Faye.

Carol buckled strap after strap. Straps went around the tops of Faye's thighs, around her waist, up over her shoulders. Two straps encircled each of her huge breasts. Vertical straps connected the thigh, waist, and breast straps, with round steel rings at every junction. Carol did up the shiny buckles, and Faye's breasts bulged taut. The long thick dildo sprang up from her loins, a shocking contradiction to her femaleness. Erect, and lifelike in detailing, it stood there as a question, promise and threat. It was a stunning sight. Faye's huge breasts bulged tautly between the confining straps, her white flesh a contrast to the blackness of the shiny plastic. She was deliciously female, yet from her groin sprang a big penis.

'You look fantastic,' Carol breathed huskily, sounding so excited she could hardly speak.

'I feel so strange,' said Faye. She thrust her hips a little, staring at her new cock. She put her hand around the shaft and moved it. 'Oh, it feels great for my pussy. And, Carol, it's so weird, it makes me feel powerful.'

'Good,' Carol sighed. She knelt down and reverently kissed the tip of the cock, gazing up submissively at Faye. 'I'm your slave,' she whispered.

David and Mary gripped one another's hands. It was unspeakably thrilling to watch these two lovely girls sharing the first steps into advanced sexual deviation. Their fundamental innocence, their fresh-faced charm and loving tenderness, their striking and exciting young bodies, all combined to make the scene both electrifying and moving.

Faye took four black plastic straps from the cupboard and fitted them to Carol's wrists and ankles. Each strap had a shiny steel ring firmly attached. Then she took out four long red plastic cords.

'Bondage,' breathed David.

'They're so brave,' Mary sighed. She found the sight of these girls deeply thrilling and poignant.

David undid his jeans and pulled them down to reveal a full erection. Mary likewise pulled down her dark-red cotton slacks. Still watching the screens, they fondled one another's genitals.

Faye took Carol's hand and led her to the water bed. They got onto its warm, undulating surface.

'Are you ready to be tied up?' Faye asked in a small voice.

'No, I can never be ready for something so strange.' Carol laughed nervously. 'But I'm as ready as I'll ever be. Go on. We must try it.'

'I'm frightened.'

'So am I. But come on. Please tie me up.' Carol kissed Faye, and then she lay back spreadeagled on the water bed. She threw her long pale-gold hair out at both sides of her head. Tongue sticking out with concentration, Faye started to tie her courageous partner to the steel rings set in the floor. Anxiety and guilt made every movement of her fingers fumbling and clumsy.

'You can do it,' Carol said encouragingly.

'It's so strange,' Faye replied. Eventually she succeeded. The metal rings attached to Carol's wrist and ankle straps were tied by plastic cords to the metal rings in the floor beside the water bed.

'Oh, how strange!' Carol exclaimed, testing her bonds. 'I can't move. I'm your prisoner. It feels so sexy, I can't believe it. I want to come so much. But you have to tease me. Don't make me come even though I'll beg. Don't let me. Make me beg.'

'I'll try my best,' said Faye. She poured more baby oil on Carol's breasts, belly and thighs, massaging and teasing her, rubbing her own breasts on Carol's and kissing her mouth.

'Please, please, make me come,' Carol pleaded. 'Put your big dick in me and fuck me hard. I need it so much.'

'Oh, you dirty girl,' Faye replied, pretending to be shocked. 'You're so bad. If there were three men here you'd beg them to fuck you and come all over you, wouldn't you?'

'Yes, yes, I couldn't help it. Oh, Faye, if you love me really you have to fuck me now or I'll go mad.'

'I don't want to fuck you now, you're too bad. Dirty, bad girl. You don't deserve an orgasm. Besides, it's fun to tease you. I'm going to enjoy myself and you'll have to suffer. The more you suffer, the more fun I'll have. Serves you right. You're so bad you wanted to be tied up.' Faye held the dildo in her right hand and moved it back and forth, around and around, pressuring and churning her own pussy. The knobbly stem at the dildo's base was in her vagina, and soft rubber ridges engaged her labia and clitoris, so she was giving herself unusual and strong stimulation. Arching and squirming, sighing and moaning, it was obvious that the forbidden fruit she and Carol were consuming had aroused her to an extreme.

Desperation became all that Carol knew. The big strong girl, her taut lean body glossy with oil and sweat, writhed and shuddered in an exquisite agony of lustful tension, arching her long back, and straining her limbs in a fruitless struggle to escape her bonds and slake her overpowering lust. Only after many more minutes of teasing did she get what she demanded.

Lying on Carol's lovely body, clutching her broad shoulders, Faye pushed in the big dildo. Carol groaned and grunted, arching her back as the cock sank deep. Faye fucked her for all she was worth. Carol moaned with relief, and came quickly. After a long hard fuck, Faye tossed her head and gave a series of choking gasps as she too reached the heights of ecstasy, and Carol came again with loud cries, pleas and swearing.

Faye collapsed and could not move for several minutes. Then she untied Carol.

'Are you all right?' Faye asked anxiously.

'That was great!' Carol gasped. 'I can see why Mary and David play these games. It's just amazing to be tied up and helpless. We must keep on doing it, really. I have all sorts of ideas. It's so interesting, and you come like hell when you're tied up. I love being teased for a long time and then coming. Ordinary sex is great, but there's only so many things you can do. With domination you can do hundreds of different things.'

'Oh, I'm so relieved you liked it,' Faye exclaimed. 'I was so afraid I was doing it wrong, or you wouldn't like it, even though you made the plan and told me it'd be great. I enjoyed it too. I had such a weird sense of power, I feel like a new person.'

Babbling happily, the two girls undid the straps of Faye's body harness, taking it off, gently removing the dildo that gleamed with Carol's juices.

'They did great,' Mary told David. 'Amazing!'

'They have a natural talent for this, Mary,' he replied gravely. 'I feel sorry for them. Now that they've started, they won't be able to stop.'

'You don't feel very sorry for them.' Mary laughed, squeezing David's huge and rigid cock in her hand. 'Mainly you want to fuck them.'

'Them and you. Let's do it now, and watch the girls at the same time.'

David and Mary quickly stripped naked, and soon they were screwing on the big sofa, flowing from one position to another, massively stimulated by Faye and Carol's actions.

On the screen, the girls got into the red bath, which had been filling for a long time, and was brimming with water and banks of foam. They sighed and exclaimed in delight as they explored its remarkable length, breadth and width.

Happily, they played, hugging and kissing, stroking and squeezing, until they were burning with renewed youthful lust. Overcome with need, Faye lay back and braced her hands and feet against the sides of the scarlet bath as hot and wet and slippery as a cunt, offering her big breasts and slender beauty to her big strong partner, tensing her body so it rose from the water arched like a bow, gleaming so shiny and quivering with yearning. Grunting with lust, Carol mounted Faye, mashing her belly and tits against Faye's in a frenzy of mindless female hunger. It was a magnificent sight to see Carol's big powerful body in action, her broad and globular ass all muscle, as it rose and fell and humped with spectacular force.

Surely, both girls must come – but Carol stopped abruptly, pulling away from Faye.

'I'm going to tie you up and tease you now that you're all worked up,' she laughed excitedly. 'I'll do strange things to your breasts. I'll jerk off! Are you scared?'

'Yes,' Faye replied quietly.

'So you should be. I'm going to gag you too.'

Hearing these words from Carol, Mary too suddenly felt afraid, of David and of herself.

Five

'This is all very cosy,' David said at breakfast next morning. 'You and I together, like a sitcom. But you realise you're leaving today, right?'

'Whatever you say,' Mary replied, without the faintest trace of sincerity. 'But come on! You have to admit it was fun seeing Carol and Faye fool around in the bathroom.'

'It was fun if you like tricking innocent girls.'

'Which you do!' Mary exclaimed. 'Don't try to be moral, David. It's never quite convincing, coming from you.'

'I suppose not,' David agreed, with a brief flash of his old, childlike smile that Mary had once loved.

Or liked. Or been tricked by, she told herself. Anyway, no reason to feel warm and gooey from a glimpse of his smile, a fragment of his old, lost self like a tiny chip of bright stone from an ancient mosaic washed away by ancient cold rains.

'You're right, it was fun,' David admitted. 'But it was bad. I have to stop doing bad things because I go too far.'

'No, you don't have to stop. Trying to stop makes you depressed and lifeless. You have to indulge yourself, then you'll feel better. Let's do one more thing together, then I'll leave.'

'The same old story!' David said sharply, spearing a piece of bacon viciously with his fork. 'Just leave, Mary.'

'I'll tell you my idea anyway. Let's try to get Carol and Faye to join us for a scene in the bathroom.'

'You're nuts. They'd never do it.'

'Oh, I think they would. They're absolutely fascinated by what they can do in the bathroom, you saw that. They trust us and they're curious about us. They're in an experimental period. They feel isolated because they're two girls in love with one another. What more do you need? A printed invitation?'

'I suppose they might actually do it.'

'Sure they would! The first time, you'll promise not to touch them, because they're lesbians. Or they think they might be lesbians. Later on, the second or third time they join us, they'll be fooling around with you. The fifth or sixth time they'll be trying bondage and domination.'

'Whoa!' David exclaimed. 'You're making plans to stay weeks, then months, then years. I see it all. No way. You're leaving today.'

'OK.' Mary stayed quiet, though she was seething with anger and desperation and sadness and frustration and twenty or thirty other things. She stayed quiet for nearly a whole half-minute before she began to erupt. As soon as she started she felt like she had wanted to erupt for a long time. 'You make me sick! I come here and the place looks like shit and so do you. I cook and clean and I fuck you and I get Faye and Carol into your bathroom and I even get you some old science-fiction paperbacks, and what thanks do I get? All I get is you telling me to leave, every day.'

'If you'd leave I wouldn't have to say it every day, Mary. Anyway, thanks for the books.'

'It's too late to say thanks! And you thanked me for the wrong things of course. You must have done that deliberately.'

'Just a little bit. Mary, I –'

'Oh, shut up. Who wants to hear you talk? You're just a shadow of yourself, it's embarrassing to hear you talk now. You're so determined to be celibate and not be a dangerous sadist and not be involved with any human being. That's pathetic! You used to be a real man. Or at least you used to be some kind of a man. Maybe you were a shit, but all men are shits, you were just more open and honest about it.'

'I was an arsehole.'

'I know, but at least you were a strong and determined and confident arsehole. Or you gave a good impression. And you weren't totally an arsehole. Sometimes you were nice, you were almost human at times. In a certain light. Maybe deep down you're very good, a really nice guy, too good for this world, so you had to be a sadist to show what you thought of the world. To show your contempt, your hatred of all the crap in the world. I always suspected you were good despite all the evidence to the contrary, and despite my best efforts.'

'Jesus,' David murmured. He ate toast. Mary was annoyed that he could eat when she was pouring her heart out like this. She would stop him being so cool and calm like an ice Buddha. She would break through his reserve and make him angry just to show she could, just to prove she was as good as him, and not some crazy woman he need not get excited about. She would make him angry if it was the last thing she did, which knowing David was always a possibility.

'You are wrong, Mary. I'm bad. There's no good in me. That's why I have to give up all that bathroom domination stuff. It's too risky because I'm bad.'

'OK so you're bad, who gives a toss? The point is that at least in the past you had a kind of strength. Maybe it was a crazy and bad kind of strength, but that's a hell of a lot better than no strength at all. Look at you now! You can hardly get out of bed, and then you're so depressed and weak and aimless you don't know what to do with yourself. Whereas in the past you had strength. If you don't have strength and energy you don't have anything, and now you don't have any strength, because you're trying so hard not to be true to your own real self. Nothing can exist without strength, energy, power, so these things are the only really good things, because they make everything else exist, so you have to get back to the roots of your own strength and be your real self again. You have to be a sadist.'

David stared at Mary with some intricate mingling of fear and anger all mixed up and feeding on one another. She liked it when she got through to him like this and made him stop ignoring her. Let him do what he damn well pleased, but he could not ignore her.

'I think you're drinking too much coffee,' said David, obviously trying to stay cool. 'Your argument is the heart and soul of fascism.'

'So what? Why don't we go to the bathroom right now and do something perverted?'

'No way.'

'You're so pathetic nowadays. I can't stand it! You used to be something and now you're nothing. I won't allow it. It's nonsense. And it makes nonsense of my life as well as yours. Now you don't even have a life. You're too cowardly to listen to your own heart, let alone mine. Everybody has to be what they truly are, or there's no point in anything, anywhere, anytime. You have to be a sadist because that's what you truly are. Don't be frightened. You can do it. It'll be OK. Everything will be OK, I promise. Let me help you be what you are.'

'This is crazy,' David protested. 'You want to be Baron Frankenstein. You want to revive the monster, like in a Frankenstein sequel. All we need is a lightning storm.'

'Yes, that's a great idea! I love the classic Frankenstein movies. Do you remember when we watched *The Bride of Frankenstein* together? We used to have such fun in all kinds of ways. We love the same movies.'

'Don't get nostalgic, Mary. I can't stand nostalgia.'

76

'Oh, you can't stand anything nowadays. So, you're Boris Karloff and I'm Baron Frankenstein, and I've found you frozen in a block of ice and I'm going to revive you.'

'Don't you realise what a disaster that would be? Haven't you ever noticed that in every Frankenstein movie nothing good ever comes out of making or reviving the monster?'

'I know, but the Baron has to do it anyway, he can't help himself.'

'You'd end up as the bride, not the Baron. And look how Elsa Lanchester ended up. She was crazy, the monster was disgusted, and he destroyed the castle. Everybody died.'

'Oh, it's just an analogy,' Mary said dismissively. 'The point is you were strong in the old days. Think about what you did! You restrained me, you took all responsibility and choice away from me. I've never been so free as when you restrained me because I didn't have to do anything. And you were strong enough to chastise and punish me. Nobody else has ever had the guts to do that to me. You made me afraid, and so everything became a hundred times more intense and real and vivid, and an hour stretched into an eternity because I knew fear and humiliation and helplessness. All of the rest of my life only seems to occupy a few minutes compared to the millions of years I was your prisoner, your slave.'

Mary paused for breath. She was on the verge of panting. David had finally stopped eating, and his hands held his knife and fork in a motion half completed, so that he looked like a still from a film of a man eating breakfast. His eyes stared at Mary so intensely it looked like he could never blink again.

'You hurt me and humiliated me and made me so afraid, and so my old self, the normal boring person I used to be, broke up and shattered and all the pieces flew away so I could never have put them together even if I had wanted to, so I had to start again from scratch and make myself out of nothing, so I could be what I wanted to be. I can never be the sort of woman my parents and everybody else says I should be. And for that I thank you. Thank you, thank you.'

Mary laughed abruptly. Suddenly, she felt happy. Her laughter did nothing to reassure David, she was glad to see.

'You made me know myself. I could feel like we could feel the heat if the top came off hell, and there it was, hell. I came to know my every bone and muscle and organ and nerve. Gagged and whipped and confined and compressed by thirty leather straps and probed and caressed, mocked and teased and hurt, I couldn't daydream or sleepwalk or be anything fake like they said I should, they said I had to. No, when you made me helpless I knew I was real, it was me all alone inside this body of mine, and so I met myself and became myself and I knew nothing else existed, it was all lies and crap, there was just me and all my nerves tingling and nothing mattered any more except the next breath, one more long slow breath, and an orgasm as big as death seeming to get further and further away even as you forced me towards it slower and slower so it got further away and bigger, until finally, after a million years you made me come, and I was so helpless and so breathless, and it was bigger than death. So together, you and I, we beat death.'

Mary finished her coffee and shrugged, to show David how much she was in control of herself, how calm she could be even though she was insane. And she gave him a nice smile.

'I don't care if you think I'm crazy for talking like this. That's another great thing you taught me about myself. Now I know I really don't give a shit about anything, that's lovely. After what we did together, who cares about anything? It would be ridiculous.'

'You're not crazy,' David said quietly. 'That's what scares me.'

'I don't care either way. I was young and innocent and then I met you and your big cock and your bathroom and your collection, and then I wasn't so young and innocent any more, and that was good, because being so young and innocent was such total crap. End of story. That's all there is, there is no more. I'm whatever the hell I am and you're tired and depressed, washed-up. So according to you it's all over. Now there's just the boring real world where everybody goes to work when they don't want to and has children they hate. And they get into debt and think about what to buy next. And women read books on relationships. Boy, do we ever read a lot of books on relationships. And they get old and they die. You and I had everything once. We had it all in that bathroom, we had a world of our own and it actually was our world. Infinity, eternity, we had the lot. For a brief moment you and I were one, because you dared to be my master and I dared to be your slave. We weren't bored and lonely. Well, everything good comes to an end very quickly. The brave and the bold, the bright and the beautiful, all burn up in a flash and leave a lot of ash. What a mess. Crap wins. Loneliness conquers all. How sad it all is. How sad.'

Mary fell silent, having said everything she had held inside her all locked up and secret. She had brooded for many a day and night, and she had wept. Now she had given voice to all her pain and joy, and it felt good to have spoken once in all sincerity and without fear of being judged. Once and for all she had given voice. For the first time, she no longer cared what David thought of her, or what he did. She did not want revenge or an apology, she did not want love or suffering.

'So,' said David, 'you understand nothing. You don't understand me or anything I've said. You don't see any dangers. You just think I'm weak. Instead of congratulating me on my strength of will, you say I'm weak. Thanks. Thanks a lot.'

Mary was surprised by David's bitterness. She had thought he was invulnerable and beyond her reach, but now here he was getting pissed. Good. Progress at last. At once she lost all her indifference and her short-lived peace of mind.

'Why can't you praise me a little for trying to give up all that bathroom domination crap?'

'You're whining,' Mary sneered.

'OK, that's it,' David yelled. 'Come to the bathroom now and I'll show you how bad I am and how stupid you are. Submit to me.'

'No,' Mary replied.

'What? Why the hell not? That's what you've practically been begging me to do.'

'Well, now I've changed my mind. You haven't said anything nice to me, you haven't shown me any respect. You haven't even been polite. You should know that without politeness there isn't anything except garbage.'

'You crazy fucking bitch!'

'Thank you for proving my point.'

This, thought Mary, was it. This was the moment she had been waiting for. It was perfect. David wanted her now with all his heart and soul and cock. Now was the moment she had to leave once and for all, never to see David again. Then she could look back for the rest of her life on this, her final and crushing victory.

But she could not let go just yet. It was too interesting. Here was David all worked up. She was getting to him at long last. There had to be some way she could turn this to her further advantage and so win an even more stunning triumph.

An idea came to Mary that was so perverse and risky she knew she had to do it. She dug in her pocket, took out a dulled pound coin, and tossed it on the table. It bounced and spun, until it hit David's coffee cup with a satisfying ping. Shivering, it lay down and died.

'Toss you for it,' said Mary. 'Heads I submit to you and you can do what you like to me. Tails you submit to me and likewise.'

'You're even crazier than I thought. I never submit.'

'Up to you,' Mary said with an irritating shrug.

'OK, we'll do it,' David exploded. 'And you'll regret it. But that's your problem, not mine. You toss the damn coin. If I do it you'll say I cheated.'

'You would.'

Mary tossed the coin. She had a strong feeling it must be tails, because she was on a winning streak and she felt good, full of beans and piss and vinegar. The coin flew up into the air, flashing again and again with renewed life. Mary decided that if David submitted to her, she would not hurt him. Instead she would make him come again and again, so that he would miss her when she left. That would be a fine revenge. The coin nearly hit the ceiling, then started to fall. Mary caught the coin. She would win. She slapped the coin onto her left hand and held it out. It was heads. Quite a surprise. Yet it must be fate.

'Congratulations,' she said to David. In fact, she decided, this was just as good as tails, if not better. Now David would dominate her, and he would once again be an addict. Then she would leave him alone with his revived addiction. That would be another kind of win.

But when she saw the look in David's eyes she began to be afraid.

'Let's go,' he said.

Mary nearly refused. She was bigger and stronger than him after all, he could not force her to do anything. But she knew that if she left the house now she would feel she had been chicken. Never could she see it as a victory.

'All right,' she said.

So they entered that bathroom once more, where too much had already happened. Mary was afraid, but she was suddenly, almost sickeningly, aroused. My own body, she thought, is a traitor.

'Strip,' David ordered.

He and Mary undressed in silence. The bathroom was warm and bright, with sunlight gleaming on tiles and taps and stainless steel rings. When the man and woman both stood naked, David tossed and kicked their clothes and shoes out of the bathroom and closed the door. It was all too obvious that he was terribly angry, and Mary felt a tingle of fear that shuddered along every nerve of her body in a way that was intensely voluptuous. David's cock was fearful in its massiveness and quivering rigidity. Never had it looked so much like a dreadful weapon.

'Put this on,' David told Mary, taking a belt from the big cupboard that contained most of Mary's old nightmares.

Fingers fumbling with nervous clumsiness, Mary fitted it tightly around her waist. It was a broad, thick belt of strong, shiny black plastic, and firmly attached to it were eight shiny steel rings.

'Put these on,' David stated coldly. 'Ankles and wrists.'

Mary fitted the four black leather straps he gave her. Each of these also had an attached steel ring. Then David took four red cotton cords. He had Mary stand in the slanting patch of sunlight near the windows at one end of the bathroom. Her heart was beating very fast. This was it. She was once again submitting to this man. He had her spread her legs, and he tied the rings of her ankle straps to rings set in the floor. Then he told her to stretch her arms out as far as she could to either side and tied a cord to her right wrist strap. He passed it through a ring in the wall and pulled hard, then harder still, forcing her to lean forwards. She felt the stirrings of panic. Then he fastened the cord. David repeated the process for her left arm. Mary was forced to lean well forwards. It was already an extremely uncomfortable position.

How, she asked herself, could she have been so dumb as to submit? She regretted her compliance, and almost asked him to release her. But she knew he would not. In his eyes glittered a terrible excitement. She had awakened all his old cruelty. David had suppressed it and renounced it, and for many months it had been building up behind the dam of his willpower. She had finally shattered that dam, and there would come an appalling flood. It would wash her away like a dead leaf.

'You stupid bitch,' sneered David, as if he had been reading her thoughts. He tied two thin white ropes to rings on either side of the broad black belt she wore, and he pulled the ropes tight and tighter. And he pulled them tauter and tauter still, each in turn, and he fastened them to large steel rings set into the floor under her torso. Mary shuddered with fear and gave a little whimper.

David fetched a large black rubber gag attached to a set of black leather head straps.

'No, I'm afraid,' Mary whimpered. 'I've changed my mind, David, please, let me go. You were right, you have to try to give all this up, and I – mmph! Umph!' Suddenly he had thrust the gag home and stopped her panic-stricken babbling. It was huge and bitter in her mouth. With quick efficiency he fastened the straps that held it in place, reducing her voice to the mumblings of an idiot, meaningless and pathetic.

Locked straight and unbending, her long and shapely legs angled forwards. Her waist was held firmly down, so her magnificent ass, like two soccer balls side by side, was thrust out and up. Her stretched-out arms were rigid and high, raising her superb tits in total vulnerability. Encased and stretched in a network of straps and ropes, she was all rigidity and tension and sublime obscenity. Her brown eyes were wide as wide could be in amazement and fear. She gave David a beseeching look and burbled through her nose and the huge gag in her mouth. No, she could not stand this contortion for another moment. Such tension and distortion was an impossibility!

'You really are stupid,' David sighed. 'That's what's so depressing about life, the fact that people are just so hopelessly dumb. You let yourself be tied up. I can do anything I like to you now, anything at all. You should be ashamed.'

Lust pulsed dizzily in Mary's swollen, gaping genitals thrust out at David in utter submission and blatant invitation. She prayed he would use her helpless body ruthlessly, occupying her weeping, twitching hole with his huge and rigid cock. How could he resist? Now he must hurt her, punish her with absolute severity, and he would fuck her and fuck her, making her come again and again. She could come even from pure punishment. His strong hands cupped her full, sweating breasts, stroked the full, hard curves of her buttocks, and caressed her sensitive thighs and belly. Expert and ruthless, his cruel fingers pinched her huge rigid nipples, swollen cunt lips and hard, hungry clit. Moaning, she prayed for the stimulation of his cock or a whip. Agony or pleasure, she could ride either or both to the same goal.

'I'm not going to fuck you or whip you, you stupid bitch,' David stated harshly. 'You're too disgusting and stupid. You think you're so magnificent that no man can resist fucking you and whipping your bum. Even tied up and gagged you think you're the queen. But you're nothing to me, Mary. Absolutely nothing. I'm not even interested enough to feel disgust.'

Hands pumping his cock, David moved around Mary with clinical detachment, studying her purely as an image to serve his pleasure. He rubbed the huge shiny helmet of his cock on her belly and arse, but he did not enter her. He tweaked her nipples, twisting and pulling and squeezing, using his left hand, while serving his own cock with his right. Cruelly, he thrust his massive, hard penis against her sensitive breasts. Arms stretched taut upwards and outwards, waist held down and rigid by the belt and ropes, legs locked straight, Mary could only suffer. Laughing nastily, David moved to her arse, savouring the view, knowing he could do anything he liked, yet choosing to jerk off over her, to prove that she was not worthy of his cock or a whip.

With a terrible shout he came, showering Mary's bum and back with endless floods of cream, spraying and hosing her lovely body with absolute contempt. Mary wept. This was worse than anything she had dreamed of. How delightful in comparison would have been the thrust of his cock, or the burning sting of a whip!

'You see, I don't need you,' David gasped, after the last spurt of his incredibly prolonged climax. 'You're nothing to me. You're not good enough to be given anything.'

Sneering, he slowly massaged his deluge into her tits and over her back and arse. She was coated with cream, and her nostrils filled with the smell.

'You filthy bitch, you dirty slut,' David snarled. 'Flaunting your tits and arse and cunt like this! You love being helpless. You'll take anything from me, no matter what, so long as you have my attention. You don't want me to do anything worthwhile or to think clearly or to try and be a better person. You just want me to think about you all the time. The puritans were right, women are a snare.'

Mary saw that his cock showed no sign of subsiding. Instead, it was huge and pulsing and absolutely rigid. It was a machine out of control, an object to inspire terror.

'I've just come, yet I can't get soft, I have to come again and again,' David said with absolute loathing and disgust. 'Well, so what? It's meaningless. I'll just keep jerking off. I don't need to touch you. I don't need you in any way, Mary. When you're gone I'll remember how you look now and I'll jerk off when I have to.'

Abruptly, he fetched a black leather blindfold and fitted it to Mary, putting her into darkness. Then she heard him leave the room, though he quickly returned. Shockingly, she felt a ferocious burning between her buttocks.

'Relax, it's only an ice cube,' David sneered. 'Let it in right now. Don't fool around.'

Mary was too afraid to resist. She somehow managed to relax her muscles, and David forced the slippery, bitingly cold thing against her flesh, forcing entry. It felt huge! Crying out with shock and disbelief and pain, she felt it suddenly slip inside her, chilling her inside. The icy penetration horrified her, it was a total violation. Then he did it again. She heard a gurgling sound, and it was her. David was conquering her depths. With a third cube, he caressed her nipples and the head of her clit, making her every nerve scream.

'Don't let there be the slightest leak,' David ordered his gorgeously tensed and distressed victim. 'Don't you dare make any mess on my bathroom floor.'

Urgently, he masturbated and, in a surprisingly short time, he came again. His groans were terrible, making his orgasm sound like death.

'You bitch, you dirty whore,' he groaned, touching her all over. 'Why do you have to be so beautiful and so helpless? It's disgusting. You're pathetic. God, how I hate you.'

For some minutes Mary heard David walking around in the bathroom, sometimes muttering to himself and sometimes insulting her. He urinated. He took stuff from the cupboard and put it back. He took a shower. Cold.

'Damn you,' he said. 'I have to come again. And it's

all your fault. Why couldn't you just leave me alone? Was that so much to ask for?'

Mary was so frightened that she could not control her bladder.

'You filthy whore,' David snarled. 'You did that deliberately!'

Retaliation came swiftly. A sharp crack resounded in the room. Mary squealed and wept and struggled in blind panic, but for all her ludicrous exertions she could not move an inch or even beg for mercy as a series of vicious blows landed on and between the taut ripe cheeks of her superb arse. Fire burned through every fibre of her body and soul, nothing existed but over-powering pain. Never had Mary known such pure, fiery agony. With every terrible blow, she prayed he would stop, but he went on hitting her like a machine, incapable of knowing exhaustion. He struck all her totally vulnerable nudity. Mary's every muscle ached from her writhings and spasms, the pointless struggles that made her body the picture of female failure and futility.

Thousands of years later, it seemed, David threw down his leather tawse and thrust his massive cock into the dark red and hugely swollen lips of Mary's blatantly displayed cunt. Endlessly, he fucked her with ruthless male power, churning the depths of her body and soul with the irresistible force of his solid, weighty penis. Unwilling, horrified, Mary nevertheless came quickly, and was stunned and appalled by the length and force of her orgasm. She was ripped apart by shattering ecstatic explosions, and rebuilt in strange forms. And soon she came again, no matter how she fought her own rapture.

At last David came, with fearsome cries and a long drawn-out croaking, choking sound in his throat like a hideous death rattle. When he had finished, he set about freeing her and tried to hide his nervousness. What if she went for his throat?

Mary hurried to the nearest shower on her release and sobbed and grimaced as she used floods of cold water to ease the fiery stinging of her abused body. Quickly, she regained control of herself by a determined act of will. It was vital that she did not break down in floods of tears or lash out at him. She had to capture David's imagination by not doing what he expected.

'That did us both some good,' she said casually after turning off the shower. 'And it'll be even more fun when I get Faye and Carol in here to join us.'

'You're insane! They'll never agree, and if by some strange and stupid miracle they did, I'd never have anything to do with them.' David was obviously dismayed that Mary's ordeal had not broken her spirit.

Mary simply smiled a mocking smile. Already she was feeling better. She had made David dominate and fuck her against his will. In reality she had won.

'We'll have to wait a few days before we get Carol and Faye to join us,' she said, holding her sore arse. 'Otherwise the marks of the tawse would scare them.'

'A few days!' David exclaimed. 'You'll drive me nuts.'

'Ignore me. I'll clean the house and cook. We can go shopping for new equipment. The old rubber helmets are perished. Wow, Faye and Carol in rubber!'

'You're crazy. And you're leaving.'

'OK,' Mary replied, knowing he would change his mind. He was still too depressed and confused to chase her away.

Mary had not yet begun to submit.

Six

Drizzle filled the air nearly the whole of the next day, but Mary was cheerful and busy. She did a lot of housework and shopping, as well as cooking. By the end of the day, David's house was in a much better state than it had been, and Mary felt she understood a great truth: it was good simply to work, and to feel useful. If only David had not avoided her so much, the whole day might even have been worth living.

Next day was a Sunday. After lunch, David made an announcement. 'I've got to persuade you to leave, Mary. You're in danger if you stay here. I'm in danger because you keep tempting me to go too far. Carol and Faye are in danger because of your crazy plan to get them involved with us.'

'It's not so crazy. They love the bathroom, and you'd love to have them join us there.'

'Of course, but the point is that it's all wrong,' David explained slowly and carefully, as though, Mary thought, he truly believed she was a crazy woman. How strange he was!

'No words of mine can persuade you, Mary, because you just ignore anything I say about wanting to be alone.'

'Yes, because you don't know what's good for you. And you don't even mean it.'

'You see? And it's no use my being cruel to you. You get satisfaction from that because at least I'm paying attention to you. When I dominate you, you just come and come, so that just makes you want to stay.'

'You understand me,' Mary said. 'I like that too, though I shouldn't admit it.'

'So I have a plan to persuade you to leave. I've arranged a scene at that house in London I told you about once. Remember?'

'Yes. You stopped going before you met me, because you preferred intimacy to group scenes.'

'Right. Now, you have a straight choice. You can leave me today, or you can come with me to this house, to be dominated by a bunch of silly upper-class prats who think of themselves as an elect secret society. The experience will be so bad that it'll make you determined to leave me.'

'What if I refuse both alternatives?' Mary inquired.

'Then we get involved with the police, and a court case which would be incredibly messy. But if I'm forced to prosecute you for illegal occupation of a dwelling, stalking or whatever, I promise you I will.'

'Difficult. This is difficult,' said Mary, feeling sad that David could be such a fool. It was disappointing. Why could he not simply be glad that she was there, and beg her to stay?

'We can't go on like this,' David said abruptly.

'Yes, yes, I know everything you're going to say,' Mary told him. 'I'm an evil woman who leads you back into the radioactive badlands of sadomasochism, and you're the good man who wants to dedicate his life to celibacy, carpentry and collecting science-fiction paperbacks published before 1971. You're good, I'm bad, you don't want to screw up Carol and Faye's tender young minds, and you want me to go away. Why do you keep saying the same things all the time? It's pretty boring. I suppose you want to pretend you have a conscience.'

90

'You're right, Mary. I do keep on saying the same old things to you. But this is different. This time it's for real. Make your decision. Leave or be dominated by a group.'

'I need a week to make a decision like that. Not that there are any decisions like that.'

'Of course you need a week. What you actually have is five minutes.'

'Please, David, at least tell me a little about this scene. What are the rules? The limits? Is it dangerous?'

'Of course it's not physically dangerous for you, because that's just what I'm striving to avoid,' David replied, clearly trying hard to keep his temper. 'Give me credit for some sense. I'm not stupid. Of course you won't get any permanent marks or be in physical danger, including the danger of disease. No man will penetrate you, but you'll have to serve men and women. If I go into all the details the scene will lose all its effectiveness, so no more details. The end. Decide.'

'OK. I agree,' said Mary, though the words seemed to stick in her throat. She felt dazed and afraid. 'Wait a minute, you're going too fast. What happens afterwards? What if I insist on staying here – or try to stay here, with you – after I've endured this ordeal?'

'Then we'll visit this group again. A week later, say. Until you've had enough. But I think once will be enough to persuade you to leave me alone.'

Two hours later, they left David's house and drove to London. Mary was very nervous, yet she still had some hope.

Hope was something she kept coming back to, after every lousy and hopeless experience of her life, so even now, sitting in the car on the way to what David assured her was sheer nastiness, she still found some kind of hope in the idea that, if she submitted to strangers and suffered terrible humiliations and chastisements, then David would come to regard her with some genuine emotion, whether it was pity or admiration. Or even disgust. Disgust was better than nothing.

On arrival at an imposing house in Kensington, a serious-looking security guard checked David's identity, then allowed him to drive into an underground car park. David led Mary to a small room with three white doors on the ground floor. It had a look of bareness. He carried a briefcase.

'Here we can get you ready,' he told her. 'It's still not too late to change your mind, but soon it will be too late. Once it's started, that's it. It'll go on no matter what.'

'I understand,' Mary replied. She was almost shaking. 'But I can't back out now. I'd despise myself. And I'd always be curious. I know, I know: curiosity killed the cat.'

First they undressed, and then they used the shower and toilet in the tiny adjoining bathroom. David opened his briefcase, and took out a gag, a helmet, a pair of gloves, and a pair of pants, all in scarlet rubber. Mary shivered. At the urging of David, she drank some water, and ate some biscuits for energy, though she could hardly swallow. Then David dressed her for her ordeal. First he put on her thin, stretchy rubber pants, which had very tight elasticated waist and legs. They also had a fitted, flexible dildo inside. Mary accepted this into her vagina without pleasure. Then she placed into her mouth the rubber bulb gag, which had a short breathing tube through its centre. Then the rubber helmet. This had holes for her eyes, nostrils and the tube of the gag, and a larger hole at the back for her hair to pass through. David carefully fitted the helmet so it was smooth. He put a band around her shoulder-length dark-chestnut hair to arrange it in a neat ponytail. The long neckpiece of the helmet lightly embraced her throat. Lastly, she put on the long latex gloves, which had no fingers, simply a closed end which made it difficult for her to move her fingers at all, as it was so tight. Oddly enough, this minor detail disturbed her more than the gag, helmet and pants with internal dildo. The gloves were tautly stretched around her arms and hands like big condoms, and felt strangely dehumanising.

In the large adjustable mirror that stood in one corner of the small bare white room, Mary gazed at herself in awe and fear. She looked like pure sex, a delectable victim, so tall and shapely. And just like this, she was going to present herself to a group of strangers. Perverts. How she would turn them on, whether she wanted to or not! David was already highly aroused, his cock huge and upright, like a police truncheon.

'Put on a good show, Mary,' he encouraged her. 'Don't embarrass me and yourself in front of all these people, even if they are phonies and twats.' He could not help smiling at his own contradictory feelings towards the group. 'First off, you'll bring off a few men by hand. Make them come over you. Do it well, OK? Be sexy, try to please them and excite the audience. They've seen and done it all, so they'll be bored and angry if it's a dull show. Better to keep on their good side by being a star turn, right?'

Mary nodded in agreement, feeling more afraid by the second. She felt she had made another stupid mistake in agreeing to come to this place, but she was too stubborn to try to back out now. How cowardly it would seem to her afterwards! Perhaps David had expected her to refuse, and the whole thing might be a bluff. That would be funny. She looked into his eyes and saw his anticipation. No, it was not a bluff.

He picked up the phone, said that they were ready, listened. 'We'll wait a few minutes,' he told Mary. 'Have a seat.'

They waited for what seemed to Mary like a long time, and she began to feel like crying. The phone rang. David picked it up, listened briefly, put it down.

'You're on,' he told Mary. 'Walk tall. Look proud. Win the crowd of fools over. Follow instructions instantly.'

He opened one of the white doors and led Mary through it and along an empty passage, then opened another white door, ushered her inside a totally dark room, followed her in and shut the door behind them. Mary could see nothing in the darkness. She stood there in mounting terror.

Abruptly, several lights came on, and they all seemed to be directed at her. At first she was dazzled. As her eyes adjusted, she saw that she was in a large room, facing over thirty people, more than she had expected. Most were naked. They sat or lay on armchairs, sofas, heaps of cushions, all of which were black, as were the curtains, carpet, walls and ceiling.

'This is Mary,' said David. 'Such a beautiful body, and such an annoying character.'

Mary remembered to stand up straight, and tried not to show her fear. Murmurs of appreciation spread around the room, and Mary heard favourable comments on her superb breasts, narrow waist, long, powerful legs and firm round arse that helped her regain a little of her usual confidence.

'Play with yourself, Mary,' said David. 'Arouse us all.'

It was terrible for Mary to do anything in front of so many people, but if she showed shyness or fear she sensed their mockery would be savage. She and David would both look foolish. Besides, several naked men and women were already caressing each other or casually masturbating, which helped. So Mary began to put on a show. Caressing her breasts, pulling on her big nipples, rubbing the crotch of her rubber pants, thrusting out her rear and stroking it, she gradually aroused herself as well as the group. The dildo began to be welcome.

'Now bring off a man or two, Mary,' David ordered.

Two naked men came towards her as David led her to a black rubber sheet covering soft cushions. He took a large tube of lubricant gel and squirted some on her hands, breasts and inner thighs. One of the men who approached her was middle-aged and overweight, the other younger and muscular. They began to caress Mary and, after a moment's hesitation, she touched their cocks, which quickly grew rigid. Never, despite all she had done with David, had Mary imagined she could ever do such a strange and whorish act, but now she did it. What else could she do? She tried to think of it as a gift for David even if he did not deserve any gifts, a proof of her obedience. Never would he find a more exciting woman. She would be so dirty and thrilling that he would eventually have to beg her to stay with him forever.

Such thoughts helped her, and she threw herself into the task of pleasing two men. She handled their cocks with enthusiasm and skill, stroking and squeezing them tightly. Kneeling before them, she rubbed both their knobs on her breasts at the same time, using her huge hard teats to rub against every part of the big gleaming heads of their cocks, while holding their shafts tightly, one in each hand. Then the elder man lay down, so Mary went on all fours and took his penis in her rubber-sheathed and lubricated hands, proffering her arse to the younger man, who rubbed his tool on her rubber pants, then put it between her shiny thighs and humped back and forth with moans of delight. After trying several other positions, the elder man had Mary jerk him off over her breasts, deluging them with floods of sticky cream, and then the younger man came all over her back, crying out loudly as he hosed her long, lean torso with powerful leaping spurts.

Shuddering, Mary felt degraded. This was disgusting. But it would be stupid to stop now, before she had even come. Besides, she saw that David was staring at her in fascination, idly handling his cock. She had to capture his imagination. She would not break, as he doubtless thought she would. To her surprise, a gorgeous nude woman who looked like a model came and licked her back clean, then kissed the young man who had come there. A loving couple. Then three men came to Mary. One lay down and arranged her so she lay on top of him, face up, his penis between her thighs, while the other two knelt on either side of them. She handled their cocks well and, to her surprise, realised she was becoming strongly aroused. It made her feel she must be truly crazy and bad, like David seemed to feel she was, but there was no getting away from the simple truth of her need.

Nobody spoke to her, not even to mock her. Instead, they treated her as if she were mindless, a body without any personality. Nobody even looked her in the eyes, except David. It seemed everyone was following some kind of script, probably written by David, and the only person who knew nothing about it was Mary herself, a thought she found frightening. One of the men in her hands came over her breasts, then two women, one naked and one in red underwear, came to suck and caress the other two until they came, spattering Mary from her knees to her head with leaping spurts.

Feeling dazed by her dehumanising treatment, Mary was then taken to a large bathroom upstairs and thoroughly washed in complete silence, as though she were a laboratory animal being prepared for an experiment of some nastiness. When they returned to the black room, Mary noticed that the party was really getting somewhere, with several couples screwing, other groups caressing each other, and a few men and women casually masturbating. Then she had a shock: David sat on a couch with a naked woman on either side, and they were handling his penis while he caressed their bodies.

Mary told herself it was ridiculous to be shocked. Obviously, David had planned to do something with other women, to make her, Mary, feel lousy. Obvious, yes, but Mary had somehow assumed he would only touch her. She had not expected him to ignore her. Yet she was angry with herself, not David. How could she have been so naive?

Gently but firmly, the four women lay Mary on black silk sheets, under which were cushions. A large woman in her forties wearing black bra, panties, suspender belt and stockings, got on top of Mary and sucked her nipples in turn, turning her on so much she hardly noticed that her arms were being stretched out above her head. Abrubtly, leather straps closed around her wrists. Startled, Mary instinctively struggled, but the woman on top of her was too heavy to throw off. She rode Mary, baring her teeth in a chilling grin of animal excitement. Almost before Mary could even grasp what was going on, her legs had been forced well apart and immobilised by ankle straps attached to chains that were fixed firmly to the floor. Mary was tautly stretched out and utterly helpless. There was scattered applause for the four women who had put her into restraint.

Struggling uselessly, Mary tried to call for help, but her gag made her words into a meaningless animal cry. She told herself not to become hysterical, as that would only make her suffering worse. It was obvious not one person in the room would help her. Indeed, most of them were not even watching her, including David, which was deeply unpleasant. If she were foolish enough to offer herself as a victim to these nasty perverts, they should at least have paid rapt attention to her suffering. She told herself to relax. Not panic.

Grinning wolfishly, the woman on top of her rubbed her breasts and pubes on Mary's, grinding down on her helpless body. Mary speculated about how normal and polite this nasty bitch surely was when she was in the outside world, pretending to be sane.

Grunting, the woman on Mary came. Then she spat several times on Mary's body and helmeted head. Immediately, two of the other women, young and naked, one big-breasted and the other flat-chested, applied clear plastic hemispheres about three inches across to Mary's breasts. A tube led from each to a rubber bulb with a valve, and when they squeezed the bulbs, air was sucked out of the hemispheres and her nipples expanded greatly. It was not painful, but acutely alarming. Mary struggled fruitlessly and made noises through her gag, then forced herself to stop. To panic would indeed be dreadful. The big-breasted woman, a beautiful blonde, got on top of her and rubbed her body on Mary's with the breast suction devices in place. Two elderly men, aroused by their sadism, came to caress their bodies and gloat over the prisoner's helplessness. The discomfort of Mary's teats increased by the minute, and she suffered too from the heat generated by her latex garments and her own fear. Then they removed the suction cups, though her nipples remained huge. And then she heard David's voice, and it was the start of the real horror.

'I'd like to thank everyone for coming here today,' he announced, like the chairman of some boring meeting. 'I'd like to explain about Mary, over there, and myself.' His voice was loud and clear, and everybody paid attention to him even if some of them were having some kind of sex at the same time. 'I first met Mary nearly three years ago, and I dominated her. She took to it like a fish to water. Unfortunately for both of us, I went too far. She was so beautiful, so submissive. Sexually submissive. Usually she's stubborn. About two years ago she left me. I'd been too cruel. She did the right thing. Since then I've been trying to break myself of my old habits. But recently she came back to me, and she

98

tempted me. She encouraged me to start again. So submissive, yet so determined as well. So stubborn. She wouldn't leave me alone. She even had a crazy plan to seduce two innocent girls, to dominate them. You see, Mary just wants me to be my old self: a sadist. It's dangerous for her, and for me. But she's stubborn. So I brought her here to learn just how bad I am. And what contempt I have for her. Because really, she's an annoying bitch.'

Mary screamed through her gag and struggled to break her bonds. Gasping with excitement, the woman on top of her rubbed her body harder and harder on Mary's, and came, so turned on was she by David's story and Mary's absolute humiliation. She rolled off, panting. The big woman went on all fours, over Mary, her rear above Mary's head, and a very hairy man took her from behind, their coupled genitals inches from Mary's eyes. Never had Mary dreamed of such suffering, such insane humiliation. She had been able to endure reasonably well until David started speaking, but now it was unbearable agony to have so many people listen to David saying she was bad and crazy. All the physical suffering she had ever endured now seemed a trifle compared to this spiritual horror.

'Of course,' David continued, 'Mary, if she could speak, would tell the same story in a completely different way. That's the funny thing about stories. She would say something like this: I introduced her to domination, and she liked it. Before that she'd hardly thought of it, the whole scene was outside her experience, and she would have gone on as content as anyone else if she'd never had any experience of it. I disturbed her equilibrium, I messed up her life, by giving her a taste for domination. That's the first point Mary could make, and it's perfectly valid. Then she might talk about how she came to see me again a week or so ago, and she found me living in solitude, with the house a mess. I admit it was a mess, but I was going to clean it all up soon anyway. It's my affair if I choose to do housework once every month or two instead of wasting time doing it every day.'

Mary wanted to say that he was lying, that he would never have tidied the house, but gagged and bound as she was, underneath a copulating couple, her opportunities for communication were distinctly limited.

'So from her point of view, she felt she ought to stay and help me, as my house was a mess and I seemed depressed,' David continued, calmly, the voice of reason in a big black room full of unreason. 'Of course, she probably had some subconscious reasons as well. Sexual motivation. But she could say that she was trying to help me, to wake me up a bit, to make me happy. Mary might well say that I'm an ungrateful pig not to be grateful to her, and in a way she'd be right. But the point is, I really do want to be alone. I want to live as a hermit, having nothing to do with her or anyone else. We should all have the right to live as we choose, or what's the point of being alive? Perhaps one day next month or year I'll get fed up with being a hermit, and then I'll do something else. Whatever I choose to do. But it's my life and my decision to make, not Mary's.'

While David had been giving his version of Mary's point of view, a version that was a parody to her mind, the big woman and hairy man screwing above her had both come. The man pulled out and the woman stood with open legs over Mary's head, dripping like a faulty tap while two men caressed her. Finally, the hairy man licked clean Mary's helmet.

'So there you have it,' said David. 'I want Mary to leave me alone, and she keeps refusing to go. I brought her here to help her make up her mind to leave, and it's good of you all to help bring her to her senses. Now perhaps some of you would enjoy telling Mary what you think of her.'

100

Mary's nightmare now reached a new depth of horror. About twenty people, mostly naked, formed a ring around her. Most of them were groping, kissing or masturbating. Excited and aroused, they were like a gang of bullies at school, only much, much worse.

Taking pleasure in their own nastiness, they began to deliver their verdicts.

'What kind of woman annoys a man by hanging around when she's not wanted? Have some sense, woman.'

'Like a bitch in heat. Why don't you see a shrink?'

'There are three billion men in the world, for God's sake. Surely you can find one who actually wants you?'

'I actually want you. Have me instead of David.'

'She's fixated on David, darling. She doesn't want you.'

'Stupid cunt. Every cock is just a cock.'

'She's just stubborn. Admit it, you're just stubborn. It's stupid.'

'It certainly is stupid. Look at her. You can see how stupid she is. It's written all over her.'

'Silly, sad, pathetic slut. Ugh.'

'So what if you have a great body? Stop being so arrogant.'

'Yes, it's sheer bloody arrogance to act like she does.'

'You're a stalker, dear. And everybody hates stalkers.'

'You see where throwing yourself at a man has got you? He doesn't want you. Get that through your thick head.'

'Face facts, love. It's all over. Really it is.'

'Stop being so totally pathetic, you silly pathetic bitch.'

This went on for many minutes, with people leaving or joining the ring around Mary as they chose. Some of them poured their drinks over her, and a few spat. Two more men came over her, and it became a popular game to fire rubber bands at her, aiming for her nipples.

Eventually David said something, and a black sheet was taken away to reveal a huge wooden frame with metal rings inside its four corners. It stood against a wall, and Mary knew its purpose. She struggled as her limbs were freed, but so many people, laughing with cruel amusement, held her arms and legs that all her efforts were useless. Then her rubber pants were pulled off, and she was quickly placed inside the frame, standing on its leather-padded bottom strut. The chains from her ankle and wrist straps were connected to the rings at the corners of the frame, putting her into helpless restraint and, as a final degradation, big black cushions were piled between her body and the wall so that her arse was thrust far out, and she stood there presenting her buttocks and genitals to a roomful of sophisticated perverts with her arms, legs and torso in high-tension bondage.

Stomach churning with fear, she tried to plead for mercy through her gag, amusing her audience with animal sounds. A remarkably tall black woman came slowly towards her, carrying a leather cat-o'-nine. Cheers and applause greeted her. She wore only a white leather domino mask and matching long gloves, and her slender body was all feline grace. What sickened Mary was not so much the threat of the whipping as the fact that it was to be done by a stranger, not by David. She knew that this was his way of proving he was through with her. It showed his contempt.

But when the black woman struck Mary across her arse with no warning, no teasing preparation, Mary stopped thinking about David, because it was impossible to have anything in her mind except the pain of the blow. It burned and stung intolerably, yet she had to tolerate it because she had no choice. Appalled by her vulnerability, she shuddered and moaned. Sweat poured down her skin. Her buttocks seemed to be on fire, yet that was only the first blow. Never had she felt so nude, so helpless. It felt impossible that any human being could be so well trussed, so entirely naked. She was a vulnerable bound animal in high-tension restraint, presenting to a cruel crowd her buttocks and genitals. All these people were taking pleasure in her torment.

Minutes passed. Mary might almost have welcomed more blows to end the terrible tension of waiting, but instead she was untouched for a long time. Men and women clustered around her tormentor, exchanging kisses and caresses, and many of them started screwing near Mary, facing her so they could witness her suffering and enjoy it as a stimulation.

Suddenly, the cat cracked, and the very ends of the hissing tails touched Mary's right thigh, making the slightest and briefest of contacts, yet stinging and burning Mary's skin like a touch of fire. Then followed a dozen feints, none of which made contact. Mary's flinching caused great amusement. The next three blows made the slightest of contacts with her arse, and the four subsequent strikes grazed her back with fiery kisses. Five feints, and then six strikes to her thighs, heavy and harsh blows indeed, rapid and loud. An elderly man kissed the black woman's feet, while a fat man licked her buttocks as a thin Indian girl suckled on his penis.

Ice was applied to Mary's thighs, and at first it was soothing, but soon her skin burned terribly, and she guessed that the ice was frozen vinegar or lemon juice. Then the tails of the cat hissed up between Mary's legs, making slight yet fearsome contact with her sensitive flesh. Eight blows came to her buttocks next, at unpredictable intervals. An old man crawled to lick her reddening arse, and masturbated to orgasm. A woman in her forties, with a neurotic appearance, touched Mary's buttocks, then sank to the floor to be fucked by her husband, while pretending to resist.

What skill the woman with the cat displayed as she sent the leather tails hissing around Mary's sides to land the slightest of kisses on her breasts! Slight, yet intensely painful, owing to the high velocity imparted to the tails. Everybody in the room, with one exception, admired such finesse, so complete a mastery of technique. There followed seven heavy and shocking blows to Mary's arse. Wriggling and weeping, howling through her gag, sweating and straining, Mary burned in a hell of suffering. Mindless, she was utterly overwhelmed by pain, humiliation and degradation.

Moans of ecstasy filled the room as several couples tensed in the rapture of orgasm that so closely resembles agony. Mary was left to burn for several minutes before the black woman landed one last telling blow, perfectly aimed, between her buttocks. Gleaming with sweat, the superb sadist dropped the cat and lay down to receive lustful tributes of flesh from her many admirers.

When David came to stand behind Mary, she could hardly pay any attention to him, so wrapped up was she in her own body. Even though two gorgeous young females jerked him off over Mary's buttocks, she could not hate him, or even truly notice his presence. He and everything else in the world had lost all their former importance, which now seemed spurious, mistaken, perhaps even a series of lies told to her by the world about the world. Now Mary could only believe in her own suffering.

David groaned. He spurted. His huge cock painted the symbols of his victory in vivid white on reddened, abused, curvaceous flesh.

'Now then, Mary,' panted David. 'Let's call it quits. You see everyone here is full of beans. This could go on all night. Be sensible. I'll remove your gag. You promise to leave me alone. Then you can go. If you say anything else, the gag goes back.'

It was clear to Mary, even in her state of near panic, that she should promise to leave David alone. By now that was all she wanted to do anyway. Never to see him again would be fine. Besides, she could always break her promise if she wanted to – what could David do, sue her for breach of contract?

So she would promise. He removed her gag. She bit his right index finger and he howled. Only when somebody struck her across the arse with the leather cat was David able to pull his finger away from Mary's vengeful teeth. Three women rushed over in a fury, and replaced Mary's gag.

'Take her to the next stage,' David gasped, clutching his finger. 'You're an animal, Mary. But you're going to be cured of wanting to be in my bloody bathroom.'

When Mary's arms were released from the wooden frame, she resisted, but was helpless in the clutch of so many hands. Her wrists were shackled behind her back and, when her legs were released, the crowd soon transferred her ankles to the restraint of a dark, heavy wood leg stretcher, which held her legs far apart, forcing her to display her swollen cunt. Then the excited men and women carried her off like a trophy to a large bathroom, dominated by a huge black bath sunk into the floor. It was full of foaming hot water. A pair of ravishingly beautiful young women with long blonde hair were in the bath, playing with waterproof vibrators.

Laughing like cruel mermaids seeing a sinking ship, they welcomed Mary as a new toy to play with. Her gag was removed, and a swimming mask was put over her eyes and nose. She opened her mouth to speak, but could only shriek as she was picked up by a dozen hands and placed into the deep waters of the bath.

Seven

Slowly, very slowly, Mary came to her senses. She was lying in bed. She reviewed the beds of her life: was she in her parents' home? No. Her flat in Leeds, or David's house? No and no. All at once the events of the day and night before hit her mind like a blow, the hammer blow of wakefulness, the end of sleep, the resumption of suffering. She lurched out of bed and staggered to the window with its closed curtains of green. Her movements were slow and clumsy, her thinking a chaos of humiliations, her limbs ached, her pussy and nipples were tender, and her thighs, arse and back were smarting.

Opening the curtains she saw an unfamiliar view. Trees and fields on a lovely summer's day. It would have been better if it had been cold, grey and drizzly, to reflect her mood. Suffering was always harder to bear when the weather was good, and what made it even worse was the feeling that somebody somewhere was happy, the selfish bastard. Mary thought that she herself might have been capable of great joy if only everything in her life had gone differently, from her birth to the present moment. Was that so much to ask?

Dazed, she looked around the unfamiliar room and saw a large sheet of paper on a desk next to her bag. The large, confident handwriting on the paper was also unfamiliar:

Dear Mary,

Thank you for a wonderful time. I paid for five nights in advance, so you can stay here and have a good rest. The money is in your bag, and your car is in the car park. I tell you all this because you had a bit too much to drink last night. This hotel is near Reading, in case you forgot that as well.

Thanks for everything,

Rex.

Mary put down the note, looked in her bag, and found a thousand pounds in fifties. Her first impulse was to flush the money down the toilet, but then it struck her that if she were ever to take revenge on David, it would be of real use. She had to think clearly first. Now she could not think at all, let alone think clearly.

Her mouth was very dry. She saw a small fridge and opened it, to see cheese, butter, salmon, ham, her favourite chocolates. And there were two large loaves of wholemeal bread on top of the fridge. Mary drank some water, sat on the bed, and was asleep again before she knew it. When she awoke again, she found her watch and saw that it was nearly five. She felt a little less dizzy and confused. It dawned on her that she had been sedated in order to get her here without her being able to make a fuss. At the end, had there not been an elderly man who assured her that he was a doctor, and given her an injection?

Tea. She wanted tea. When love has gone, and gone in stereo at that, Jack and David as twin speakers, and you have lost all faith in the human race and in life itself, when you hate yourself and see clearly that all the world is just evil, stupidity and suffering, nothing but a big piece of shit, there is still tea. So Mary pulled on some clothes, rang room service and had a pot of tea brought up.

Sitting alone again, she looked out of the window at the lovely blue sky with fluffy white clouds, at the trees and the birds and the fruitful fields, and she suddenly decided not to fall into complete despair after all, no matter how tempting and basically right and true it was to despair. This, she thought, is the only truly important decision it is possible for any human being ever to make: I decide not to despair. All other decisions, by comparison, are just yesterday's vomit.

Appetite had she none, but she ate anyway. Surely life was nothing but a miserable, lonely and pointless fight to the death against overwhelming odds, but so what? She would eat to keep up her strength for the fight.

Her bum and thighs stung a little, but not too badly. She undressed to study her skin, and saw only some reddened areas, nothing dramatic. If she went to the police, they would think she was making a fuss about nothing. The marks did not seem as bad as Mary expected, remembering more details of last night, and she wondered if some soothing cream had been applied after she had been sedated. Those perverts really were methodical to a fault, indeed a whole bunch of faults.

Really, there was no point, Mary decided, in going to the police. It was not simply that she could prove nothing about her terrible ordeal, but also that she had in fact consented to it. David had set out the terms, she had agreed to them and the terms had not been broken. Besides, she was not even truly angry about the physical, sexual domination she had voluntarily endured. Rather, it was the way David had so thoroughly humiliated her in public and then discarded her like a piece of dirty rubbish that shocked her to the core. She could have enjoyed the whole thing if it had been done by David with love instead of hate – no, contempt. Hate is a fresh and invigorating emotion compared to contempt.

Wonder and a kind of pleasant fear filled Mary as she realised she was not sure what to do now, or even where to go. Everything had come to an end. That was frightening, but it was also a kind of liberation. She had always loved freedom, and to bring everything in her life to an end was freedom. Her job had come to an end when she lost her temper, Jack had been well and truly ended when she dominated him in that hotel room, and now the story of her and David had gone from her mind because he had brought the whole thing to a shattering climax. Usually people thought it was sad when anything came to an end, but even in her dazed and unhappy state, Mary wondered if there might not be at least as much good in ends as beginnings. An end was the end of suffering, a beginning was only the bloody start.

What did you do when everything came to an end? It seemed to Mary that she must not fall back into old ways and habits, but instead be new, fresh. Not start anew, as she could not even think of anything to start, but be new. That was fine, but what was she actually going to do, and where was she to live? The idea of going back to her flat in Leeds seemed ridiculous. Even that flat seemed to have come to an end, she could hardly believe it still existed. She felt she had no more reason to be in Leeds than anywhere else. As for people, who the hell cared about people? It was so much better to be alone. The human race? What was that? A lot of people straining their guts out to win and so make everybody else look and feel bad? What were the prizes for this race? Who were the organisers, where was the audience? It all seemed pretty fishy to Mary, this whole business of the human race. The fix was in, some of the runners were doped, the handicapping system was a fucking joke, the whole thing was rigged. She refused to believe for one more second in this crap race from the rubbish tip to the graveyard, from being bullied at school to being drugged and mistreated in an old people's home. A race against time, the race of the century. Fuck off, fuck off, fuck off.

Before 10 p.m., Mary was asleep again. When she awoke next morning she had a hearty breakfast, then went for a long walk. Her various aches, her soreness and tenderness, had almost faded completely. How full the world was of things to look at, touch, smell, and listen to! And there were people everywhere, though most of them seemed tired and discontent. What stops us, Mary wondered, from being happy, right here and now? Are we missing the point? Why are so many people, especially me, so well and truly fucked up? She decided to be strong and competent from then on, but when she got back to her hotel room she felt so lonely and depressed that she cried for an hour, then ate a lot of chocolate and had a nap. For the rest of the evening she stayed in bed, thinking about all the people she had ever known.

David, for instance. Of course he was a crazy, evil sadist, but how hard it was to hate the little creep, or even to despise him as he deserved. Other people seemed so boring and stupid by comparison, even if they were good. She would just have to try harder to hate him, or forget and ignore him, or to take on him a sickening revenge, not that he was even worthy of her vengeance. And all the other people? It was hard even to think of her friends in Leeds, they seemed so ordinary and foolish that they hardly seemed to exist. Everyone she had ever known except for David, Carol and Faye seemed just silly and pointless.

No wonder she had always found David so fascinating. He was not the same as everybody else, and nearly everybody else was so bloody boring and stupid.

Carol and Faye stood out in Mary's mind too, for being so good, so nice, so happy with one another. Maybe she would visit them, since they were the only people she still liked, and she had nothing else to do and nowhere else to go. So what if they lived near David? She was a free agent, she could go where she liked. He

110

was nothing to do with anything in her life, not any more. It was all over, and she would never think of him again. Forget the past. Burn it. Follow a scorched earth policy, leave nothing behind. Destroy everything.

Think of all the things he had done to her! No, better not to, it would make her horny. Too late. Mary decided she would masturbate while thinking of David one last time, to say goodbye to all that, to methodically clear it from her mind once and forever. David and all those creeps in that house in London where so much had happened. Truly her mind and body were full of that experience, and she had to have an orgasm just to be able to think clearly about other things and come back to herself. So for nearly two hours she masturbated in every way she could think of, and it was refreshing.

She used her fingers, her toothbrush, the shower. She rode two pillows as if they were a man, and she bound her breasts, waist and thighs tightly with a sheet. She masturbated in positions she had never masturbated in before, and after she had come three times she rated the operation a success, and slept the good sleep of the orgasmed.

Next day, Mary drove around and did some shopping, though she was careful not to spend much. One of the things she bought was *Space Opera* by Jack Vance, David's favourite author. It was not that she wanted to understand David better, she told herself, rather she needed to broaden her horizons. Just because David did something or liked something was no reason for her to avoid it. That would be petty, and giving David too much importance. She found the novel insane and funny.

It was raining hard when Mary awoke next morning. She performed her routine exercises, a habit she had briefly allowed to lapse. She resolved never to be so distracted and confused again. Discipline was the key to

111

life, self-discipline and methodical behaviour. All those other things people talked about, like being nice and helpful and sociable, and all that New Age pigshit about magic, astrology and so on, was all crappy lies, which was why so many people liked it. What counted was self-discipline, method, skills and strength.

Mary slowly ate a hearty breakfast while staring out of the window at the rain-drenched landscape of England, and even more she stared at the window itself, visible with drops and rivulets of water that trembled, shivered, flowed and merged, glistening with light, heading down and down. As a child, Mary could look at rain on the windows for hours on end, which was one of the reasons her parents secretly thought she was a bit touched. But really, Mary thought, watching rain on the window is far more interesting than most of the things people do. It struck her as strange that nobody ever told you the useful facts that life is only a solitary fight to the death against overwhelming odds, but that sometimes you can have a rest by watching rain on a window. Who gained the advantage from keeping the truth a secret?

After she finished breakfast it was still raining hard, so she practised karate moves for a while, then showered, dressed, packed and checked out. By then it was only drizzling.

As she drove along, she had an idea that filled her with true horror: what if all her experiences with David were the most exciting part of her life, her whole life? What if, after David, there was nothing but trivialities, normality and boredom?

Eight

Drizzle was so English, Mary thought, as she arrived at Carol's family house. It went on and on for no reason, it was neither one thing nor the other, it veiled everything in vagueness to avoid any unwelcome clarity, and it was so cold and damp and depressing that it made you wonder what the point of anything was. It was hypocritical and puritanical. Mary had recently read that Spanish women had the most orgasms of any women in Europe. Of course they do, she thought, and why not? Spain is noted for its lack of drizzle.

Everything about the big house and garden said money. A former farmhouse swallowed up by the suburbs, it had been largely rebuilt. Carol's parents were both geneticists, and Mary knew they must be as good as Frankenstein to afford such a great place. Carol and Faye's parents alike were away, but the two girls were spending most of their time at Carol's, as it had everything, and everything it had was the best. Mary thought it would be a good place to recuperate and regroup, but she was determined not to repeat the mistake she had made with David. This time, if she were not sure she was welcome, she would leave at once. There was plenty to do back home in Leeds. Such as the washing-up she had abandoned in the sink.

'Mary! Good to see you! Come on in,' Carol exclaimed when she opened the door.

Mary had been prepared to leave rather than make a nuisance of herself all over again but, to her surprise, Carol and Faye really were pleased to see her, indeed they even seemed excited. The strong welcome filled Mary with suspicion and, ironically, she felt like making her excuses and leaving.

The three of them sat at a table in a beautiful room where everything seemed to be made of golden wood. It was, thought Mary, like being inside an advert for something. Life, perhaps. Over tea and biscuits they talked: Mary said that she had argued with David, and they had broken up for good. To her surprise, she suddenly started sobbing violently, though it would have been hard for her to explain exactly what she was crying about. How kind Faye and Carol were, how well they tried to console her and reassure her! They hugged her, patted her, said all the right things, held her hand and kept saying she had to stay with them for a holiday, she really had to. Both Faye and Carol would make great mothers one day, Mary thought, and she felt tempted to give up for a while and pretend to be their infant daughter. It would be nice to abandon the hardships of adult life, just temporarily, and be a child again, though not of course with her real parents. She was not that crazy.

'Stay here for a long time,' said Carol. 'Please say you will. My parents won't be back for another four weeks, you know. They're going to a conference and then they're taking a tour of America before they come back. They'll visit some institutes and universities as well, it's partly a working holiday. This house is so big, there's tons of room. And we can use the swimming pool when the weather improves. And we'll go out. The three of us can have a nice time.'

'Please stay, Mary,' Faye insisted with shy and charming intensity. 'It'll be good for you, I can sense it. If you go away now you'll only get depressed. Remember when we told you you were the only person we trusted? We really meant it, you know. And we like you so much.'

'If you're sure I won't be a nuisance, I'll stay a couple of days,' said Mary. She wiped her face and blew her nose. Already she had an instinctive feeling that she had come to the right place, the right people. Mary trusted her instinct even if it did get her into one mess after another. What else was there to trust?

So charming were Carol and Faye, and so splendid the house and garden, that Mary, over the next two days, began to feel better almost despite herself. The three young women had got on very well when Mary had stayed at David's house years ago, and now they seemed even closer, sharing a basic feeling of contentment in simple pleasures, and a fundamental integrity. Intelligent and sincere, they all hated stupidity and insincerity. There are strengths, there is a kind of goodness, that can be recognised and shared without the need to speak of the understanding.

So they went shopping, drove to a wood and walked, watched classic movies on a stupendous home theatre and did some housework. Mary sensed though, that Carol and Faye had something they were holding back for the right moment, something they wanted to talk about. She guessed it probably had to do with their strange adventures in David's bathroom, and hoped her guess was wrong. Not only did she want to forget David, but she felt terribly guilty about getting these nice girls into that creep's weird bathroom so he could put them on tape. She must have been insane. How could she have been stupid enough to think up such an immoral idea just so David would find her more interesting? It was pathetic.

But Faye and Carol had certainly been fascinated by David's bathroom and his equipment, and they probably needed to talk it over with Mary. They would find it difficult to talk about with anyone else, that was for sure, as bathroom domination was such an odd combination of fetishes. Mermaids and masters, serious bathing, wet and hot and slippery, floating and coming – no, she would not even think of it, let alone ever get involved in it again. She was nothing like David, she was not crazy.

'What are you brooding about, Mary?' Faye inquired.

'Nothing,' Mary lied, nearly dropping the cup she was washing.

'You were thinking about David, weren't you?' said Carol. 'Don't deny it, I've been hearing you think for the last two hours at least.'

'Don't worry, just relax,' Faye insisted. 'And don't think so loud, you'll give us all a headache. Turn it down.' She giggled, and gave Mary a hug. Carol joined in.

'I'll stop brooding,' Mary announced firmly. She was surprised by the strong wave of desire that swept her just because the girls' bodies were pressed tight to hers. Why, she wondered, did she have to be so easily aroused and always needing to come? What a bloody nuisance sex was. And it was all just a trick by genes anyway, so they could carry on for millions more years after she had died and blown away as dust on the desert wind. On the other hand, an orgasm would be nice.

'Let's watch a movie,' Carol suggested. 'And have a drink.'

Mary had cider, Carol had beer, and Faye chose red wine. Carol and Faye hardly ever touched alcohol, so seeing them drink now made Mary wonder if they were trying to create some kind of special occasion. Carol put on a DVD, a French lesbian movie which had the merit of not looking like teaching material for a course in gynaecology. Mary felt more and more aroused. She wished Faye and Carol would make a move. Even a tiny one.

'Did you ever make love with another woman?' Carol asked Mary, putting her arm round Mary's shoulders and gazing directly into her eyes. Her gaze was cool, clear light blue, full of confidence.

'Yes, and I enjoyed it,' Mary replied, giving the shortest possible answer so she could cut to the chase. She kissed Carol, who responded passionately, then turned to Faye, saw her excitement, and shared a long kiss with her too. Mary's hands were drawn at once to Faye's huge breasts. 'But,' Mary gasped, 'I never did it with two really nice girls before.'

'This is amazing,' Carol moaned. 'It's so different.'

All three women shared the same surprise and excitement, finding the reality of a threesome more intense and thrilling than they had anticipated. Hands seemed to be everywhere. Like echoes, their excitement bounced back and forth, and like mirrors they reflected each other's arousal. For a long time, Mary had been struck by Faye and Carol's attractions. Now she was freely enjoying herself with them, such nice girls and old friends, and it was a wonder and a delight to kiss those mouths she had seen many times, and to hear the rapid breathing and muted sighs of their ardour.

Soft and big, the sofa of dark-red leather that they squirmed rather than sat on served them as a fine playground. Kissing and caressing, they undressed very slowly because they could hardly bear to break away from one another even for a moment. Mary came when still in her underwear, lying on the sofa with Faye on top of her, fully dressed, while Carol alternately kissed Faye and Mary, and masturbated by rubbing herself on a pair of large cushions she straddled.

Amazement filled all three women after they had come, and they chattered excitedly. They had known intellectually that three women could do all kinds of things together, but the reality was overwhelming, and presented so many thrilling sensations to them that their minds and bodies seemed to buzz with energy like a hive of bees vibrant in the summer's warmth. Simple joy surged through them, as they cuddled and kissed, sharing skin with reckless generosity.

Nowness felt like lightning. All was known, everything was real. The three women struggled out of their remaining clothes and saw dizzying potentials in so much nudity: kissing and groping, licking and touching, flying and floating away, they laughed from sheer happiness.

'How beautiful, how beautiful you both are!' Mary cried out, almost sang out. Suddenly there seemed to be songs everywhere, in everything she was and knew.

'You two are perfect, but my breasts are much too big,' Faye murmured.

'You're crazy,' Mary protested. 'I love your breasts.'

'So do I,' agreed Carol. She and Mary simultaneously suckled on Faye's gigantic, yet surprisingly firm, udders.

Faye shuddered. 'Oh, my God, that's incredible,' she moaned. 'It's more than twice as good. Stop, please, stop, I can't stand it. No, no, don't stop, I'll die.'

Fascinated, the three women studied and played with each other's bodies, and exchanged sincere praise. All of them exercised, and enjoyed various sports, giving their bodies a pleasing tautness, strength, co-ordination and grace, a fine confidence and correctness in movement. Faye laughed with delight as she fingered Mary's nipples, so big and hard, and then showed Mary how big Carol's clit was. Carol and Faye kissed Mary's superb, strong round arse; Mary and Faye licked and stroked Carol's impossibly long legs; Mary and Carol played with Faye's huge breasts again and again. Everything was just so fascinating.

To Mary's horror, she found herself thinking how wonderful the girls would look and feel in restraint, and how much fun she could have teasing them, ordering them to serve her, and making them come and come.

Then they could bind her and take a gleeful, playful revenge. No, she was insane to imagine such crazy stuff. Surely David had not screwed her mind up that much? She would be normal or burst, Mary resolved, even as she imagined fastening straps around Faye's exceptional breasts and touching their bulging tautness.

Lust mounting, they began to rub their bodies together, and to suck breasts and cunts, all so round and delicious. They played on the big soft sofa and, by putting cushions on the adjacent deep, soft dark-purple rug, they made an extended playground, moving from rug to sofa, sofa to rug, trying every position they could think of with mounting wonder and delight. Skins gleaming with fresh sweat, Mary mounted Faye, Carol mounted Mary, and so on in all six ways, and six ways too for mouth to pussy, but that was only the start of the algebra and geometry of three young female bodies straining themselves to splendid achievements: the opening lines of the introduction to tripleness.

There were so many ways to form threes: mouths to pussies to make a triangle, lying on their sides, or one lying across two, rubbing pussies with one partner and kissing the mouth or breasts of the other. Two lay face to face on their sides, pressing flesh to flesh, while the third straddled their waists, hips, or thighs, holding the pair together with arms and legs. So many joys that it made a couple seem so limited, some kind of a trick played on them by a society that always talked about two and never about three, as though two were not less than three, but more. And even if three chanced in the warm flow of events to become two and one for a while, the one could happily masturbate, or ask for a free hand or mouth. For hours that night, Mary, Carol and Faye learned a lot about the power of three, which is not a mere addition of one to two, but a surprising multiplication.

Awaking in the same bed next morning, they had the deep and true happiness of knowing each other's bodies and pleasures, the extra sparkling energy and freshness which comes from stealing a few orgasms from fate. At first, each was a little shy, almost afraid that she had enjoyed herself more than the other two, so they would think it strange if she was sincere in her joy, but then each looked into four eyes, and saw that she was not alone and peculiar in the depth and strength of her pleasure, and they all three knew that what they had started would go on growing, for it had special roots and unique strengths.

Breakfast seemed delectable, with the most ordinary of foods taking on a new flavour. Eagerly, the three women talked over the events of the day before, and soon felt hungry for more.

'Let's have a bath together this afternoon,' Carol suggested.

'Yes, that'll be lovely,' Faye agreed. 'There's so many things we can do in the bathroom. Slippery, warm, wet things.'

'We have a nice bathroom here to play in,' said Carol. 'Even if it's not such a good bathroom as David's.'

Mary felt Carol and Faye's eyes on her like heavy weights as she chewed her toast, which suddenly became difficult to swallow. She felt sure the girls had been dying to talk about David's bathroom with her ever since they had tried out its unique facilities, but they had managed to restrain themselves until now. Mary did not want to talk about it, or even think about it. The whole topic seemed to her to be repulsive, as it was the story of her own stupidity.

'I'm sorry, but I'm not going to talk about it,' she told Faye and Carol, breaking the thickening silence. 'He and I are through. The whole thing was a disgusting mess. He's crazy, and the bathroom shows his craziness.'

'He wanted us to see it, didn't he?' Carol asked. 'When you and he went out and we looked after Ellie.'

Mary wondered what David had done with Ellie. The cat's fate would reveal something about David's character. Stop it, she ordered herself. I already know his true character.

'What makes you think that?' she asked Carol, her voice sounding, in her own ears, hopelessly fake.

'Oh, come on,' Faye protested. 'The door had a lock, so he could stop people seeing that bathroom if he wanted to. But it was unlocked. I bet he got a kick out of the thought of our seeing it.'

'You must have known,' Carol said to Mary. 'Obviously Faye and I would be nosey enough to look around. And you're sharp, you must have noticed the door was unlocked.'

'Well, yes,' Mary admitted reluctantly. But she was determined not to admit that the whole idea had been hers, not David's. Neither dare she admit to, or mention, the embarrassing fact that Carol and Faye's frolics had been recorded. 'Now you see what a loonie David is,' she said, though she disliked her own hypocrisy. It seemed a new low.

'Yes, I'm sure you did the right thing to break up with him,' Faye said. 'All that stuff. The bathroom. How weird can you get? I mean, just think of those –'

'Can't we just forget the whole thing?' Mary protested, pouring herself some more tea and spilling half of it.

'It's all a little too striking to forget,' Carol replied, methodically mopping up all the tea with tissues. 'And, in fact, you know, we were very interested. And we took a bath. And we even tried a thing or two. From the cupboard.'

'It's really intriguing,' said Faye. 'The psychology. The acting out. The whole look.' She was blushing slightly.

Mary felt that Faye was not embarrassed to talk about sex as such, but rather by her and Carol's liking for David's brand of weirdness.

121

'The point is,' said Carol hesitantly, 'since then, Faye and I have, I mean we've – oh, why is it so hard to talk about? Why can't we all talk about how we get orgasms like we talk about politics or the bloody weather? It'd be more interesting, and we'd all be happier.'

'They don't want us to be uninhibited and happy,' said Mary.

'It's hard to talk about what's supposed to be strange and perverted,' Faye sighed. 'But fifty years from now it'll just seem normal. It's in *Cosmopolitan* magazine already.' This last thought gave her fresh heart. 'Domination, I mean. Restraint. Mistress and slave games.'

'It's fascinating!' Carol exclaimed. 'Faye and I have been experimenting with restraint. It feels lovely! We're glad David let us see his bathroom, even though I bet he got some kind of kinky thrill out of our seeing it.'

'It inspired us. It set us on the right course.'

'I doubt it,' Mary sighed. 'Oh, well. It's none of my business what you two do. Have fun.'

'Oh, but it is your business now,' Carol protested, giving Mary her brightest smile. 'You're with us, and you must be an expert on domination, so you can help us. Join us.'

'No, no, no,' Mary said firmly. 'I've given all that up, and I'd be crazy to start again.' She suddenly realised that this was just what David had kept saying to her, a thought that filled her with a kind of horror at the strange workings of fate. Was this some kind of punishment?

'Come on, Mary, don't be a spoilsport,' Faye said in a wheedling tone, dipping her spoon in and out of her boiled egg.

'Imagine what the three of us could do together,' Carol insisted. 'Slave and Mistress games. Pure fun. Not heavy.'

'It brings out the worst in people.'

'But, Mary, even if that's true, maybe it does you good to get the worst out,' said Faye. 'So it's therapy and fun.'

'You must have enjoyed doing all that stuff with David in the past. Why should you stop doing it just because you've ended your relationship with him? Now you can carry on with Faye and me. Come on, I bet you want to really.'

'You can be the High Priestess initiating two novices into the secrets of your sect.' Faye giggled, squirming in her chair. 'Think of all the expertise you've acquired.'

'I don't want to think of it,' Mary protested, grimacing. 'I'm sorry. Thanks for the invitation. You're both so beautiful and nice. But I daren't. I mustn't. You can have fun together experimenting, but I've been through it all. For me it's over.'

'So what will you do with the rest of your life?' Carol demanded.

Mary shrank from the force of the question. 'I'll think of something,' she replied weakly.

'Never mind,' said Faye. 'Let's forget about it. What shall we do this morning? Let's go shopping.' She gave Carol a meaningful look, and Carol, who wanted to go on arguing with Mary, managed to stop herself. They have some plan, thought Mary. They are determined to get me to join in their games, they cannot take no for an answer. It shocked her to realise that this was not so much her conviction as her hope.

Sunshine was breaking through at last as they went to the shops. First, Mary bought a one-piece swimsuit. Then they went to Sainsbury's, where Faye and Carol picked up all manner of soaps, lotions and foam bath liquids, as well as two bottles of baby oil.

'For massage,' Carol told Mary. 'I want to tie Faye up in the bathroom and torment her,' she whispered. 'Just think: you and I could make love in front of her, and she'd be dying to come. If only you'd join us.'

'Oh, please say yes, Mary. We need you. We want you. We don't even know what to use for tying-up games. I bet you'd have lots of ideas. Don't be a coward.'

'You're not encouraging us if you join us, because we're determined to do it anyway,' Carol pointed out. 'Your conscience will be clear. You just have to be a little bit brave. A cowardly life is so boring.'

'I am not a coward!' Mary exclaimed, so angrily that half the people in Sainsbury's turned their heads in surprise. Oh, a bad noisy woman! Mary forced herself to be silent for ten seconds, and to breathe calmly. 'All right,' she said at last. 'Of course, I'll join you. You know I'm dying to. Thanks.'

'Hooray!' Faye exclaimed, clapping her hands childishly.

'Great!' Carol cried.

'Just don't blame me if it ends in tears. All right, let's pick up some stuff we can use.' Mary knew it was impossible for her to resist any longer. It was fate. Now she knew how David had felt when she had tempted him into resuming his old ways, and she could better understand his mixed feelings of terrible lust and resentment. Was this the hand of God, instructing her on the consequences of her actions? It was like the classic cowboy film plot: nobody will allow the famous gunslinger to hang up his guns and reform his ways. OK. Load guns. Open fire.

If Faye and Carol could not take no for an answer, if they were determined to experiment, then let loose the dogs of war, kick down the gates of hell! They would get more than they bargained for. Two young women in an experimental phase? Fine. Just what she could use. After all she had been through with David and without David, she felt like being a cruel and ruthless scientist manipulating and using two girls. Let them become her white mice.

'We'll get several kinds of plastic cords, ropes, belts, whatever,' she stated. 'Cheap stuff like that is useful because it's disposable. We can throw it away if it gets oily.'

They ended up buying a surprising amount of things for the bathroom and for domination games, some of which startled Carol and Faye greatly. As they drove home in Carol's new red Volvo, they shared a great excitement. Sensing Mary's new determination and energy, Carol and Faye were also a little nervous.

After unpacking the groceries, Mary did something to make Carol and Faye even more nervous and excited: she took the black plastic bag of domination garments and equipment from her car boot and emptied it out on the living-room floor.

'A few souvenirs from David,' she explained.

The girls were amazed, and talked excitedly as they studied the items. They wanted to strip off and try them there and then, but Mary would not allow them such a quick satisfaction.

'No, we're going to wait,' she said firmly. 'We'll have a long build-up, and then an even longer session. If we rush it won't be so exciting. Look how nice the weather is. We should have a swim first.'

Full of anticipation, the three women had a happy time cleaning and discussing the bizarre pieces Mary had brought from David's collection, as well as the many new things they had got from the supermarket, everyday items that could play a role in domination sessions. It was deeply thrilling to handle all this gear, and to know they would use it for extreme restraint and torment. Truly they felt like explorers of their own bodies, of the unknown borders of human sexuality and of their secret, hidden souls.

After a light lunch, they went into the back garden to have a swim in the pool. They wore swimsuits, as the pool could be seen from two nearby houses. Mary wore her new one-piece black suit with plunging neckline, while Faye had a red bikini and Carol a light-blue one-piece suit with a large oval cutout that showed part of her belly, flank and back. The women praised each other's appearance with sincerity.

What fun life could be! All three women were strong swimmers, and it was delicious to swim deep to exchange caresses, and to splash and laugh in the sunlight that looked so fine and brave on trees, water and bodies. A bright-red plastic inflated chair floated on the surface, and it struck Mary that it would be useful in the bathroom. So they played in the water, teasing and arousing each other. After a short rest to get their breath back, they knew they had to start, as waiting any longer felt impossible.

To the bathroom they took the chair of inflated red plastic, and all the other items Mary thought they should try in their first bathroom session. They began to fill the bath, adding plenty of foam liquid. It was nowhere near as big as David's bath, of course, but it was a good modern bath, wide and long and oval in shape, not a traditional narrow bath with high sides that seemed intended to make sex difficult. The shower was too small for their purposes, and there was a problem with the floor of the bathroom, which did not have drains and tiles as did David's bathroom. They solved this by spreading a large plastic sheet on the floor next to the bath, so they gained the freedom of being able to use oil and splash water without having to worry about damaging the floor or staining the walls. A green-painted metal chair from the garden was placed on the sheet, as a useful piece of furniture for restraint.

Feeling somewhat subdued and serious, the three women removed their wet swimsuits in Carol's bedroom. They knew they were about to do something very peculiar.

'You're willing to endure a terrible ordeal?' Mary asked gravely.

'Yes,' Faye murmured, her eyes widening.

'Why? Why should you do anything so foolish?'

Faye looked dumbfounded by the question. After hesitating, she blurted out the truth. 'Because I want to.'

'Very well,' said Mary. 'Our mission,' she said to Carol, 'is clear. We must cure this silly girl of her desire to submit by treating her so severely that she never feels such a perverse urge again. And we must punish her for flaunting her body in the swimming pool.'

'That's very good,' Faye murmured. 'Oh, Mary, you do it so well.'

'Call me "Mistress" in future. And only speak if you're asked a question.'

'Come along, you silly girl,' said Carol, following Mary's lead. 'This is going to be worse than you imagined.'

Nine

As the three of them entered the bathroom, as naked as fish, Mary almost expected to see David there. Life was so strange. Now she was following in David's footsteps, trying his own unique fetish of bathroom domination, even though she had just broken up with him for the second, and final, time. It struck her forcibly that she was going to dominate a woman in the bathroom, just as he would have done. It was as if she were turning into David, becoming him. She thought that this would help her to understand him and, in some strange way, the idea pleased her deeply, no matter how she tried to put it from her mind and tell herself that her peculiar and hopeless relationship with David was now absolutely finished. Dead.

'Sit on this chair,' she ordered Faye. Forget David. He was nothing to do with this present pleasure.

Nervously, the big-breasted young woman obeyed, sitting on the metal garden chair. Dark and liquid, her eyes were wide with fear, and Carol too was nervous, gnawing her lip. Mary knew she would have to act quickly and decisively, or else the session would degenerate into a fiasco, and all their preparation would have been a silly waste of time. And if she allowed such a failure, Carol and Faye would doubtless blame her afterwards, and tell her she should have been more determined. What a responsibility it was to dominate others! It called for courage.

'Help me secure her,' she told Carol. Quickly, the two of them fastened padded black plastic ankle straps to Faye, each with a metal ring attached, through which they passed red plastic cords. These they tied tightly to the front legs of the chair. Next they fitted a remarkable bra, consisting of three interconnected black plastic adjustable straps, which encircled each of her huge breasts, with her stiffening nipples protruding through metal rings.

'Don't make me wear it too long, will you?' Faye pleaded in a small voice. 'It's not comfortable.'

'Be quiet,' Mary snapped. 'Be a brave girl. Stop whining.' She had never complained like that to David even during severe treatment, so what right did Faye have to whimper?

At the sides of the bra were two padded black plastic cuffs on short metal chains, the ends of the chains being firmly attached to the strong, thick plastic of the bra. The whole thing was an ingenious piece of work, which had its own weird beauty. Faye's wrists were strapped into the cuffs. Now, owing to the shortness of the chains, she could caress her own breasts, but not reach down to her own belly, let alone her pussy, and neither could she reach up high enough to remove the gag Mary planned to fit later. The bra with attached cuffs was a marvellously cunning device, and using it gave all three women a deep, forbidden kind of thrill.

'Now you may worship our pussies,' said Mary. 'And our arses.'

Carol and Mary kissed and fondled one another while they presented parts of their bodies in turn for Faye to lick and suck, and they found it a pleasant experience indeed to have their very own sex slave.

'Now she's ornamental and useful too.' Carol giggled.

'How nice it is,' said Mary, 'to have a prisoner.' She took another red plastic cord and used it to fasten metal rings at the back of Faye's bra to the chair on which she sat so attractively, so that now she could not stand. Then she poured baby oil over Faye's remarkably large udders.

'Caress your own breasts,' she ordered. 'Perhaps after an hour or two you might even be able to come just from squeezing your breasts and clenching your thigh muscles. It's certainly an interesting form of masturbation.'

'Restricted masturbation!' Carol exclaimed. 'What a great idea. That's really clever, Mary.'

'I'll go mad,' Faye protested. 'I need to come already. I can't stand it if I have to watch you and Carol fool around and come, if I can't come myself. Let me go!'

'All right, all right,' Mary said soothingly, moving behind Faye as though to release her. Instead, she snatched up a thick black rubber cylindrical bit and pressed it into Faye's mouth, between her teeth, as Faye reflexively opened her mouth to protest. Carol held Faye's head steady so Mary could fasten the black plastic straps, attached to the ends of the bit, around Faye's head. It was soon done, and Faye's power of speech was reduced to an ability to imitate animals.

'Don't be silly,' Carol told Faye. 'We can't stop now. It's such fun. Calm down. You'll thank me when it's over.' She paused. 'Well, maybe you won't, but we're going on with this anyway. You kept saying you wanted to be dominated.'

'Just relax and enjoy it,' Mary said gently, pouring more baby oil on Faye's breasts and thighs. She and Carol massaged Faye without going near her pussy.

Faye stopped tossing her head and straining her limbs, and instead squeezed and rubbed her own lubricated breasts, her eyes wide with amazement. Mary and Carol laughed to see her growing lust. They massaged one another with baby oil, rubbing their breasts and pussies on Faye's thighs, as well as pressing their bodies together. Standing and kneeling in front of their prisoner, feeling her hungry eyes on them like an aphrodisiac, they played all kinds of games, thrusting out their arses and breasts, parting their legs wide to proffer their pouting pussies to each other's hands. It was hugely stimulating to squeeze and rub and press flesh slippery with oil, and to know that they could come while Faye could not, added greatly to their mounting excitement.

Sighing with delight, Mary and Carol entered the bath and caressed one another ardently, their skins singing with the feel of warm slippery water and tingling foam. Their every nerve seemed to be sparkling with sensation, their muscles quivering with fresh energy. In turn they went on all fours so the other could rub her belly and pussy on firm round buttocks and hold the yielding soft jelly of breasts while thrusting. Then they probed one another with flexible waterproof vibrators, shivering and moaning as they lay back and opened their legs as wide as they could, one after the other yielding their innermost secret flesh. Then they lay back, heads at opposite ends of the bath, and intertwined their legs, pressing their pussies together in a wet kiss, a vibrator quivering inside each vagina, their hands on their own breasts. Like this they had orgasms of surprising force almost simultaneously, arching and splashing in the water, crying out as though in feverish pain, their lovely long rounded bodies straining with delicious greed for every spasm of ecstasy.

Laughter shook their bodies as the last shivers faded, as they took in the sight and sounds of Faye squeezing her own breasts, tweaking her nipples, and tensing the muscles of her thighs and belly as she struggled to achieve orgasm.

'Now then, Faye,' said Mary. 'You're going to be allowed to worship our pussies again. What a lucky girl! We spoil you.' She released Faye from the chair, but left her hands bound, then sat down in the inflated red plastic chair, leaned back, and threw her legs far apart over its arms, displaying her open vulva.

Carol helped Faye out of the metal garden chair, and had her kneel down, still with the thick rubber bit in her mouth.

'Rub your nose on my cunt,' stated Mary. 'If you do a good job on Carol and me, we're sure to let you come soon.'

Faye obeyed immediately, and Mary sighed as the big-breasted girl pleasured her. With her bound hands, Faye was able to support her weight on the seat of the plastic chair, but it was a very awkward position for her, and it made Mary and Carol laugh to see her exertions. Overcome with lust, Faye lay down on her stomach and tried to bring herself off by rubbing her pussy on the black plastic sheet covering the floor of the bathroom, but after a few minutes, just as she thought she might well be able to come in this way, Carol and Mary pulled her up and then sat her in the red plastic chair. She moaned with frustration as her humming clitoris ceased to receive any stimulation, and then Carol straddled the chair and pressed her pussy to Faye's mouth while Mary caressed her tall, shapely body and sucked her breasts.

'This is lovely,' Carol sighed. 'Faye makes such a good prisoner.'

'She does, she does,' Mary agreed. For a moment, looking down on Faye writhing in frustration, she felt that Faye was herself, and that she was not Mary but David. She wanted to make Faye suffer as she had suffered, as a kind of revenge on the world, and even on herself for having been so stupid with David. Yes, in a way, punishing Faye was like punishing herself. And besides, it was such fun!

Next, Carol and Mary tried Faye in the bath, like children trying out the possibile ways to play with a new toy. They strapped a broad, padded black plastic belt fitted with rings to her waist, and had her sit on the ledge at one end of the bath, with her legs stretched out wide apart and her ankle straps attached by plastic cords to the shiny handrails set into either side of the top of the bath, so that her pussy was proffered, swollen and visibly pulsing with frustrated lust as it oozed juices, a sight Carol and Mary found fascinating in the extreme. To have built such desire, such a fierce hunger, in Faye's helpless body, gave them a feeling of achievement and pride.

'It's time we punished Faye,' Mary panted. 'Just a little bit at first. You should be grateful we take so much interest in you, Faye.'

'What are we punishing her for?' Carol asked eagerly.

'We'll punish her for wanting us to put her into restraint and annoying us until we had to give in.'

Faye's eyes widened again as she saw Mary pick up a long-handled brush with plastic bristles, and she made amusing pleading sounds through the bit between her teeth.

'Stop drooling, you messy girl,' said Mary. She tried the brush on the insides of the prisoner's thighs. At first Faye hardly reacted, but as her skin reddened and the irritation increased, she began to whimper and struggle uselessly.

'What a fuss you make!' Mary complained. 'A big girl like you ought to be able to stand a lot of punishment.'

'She's a crybaby,' said Carol. 'I'll be much braver when it's my turn, I'm sure. You won't be able to punish me enough.' She got into the bath with Mary, and the two women lay on their sides facing, pressing and rubbing their bodies together while alternately kissing Faye's sensitive flesh and rubbing it with the harsh plastic bristles of the brush, so that Faye hardly knew if she were suffering terribly or moving to the verge of a wonderful orgasm, so cunningly did her two tormentors mingle and vary the stimulations of pain and pleasure.

133

'Now let's have her standing,' said Mary. 'Don't struggle, Faye, or you'll get a whipping.' She and Carol had Faye stand in the bath with her legs far apart. They moved the straps at her ankles to just above her knees, then tied their metal rings to the rails at the sides of the bath with plastic cords, then freed her right hand and tied her wrist ring to a tap at the end of the bath before repeating the process for her left hand. Lastly, they used cords to fasten rings at the sides of her black plastic belt to the same handrails as her ankles were fastened to. Faye looked stunningly beautiful and vulnerable: standing with legs apart, and leaning sharply forwards with her waist held down and back so that her arse was thrust out in a spectacular fashion. With the straps above her knees fastened to the handrails, she could not move her arse downwards, as would have been the case had the straps been left at her ankles, Mary explained with some pride.

'This is wonderful!' Carol exclaimed. 'Oh, you're so clever. We can do all sorts of things to Faye like this, it's lovely.'

'I envy you, Faye,' Mary sighed passionately, and kissed the captive's thighs. 'Be happy, my dear girl, my dear friend.'

'Fuck me, fuck me, please fuck me,' Carol whispered, overcome by a strange burning desire unleashed by the perverse games they were playing, a pure hunger unlike anything she had ever dreamed could exist.

'Soon, soon,' Mary replied. 'Lie down and enjoy yourself. Soon I'll fuck you hard, you lovely dirty bitch, my darling.' She stood in the bath behind Faye. 'First, I have to give this lovely girl, this sweet little prisoner, a severe spanking. It will do her good. It might even help her to come, if she tries hard enough. You must try, Faye. I'll help you.' Mary poured water from the bath over Faye and then filled the plastic bowl with cold water from the tap and slowly poured it all over Faye's quivering body. She repeated this process five more times, alternating hot and cold.

'We underestimate the effects of temperature,' she said. 'A lot can be achieved with heat and cold. It's just another of the opportunities people usually let go by. We're all so lazy and cowardly. But now we three will be brave.' Mary bit her lip, realising that much of what she had just said consisted of quotations from David. Never mind. She would drive him from her mind by action.

'This is wonderful,' Carol gasped. She was lying back in the bath masturbating with a vibrator. Gazing up at Faye, she reached up and tweaked her nipples. 'Faye has such a look in her eyes.'

'Keep trying, Faye, my darling,' Mary said quietly, feeling a kind of love for the deliciously helpless prisoner, who might just as well have been Mary herself. She poured a final bowl of bath water over Faye's back, then squirted liquid soap over her shoulders, thighs and buttocks. Faye made animal sounds through her bit all the time: snorts, snuffles, bleats, whimpers and whines, like the sounds Mary had been reduced to making when with David, sounds she found wonderfully stimulating. How good it was to become an animal, to win the right to stop making sense!

'There, there,' said Mary, soothing Faye as though she were a fettlesome mare in harness. She unfastened the constricting bra from her prisoner, then massaged Faye all over her torso and limbs with the liquid soap, though she did not touch Faye's swollen pussy. How rounded Faye's body was! It was all curves, and so firm, fit and taut. There was a delight in stroking and gently squeezing Faye's huge breasts, feeling their female softness and sensitivity, all so soft save for her nipples, big and hard from their long period of teasing. All at once, Mary gave Faye a resounding slap on her right buttock with her open hand. What a fuss Faye made!

'Shush, shush, that was nothing much,' said Mary. 'Silly girl.' She stroked and squeezed Faye's buttocks gently, touched the tips of her pouting labia, running her soapy, slippery finger up and down the ridges of flesh, and then she put her left forefinger very lightly on Faye's clitoris and gave her a hard slap with her right hand, followed, after a short interval of tickling Faye's clitoris, by three more slaps. Faye's buttocks were now visibly reddening.

'Oh God, it's wonderful,' Carol moaned, virtually in a trance of luxurious masturbation. 'She's scared. So am I.'

Faye squealed like a pig as Mary poured cold water over her arse, then probed her with her tongue before abruptly giving her two more slaps. She had to pause to rub her own pussy, thighs, belly and breasts with both hands, greedy for the kind of powerful sensations she was granting Faye with such lavish generosity. Mary felt jealous of the melon-breasted girl – really this was all too good for her. She took the plastic brush and rubbed its bristles on Faye's buttocks, touched her pussy lightly with the long black handle, then tapped it several times. Desperately, Faye struggled to rub herself on the curving plastic even as Mary used her other hand to give her three very hard slaps on the arse. Clearly, Faye was trapped on the very brink of the climax of her life, and Mary knew she had power over Faye's future, over her very soul: she could caress Faye to orgasm, or release her, or else she could do something very cruel and wrong, something that might warp this innocent girl's whole life.

As David had warped Mary's life. So Mary began to alternate light slaps delivered upwards between Faye's legs with harder blows to her arse. Faye squealed, arched her body, tensed and struggled, going wild in the grip of her bonds, and was finally ripped apart by an orgasm that seemed appalling, as Carol reached up to hold her breasts and Mary cupped her pussy with one hand in front and one behind, squeezing out all her lust like juice from a lemon. Mary and Carol were awed by the power and length of Faye's climax, which went on and on as they held her, filling them with wonder, excitement, pride and envy. The startling power of this orgasm reinforced the three women's addiction to advanced sexual deviations. They sensed the future even as Faye was still shuddering and twitching in her final convulsions, and it made them tingle with seductive, tantalising anxiety.

'Oh God,' Faye gasped brokenly when Mary removed the rubber bit from between her teeth. 'I didn't know, I didn't know.' Her limbs were released, and she was cuddled and caressed by Mary and Carol. For minutes none of them spoke a word, as there seemed nothing that was worth the saying.

Soon they were moving against each other with increasing urgency, and they tried all kinds of positions, surging forwards from one orgasm to another with a fantastic energy.

Finally, they left the bathroom, and talked eagerly for hours about what they had done and would do. All were fired with eagerness and determination, though in Mary alone this mingled with anxiety and a nagging, subdued guilt.

Next day, Carol and Faye's strong sense of duty and devotion to their university work asserted itself, and they drove to nearby woodlands where Faye could study and photograph the forestry work, while Carol did likewise for the local geomorphology, as part of their summer projects. Mary was invited to come, but declined, sensing that for her it would be boring.

To see David in the local Tesco's should not have been a shock for Mary, as his house was less than a mile from that of Carol's parents where she was staying, and yet it was indeed a shock, as he somehow seemed to have become part of the remote past, and should, according to Mary's mental map, have been removed to a remote part of Asia where there was no chance of their ever meeting. It had never even occurred to her that they could possibly meet, and yet here he was, and their trolleys nearly collided as they came to the same corner at the end of the shelves loaded with tinned fruit. And I never even buy tinned fruit, Mary told herself in surprise.

'Oh God!' David exclaimed, looking as if he had seen a ghost. 'What the hell are you doing here?'

'Shopping. People quite often do that in Tesco's.'

'For heaven's sake. You're not following me, are you?'

'Don't flatter yourself. I'm staying a couple of days with Carol and Faye. Nothing to do with you. Goodbye. Oh, just one thing: if you don't want the cat, I'll take her. Don't have her put down out of spite.'

'Of course not. She's fine. I like having her around.'

'OK. Goodbye then,' said Mary. David muttered something unintelligible in reply, and Mary quickly moved away from him, feeling very proud of herself for not lingering to talk or shout or hit the little rat with a big tin of rambutans. She did not see him again that day. When Carol and Faye returned, they were very glad of the fine meal Mary had got ready for them, and the three of them enjoyed it greatly.

Eating ice cream and peaches for dessert, they once more started talking about what they had done in the bathroom.

'It's so exciting being helpless,' said Faye. 'I was scared, but it was a sexy fear.'

'And it's great having you helpless,' Carol said eagerly. 'Mary and I could tease you and we could come when you couldn't. I came and came.'

'And you and Mary were so cruel, but that was exciting too. Oh, when I think about all the things we can do, I want to do everything, try everything.'

'It's addictive,' said Mary. 'I warned you. It makes straight sex seem dull. That's bad really, but there you are. Once you've started it's hard to stop. Though we should.'

'I don't want to stop!' Faye exclaimed. 'I want to do something tonight. Something different from yesterday.'

'I have an idea,' Carol said a little nervously. 'But it's a bit crazy. Really I shouldn't even say it.'

Curiosity made Mary and Faye demand that Carol share her idea. She breathed in deeply and took the plunge.

'It's a hot night, right? Suppose we go for a secret, bizarre, swimming party? We start late when people in the nearby houses are asleep, and we have to be very quiet, that's part of the fun. It's secret and mysterious, you see.'

'Like superheroines going out at night,' Mary put in, her active and overstimulated imagination seizing on the idea immediately. 'Batgirl, Supergirl and Wonder Woman going out at night on a mission. We can dress up in plastic and rubber and take special equipment.'

'Oh, that's great!' gasped Faye. 'I always wanted to be a heroine in a comic. We can tie Carol up for a while, can't we, Carol? It's your turn. I must have some revenge for yesterday. We can use the ladder! One day we'll be in our own comic, I can see it now. What shall we call it? *Heroines of Restraint*, or *Bizarre Bitches*?'

'How about *Wet Women*?' Carol giggled.

'I have the perfect name for us,' said Faye, 'but "Three Silly Girls Getting Out of their Depth" is too long.'

' "Aquanauts",' Mary announced, and grimaced.

'Perfect!' cried Faye. 'Mysterious, costumed explorers of sexuality in a swimming pool at midnight! We should try to sell the movie rights.'

'Is that what David said you and he were, in his wonderful bathroom?' Carol asked Mary quietly.

'Yes. You're clever. Oh, it's stupid of me to think of the past. It annoys me so much to see how weak I was.'

'It's not about being strong or weak,' Faye insisted.

'Never mind, Mary,' said Carol. 'Fool around with us and you'll feel better. Two naive and gullible middle-class girls getting involved with sexual deviations. I mean, come on, what more could anyone ask for? Jam on it?'

'If you answer "David" I'll hit you,' Faye giggled.

They all three laughed loudly and, as they joked and talked about what they would do in the pool at midnight, Mary forgot David for minutes at a time. After washing the dishes, they gathered equipment and garments, trying things on and making plans.

Excitedly they dressed up. Carol wore a black plastic suspender belt with six straps supporting black stockings, and a stretchy black plastic top, while Faye opted for a black fishnet top and matching stockings with an open crotch, plus red rubber gloves. Mary chose thigh-length black plastic boots with elasticated tops, matching long gloves, and a black plastic halter top that left her breasts, including her nipples, almost completely bare. Happy and excited, the three women kissed and touched each other and exchanged sincere praise for their outrageously sexy, fetishistic appearance. Shushing each other, they took towels and toys out to the pool. Now they were aquanauts indeed, thought Mary, a secret group of kinky mermaids.

Midnight had just passed. It was a moonless cloudy night, with no lights showing in the nearest houses, and, by the pool under the garden's large old trees, it was surprisingly dark and eerie.

'I feel,' Carol whispered, 'more like a witch than an aquanaut. How quiet it is. Why do people sleep so much?'

'They're rehearsing,' Mary replied, 'for when they're dead.'

Mystery all around and inside them, they lit six candles and placed them around the edge of the pool, to prevent them banging their heads in the darkness. They entered the water as quietly as they could, finding it deliciously cool on such a hot and sultry summer night, and they kissed and fondled each other as they pressed their bodies together, keeping to the part of the pool nearest the fence at the back of the garden, a spot overlooked by only two windows, both dark, of one neighbouring house. The sense that they were out in the night, risking observation and eavesdropping as they indulged in forbidden acts, was a massive stimulation.

Urgently, they thrust at one another, and then they used the pool's ladder to play games: one of them squatted on this with her back to the pool, and a second lay floating face up to lick and suck her pussy, while the third went between the floating girl's parted legs to give oral service while masturbating. All three of them tried each place with great pleasure. Then they brought the inflated red plastic chair into play. Mary sat on it first, throwing her legs wide apart over its arms so that Faye could float in the water and suck her off, while Carol played with Mary's breasts, clinging to them from behind while rubbing her own clitoris on the bottom of the chair. Then Faye and Carol gave one another a foot between the thighs, rubbing and pressing upwards while pleasuring Mary. Again this was so fine that they all three tried each position, finding it fascinating and thrilling that they could form all kinds of combinations while floating in the water. Its support gave them new freedom to play games of rare delight.

'Why does nobody ever tell you these things?' Carol whispered in wonder. Her perky breasts were even more upstanding than usual, thanks to her excitement and the cool water, and she was sighing with pleasure as Mary and Faye handled them tenderly. 'Why is it a kind of secret that you can do things like this?'

'The economy would collapse,' Mary told her, 'if people ever realised how happy they could be without spending money.'

'Any kind of happiness must be a secret conspiracy,' whispered Faye. 'We're the Aquanauts. Let's take our conspiracy beyond all limits. Dream harder.' She fetched swimming masks and waterproof vibrators from the bag they had placed at the side of the pool. All three donned their blue swimming masks in serious, lustful silence, and turned on the vibrators.

Aquanauts, mermaids, secret players of wet games in the darkness, the three of them breathed deeply, then dived deep, to explore the depths of passion. It was a sweet strangeness, a dark delight, to swim and to come in ecstasy.

Panting and trembling, the three women finally left the pool for a rest, radiant with fresh vitality after their astonishingly powerful orgasms. They dried each other and rested for a while on the red chair and a blue plastic airbed. Touching and smiling, they could hardly believe their own pleasure.

'Now,' breathed Carol, 'you must tie me up.'

Pouncing on her, Faye and Mary stripped her of her black plastic top, though not her black suspender belt and stockings. To tie her to a tree with soft white cotton cords was a simple matter, and there she stood in the darkness, wrists and ankles fastened. With a cruel smile, Faye tweaked Carol's nipples and clitoris in turn, and she did this for quite a long time, while Mary sat on a garden chair watching in fascination, caressing Faye's body as well as her own. Carol bit her lip as she struggled not to cry out, or plead. She had to remain silent in case the neighbours heard, which was much more difficult for her than if she had been inside the house, gagged, yet paradoxically free to make all kinds of noises in her throat and through her nose, enjoying the luxury of exerting herself and sounding like an animal. Not being gagged left her all too human.

142

Sighing with malicious and loving pleasure, Faye teased Carol with her mouth. Carol whimpered. Her magnificent tall body with legs so long and breasts so high and jutting was straining, arching and beaded with sweat, as she shuddered and heaved in the firm grip of a restraint that held her torso and limbs in an exquisite tension, so that she was a rigid bow of quivering tautness, straining to release an arrow into infinity.

Mary and Faye made love on an airbed in front of Carol, while she could only watch and listen in frustration. Before she came, Mary had Faye caress her while she struck Carol six harsh and cunning blows to her thighs with a leather strap, and this aroused Mary so much that she mounted Faye again and came with protracted whimpering and sobbing, as though she were consumed by grief.

When Carol was released, she went back into the pool to revel in the freedom of her limbs and the pleasuring of her body by Faye and Mary, until all three glowed with satisfaction.

'We must do more and more,' Carol said eagerly when they were back indoors. 'Everything.'

'Yes,' Faye agreed. 'Strange sex. Stranger sex.'

Ten

There was a man in the house. Mary heard a male voice as she came back from the shops. For a moment she thought it must be David come to apologise, and a savage delight leapt up in her like a leaping tigress as she imagined kicking him and driving him away, taking revenge. And later, so gracious and kind, to grant forgiveness. To realise that it was only Jack was no small disappointment. She took a deep breath, and walked into the breakfast room, all varnished wood and white paint, where Jack sat at the big table drinking tea with Faye and Carol. Mary had last seen her ex in that hotel room where she had subjected him to cruel and unusual domination and then abandoned him like a piece of rubbish. Seeing your old rubbish turn up again is rarely a pleasant experience.

'Hello, Mary,' he said with nervous brightness. 'Sorry I'm not David,' he added, reading her face with his professional skill as a good salesman.

'How did you know I was here?'

'I tried your apartment, your friends, your parents and, finally, David. A funny thing: last year I copied his address from an old letter I found in your room. Like I knew one day I'd need his address. A premonition. I suppose I knew you were still obsessed by him. Obsessed or whatever word you prefer.'

'Whatever it was, it's over,' Mary replied as she put away her shopping. 'Just as you and I are finished.' She was about to ask how David had known where she was, and what exactly he had said, and how he had seemed, but then she remembered that he had seen her in the supermarket, and as for the rest of her questions, she swallowed them by a great effort of will, and reminded herself that she was not even a little bit interested.

'Let's all have lunch,' Faye said brightly.

'Yes, and then Jack will have to go, won't you, Jack?' Mary said firmly. 'Owing to his enormous workload.'

'Oh, Mary,' Carol protested, 'you can't send Jack away when he's come such a long way.'

'Never mind, Carol,' Jack said, touching her hand. 'Mary has suffered a lot. She has a right to be a little brusque now and then.'

'No, I have a right to be bloody rude all the bloody time if I want to be.'

'I can't help loving you, Mary.'

'Oh, it's so romantic,' Faye sighed.

'It's just crap,' Mary protested. 'He's just trying to impress you and Carol. He's in sales. Fucking sales! He knows all the crappy little psychological tricks.'

'She's right,' Jack told Faye. 'I'm manipulative. It's sad, really, how psychology has become more about controlling people than helping people.'

'Another trick,' snorted Mary. 'An unexpected burst of sincerity and self-criticism. Chapter seven in his favourite book.'

'Unworthy as I am, I can't stop thinking about you, Mary. That's the plain truth.'

'What you really mean is that you can't stop thinking of the time I dominated you,' Mary snarled. 'Be sincere, be honest. Anything else is just a waste of time. You want me to whip you.'

Jack, Carol and Faye all stopped eating their chicken salad with rice. Mary alone kept on munching.

'I see you have no secrets from Faye and Carol,' Jack said at last. Mary was pleased to see a definite blush on his bland features.

'What use are secrets anyway?' wondered Carol. She was delighted both by the turn the conversation had taken and by Mary's confidence, a quality in her that Carol and Faye found inspiring.

'You liked being dominated and you want me to dominate you again,' Mary said through a mouthful of food, waving her fork at Jack.

'All right,' Jack agreed. He tried hard to be dignified and calm, but could not bring it off because he felt he was being a fool. 'You dominated me, and it was a terrible, shocking experience. But it haunts me. You taught me things about myself I had never even suspected. I feel I have to be dominated by you again or I'll go crazy. Maybe I'm already crazy.'

'I know how you feel,' Mary admitted. 'I used to feel the same way about David. He dominated me and it was terrible, but I wanted him to do it again. So I could find out if it was wonderful or terrible. A dream or a nightmare. In the end I realised it was a nightmare.'

'Dominate me one more time and then I too will know for sure,' said Jack.

'Now we can see our future,' Carol said to Faye with an excited laugh. 'We'll get hooked on domination and then we'll be confused and crazy about it. It's like an addictive drug.'

'Exactly!' Mary exclaimed. 'So we all have to try to give it up. Go cold turkey.'

'But it's so exciting,' Faye protested, with a touching, childlike innocence.

'So, you two lovely ladies have experience of these fascinating, harmless games,' said Jack, eyeing Carol and Faye with real hunger.

'Leave them alone,' Mary snapped. 'This is your problem, not theirs.'

'Just being sincere and honest like you said I should be,' Jack said with a smile.

'Oh, shut up. This whole thing is ridiculous, and we have to be determined to stop it all here and now,' Mary stated. 'Let's start being mature adults. The four of us will get a grip. Let's be rational. All of this domination crap started with David, him and his damn crazy bathroom. He made me crazy, and then I accidentally made the three of you crazy. But David had the sense to know he had to stop, and we have to imitate him in that.'

'Always David, you notice,' Jack said sadly to Carol and Faye. 'I bet she was thinking of him even when she dominated me.'

'You should be glad,' Carol pointed out. 'It's all the more humiliating for you. And being humiliated is an exciting part of the game, right?'

'You really are experts!' Jack exclaimed, thrilled at the idea of two such lovely girls, clearly from good families, being so knowledgeable about domination. 'Tell me, have you two ever seen this famous bathroom of David's?'

'Oh sure,' Faye replied eagerly.

'It was great!' Carol exclaimed.

'I've heard so much about that bathroom from Mary,' said Jack. 'Now I feel like I'm the only one who's never even seen it. I'm determined to at least see it.'

'Carol and I want to see it again.'

'The three of you will get yourselves into a mess,' Mary sighed, shaking her head.

'You're like a reformed alcoholic.' Jack laughed. 'Like when they get all upset because somebody has a glass of wine.'

'Domination is a whiskey distillery my friends, not a glass of wine.'

'It's a bit late for you to come over all moral,' Carol told Mary. 'After all we've done lately.'

'It's never too late for hypocrisy,' Mary replied, and everyone laughed.

'So, Jack,' said Faye, 'you want to be dominated?'

'Yes, I can't help it,' he admitted, enjoying his own guilt. 'After what Mary did to me, I'm obsessed. I have to have it.'

'Find a prostitute who does it,' Mary suggested. 'I'm having nothing to do with you.'

'Why not?' asked Carol. 'It's only domination. It's not full sex, or marriage, or living together.'

'Exactly,' said Jack. 'It's nothing. Come on, Mary, you know you'd enjoy it. Help me out.'

'Oh God,' Mary groaned. 'I was chasing after David, and he didn't want me, and now you're chasing after me and I don't want you. It's like a bloody Dostoyevsky novel.'

'It's not as bad as that,' Carol protested. She and Faye looked at one another and exchanged nods. 'If all you want is to be dominated, Jack, then Faye and I could try, if you'd be interested.'

'Really?' Jack gulped.

'Absolutely not,' Mary snapped.

'It's not your house, and you're not our mother,' Carol said firmly. 'Faye and I have discussed dominating a man, and how interesting it'd be to try.'

'We're experimenting,' Faye said to Jack, as though that explained everything.

'It doesn't seem like such a big deal,' said Carol, 'after what we've been doing with Mary.'

'Oh, do help us, Mary. Please, please, please,' Faye wheedled. 'We'll only make a mess of it without you. Come on, you know you'd enjoy it.'

'You're right,' Mary agreed quietly, suddenly losing all her ability to resist. 'I will.' A wave of lust swept through her, all warm and tingly, as she imagined all the things the three of them could do with Jack. To Jack.

The expression on her face, the tensing of her muscles, the very odour of her body, all so strongly conveyed her sudden arousal that Jack, Carol and Faye were as aware of it as they would have been of a huge bonfire they stumbled towards after a long, hungry march across a dark and frozen plain.

'This evening,' Mary announced. There was no need for her to explain. 'A few hours to build interest.'

They finished their meal in a state of arousal that was uncomfortable and comic.

'You're excused from washing the dishes,' Mary told Jack, seeing how his trapped erection made movement difficult.

As it was a sunny afternoon, Jack went to work in the garden. He kept going to the toilet to empty his bladder and so temporarily lose his erection. The three women made plans, readied equipment, and then tried to distract themselves with housework. All were so excited that a great deal of work got done in house and garden.

Late in the afternoon, the four of them changed into swimsuits and enjoyed themselves in the pool. The women flaunted their lovely bodies and exchanged occasional kisses and caresses, arousing Jack to a point where he could hardly stand his own lust. He knew that these gorgeous females already had a plan for his domination and chastisement, his utter humiliation. They had the will, the desire, the equipment, and they possessed a youthful beauty that was, for Jack, a source and the very centre of lust, agony and fear. Yet he had to swim and play with these delectable mermaids without touching their long curving bodies, and without the aid and comfort of being held by them as a helpless prisoner in strict restraint.

A light dinner followed, and then Mary told Jack to undress, leave his clothes in the kitchen, and wait in the living room. Soon he was alone and naked in that large room, where terrifying equipment had been laid out, and the large heavy table of dark wood had been raised on end and leaned against the wall. The sight of these preparations filled Jack with crawling, shivery anxiety. It seemed to him that he waited alone for a very long time.

When the three women came into the room at last, Jack took a deep breath and held it. Their beauty and air of determination were startling. Faye wore only a black fishnet catsuit with broad mesh and an open crotch, while Carol's body was adorned by thigh-length black plastic boots and a matching belt and long gloves. Mary had on only a black leather corset. Jack let out the breath he held and gazed in awe at the women's beauty. Faye's huge breasts, Carol's great height and Mary's perfect full round arse struck him like physical blows; yet these were only the most obvious features. Everything about these women, from their hair and bright eyes to their feet, was gorgeous. Their female perfection seemed, to Jack, to demand the most extreme devotion, love, worship and sacrifice.

'First,' Mary stated, 'you must insult us.'

'What?'

'I'm sure you heard what I said. Insult us. Call us names. Be rude. Be nasty. Hurry up, you're wasting time.'

'You're telling me to insult you?'

'I told you he was a stupid bastard,' Mary said to Carol and Faye as she picked up a red leather cat-o'-nine.

'Insult the three of us,' Carol told Jack. 'So we have a reason to punish you. A real motive. A need.'

'How can I insult three such gorgeous women?'

'Because we order you to,' Mary snapped. 'Come on! If you don't insult us very quickly, we won't waste our time on you. You'll simply have to leave. And your insults must be firmly based on reality. No random, meaningless statements.'

'You can do it, Jack,' said Faye. 'You can say my breasts are too big.'

'You can say I'm stupid and crazy,' said Mary, 'because I ran after David and then got poor Carol and Faye involved with all this domination crap.'

'And you can say Faye and I are stupid naive middle-class idiots who allow Mary to manipulate us.'

'But if you don't start in the next few seconds,' Mary told Jack, 'you're out of here. I swear.'

'Your tits really are too big,' Jack insulted Faye in desperation, suddenly convinced that Mary meant what she said. 'Far too big. Ugly huge lumps of fat.'

'More, more,' Mary insisted. 'Say worse things, much worse. Really and truly insult us. With skill. Shock us to the core.'

'You run after David like a bitch in heat,' Jack yelled, half crazy with shame and lust. 'He doesn't want you, he treats like you dirt. I want you, so you treat me like dirt, that's what a pathetic loser you are.'

'Good!' Carol applauded. 'But you can do much better.'

'Use dirty words as well,' Faye demanded. 'Or Carol and I won't let you stay here even if Mary wanted you to stay.'

'Mary sows confusion wherever she goes, she's mentally ill,' Jack cried out, pained by his burning erection. 'She's fucked up my life, her own life and she'll fuck up your lives too.'

'This is better,' Mary said pleasantly. 'Now, we're starting to get somewhere.' She lay down on the rug with a cushion under her head. 'Let's all relax. Faye, Carol, you should sit on the sofa. Jack, you can stand here and jerk off. But only if you insult us far more nastily.'

Jack clutched his cock and pumped it as the three women took up position in front of him. Their eyes were bright with excitement, and their faces were lit up by the pure smiles of carnivores.

'My life is a wreck,' Jack groaned. 'Since you dominated me, all I can think of is you engulfing me in bondage and hurting me. I'm obsessed with you. You've ruined my life. I used to be normal, now I'm as sick and crazy as you. You want me, Faye and Carol to have the same mental illness as you, you crazy bitch. You're just dirty and nasty.' Now that he was masturbating, the words flowed more freely.

'Good!' Mary laughed. 'Now you're telling the truth at last.' She caressed herself avidly, squeezing her cunt with both hands as though trying to get out all the juice. 'Stop!' she ordered. 'Take your hands away from your cock.'

Her manner was so commanding, and Jack was so submissive, that he obeyed despite his burning need to come. With a slight smile on her autocratic features, Mary picked up a flexible black rubber cap shaped like a small bell. On its inner surface it had hard rubber studs and a short knobbly stem of softer rubber. She smeared lubricant from a tube on this stem, and then fitted the cap so that it encased the helmet of Jack's cock, with the stem entering his penis. He gasped in awe at the power of the perverse penetration, and revelled in the fascinated gaze of Carol and Faye who were eagerly stroking and squeezing one another's bodies. Mary next fitted a leather cock corset to encase Jack's shaft, fastening its five external straps rather more tightly than Jack would have preferred. Then she fitted a padded leather sheath over Jack's penis, after which she bound his balls and the root of his genitals with a soft red cotton cord. Lastly, she fitted a nest of black leather straps around his waist and thighs, with straps between his buttocks and on either side of his cock. Jack groaned as the lubricated rubber knob fitted to the strap between his buttocks slid home. Mary fastened all the buckles on the set of connected straps, then attached the rings at the base of the leather sheath around Jack's cock to the rings on the straps on either side of his genitals.

'Interesting,' said Mary.

'Oh, my God,' Jack groaned in awe.

'Carry on insulting us, Jack,' Mary ordered, sitting in an armchair. 'You may masturbate. If you don't insult the three of us far more severely, we won't let you stay a minute longer. We don't need you. Come on, you fool, insult us properly.'

'You cruel bitch, Mary,' Jack groaned. Desperately, he clutched his shaft, but he could hardly feel his own grip due to the two layers of leather imprisoning his penis. Only by squeezing his balls and the head of his cock, could he impart any stimulation to his genitals, and to do so was more of a pain than a pleasure; yet such was his lust that he had to embrace this suffering in the hope that it might eventually lead to orgasm.

'Don't try to remove anything from your stupid little cock and balls,' Mary told him as she teased her clitoris with a vibrator. 'If you try, we'll only overpower you and tie you up.'

'Insult us, please, Jack,' said Faye. 'You've hardly insulted Carol and me at all. Turn us on with dirty words.'

'You filthy sluts,' Jack gasped. 'Stupid bimbo dykes. Mary is simply using you because David won't fuck her and whip her and tie her up, so she's pissed off with the world. A melon-breasted dyke and a tall freak dyke. Stupid cunts.'

'Good, good,' Carol moaned. Faye lay back and Carol mounted her, rubbing hard against her soft body.

Insults are addictive. Politeness is a good habit, which like all the other elements of civilisation, can be lost with shocking rapidity. Vile words poured from Jack's mouth as the minutes passed, a flow fuelled by his lust and frustration as well as by the women's encouragement. He felt that he might be able to come despite the confinement of his penis if only he could find enough filthy words and insults.

153

'That's enough,' Mary suddenly announced. 'Now we'll put you in restraint, unwrap your cock, and help you to come.'

Mary's statement, and her cold calmness, filled Jack with fresh fear. What would she, Carol and Faye do to him after he had insulted them so much? Should he not resist, even if it meant he had to leave? But even as he was asking himself these questions, the women were urging him towards the table that stood leaning with its top against the wall, and very quickly they had tied his wrists and ankles to its four legs, using red cotton cords that went over the top of the table as well as around its legs, so that he was helpless and spreadeagled. As his back was to the table, his genitals were proffered defencelessly to the women, at their disposal.

'I didn't mean what I said,' Jack babbled. 'I was only obeying your orders to insult you.'

'What a cliché!' said Mary. 'Are you a German?'

'I couldn't refuse, right? You're a goddess. I must obey you.'

'You've failed an important test,' Mary said grimly as she began to remove the leather sheath from Jack's cock. 'You should have refused to insult us. That's obvious. Even an idiot like you should have been able to see that. You should have said we were so beautiful and good that you couldn't possibly say a word against us. Instead you revealed what you really think of us.'

'You were horrible, Jack,' Carol said angrily.

'I never thought anyone could be so nasty and stupid,' Faye sighed. 'Now I start to understand men.'

'No punishment can be severe enough for what you said to us,' Mary stated. She finished removing the bindings from Jack's genitals, leaving them naked and vulnerable.

'You know I didn't mean what I said!'

'Nobody knows anything about anybody,' Mary replied.

Jack suddenly became truly terrified. He knew he had been a fool to chase after Mary after what she had done to him in that hotel, but what proved his stupidity was the fact that he had allowed these three women to make him helpless. He would have given anything to turn back the clock. How serious and angry they looked! Surely they were mentally ill, capable of any cruelty.

'Let's play a nice little game,' Mary announced. 'The three of us will take turns playing with Jack's cock. We'll take five minutes each. Now then, Jack, listen carefully. If you can come while I'm playing with your cock, we'll let you go, and then we'll have some fun together. But if you come while Faye or Carol are playing with you, then you'll really suffer. You'll be punished severely, and you won't even enjoy it, because you'll have come already. There are too many clichés in domination, and one of these is that a man is punished until he comes. What's the point of that? The man enjoys himself because he has an erection, so it's not true punishment at all. In this game you risk punishment after you've lost your erection.' Mary smiled a warm and happy smile, proud of herself for inventing such a good game. 'You should thank me sincerely for thinking of this.'

'No, no,' Jack babbled. 'Faye, Carol, don't go along with this. She's crazy. Now I see it clearly. She's still obsessed with David. She wants to win his approval by training us. She'll end up presenting us to David, and he won't be able to resist. He's the one Mary's interested in. We're just pawns in her real game, her game with David. We'll end up in that crazy bastard's bathroom. She'll use the three of us to gain his interest. Faye, Carol, you have to – umm! Mmm!' Jack's tirade had been ended abruptly by a rubber gag. Mary had suddenly pushed it into his mouth while he had been staring at Carol and Faye, striving to convince them, and now Mary was buckling its attached red leather straps around his head with her usual efficiency.

'What a baby!' Faye exclaimed. 'We haven't even done anything to him yet. That's pathetic.'

'He comes here begging to be dominated and, as soon as it starts, he panics,' said Carol. 'It makes me angry.'

'Mind you, there's probably something in what he said about you and David, Mary. Don't you think so?'

'David and I are through. I have no plan to train you, Carol and Jack and then hand you to him as a gift to win his approval. What a silly idea! Nobody could be that crazy,' Mary stated. She paused. Thought again. 'Mind you, I'm no judge of my own motives. Who knows? Maybe David would enjoy you three.' Sincerity had always been her main vice.

'How reassuring!' Carol observed. 'You've certainly stopped me worrying. Thanks a lot, Mary.'

'Oh, who cares?' said Faye. 'We'll cross that bridge when we come to it. Or we'll take a ferry. Go another route.'

'David and Mary couldn't force us to do anything anyway,' Carol reassured herself, and shrugged. 'Who's first with Jack? I want to go first.'

'I'll go first,' Mary insisted. 'You're too eager. You'll make him come, and that will end this game too quickly.'

'Carol likes cocks,' said Faye. 'It's her guilty secret.'

'I do not! Well, not much. It's just a slight interest.'

'Tell me when my five minutes are up,' said Mary. None of them were wearing watches, but there was a Victorian clock on the mantelpiece, an ornate black and gold piece of architecture not quite as big as an altar, which seemed to witness the proceedings in the room with an enviable sense of rectitude and superiority.

Mary had a plan for tormenting Jack's penis. It was simple, and she was sure it would be fun. For her, not for Jack. She drew up a wooden chair and sat on it in front of her prisoner. How nicely trussed he was! A bound and gagged man presented so many possibilities. Now she could fight Jack tooth and nail. He deserved all the punishment in the world for not being David.

'If you come while I'm playing with you, it'll prove you love me,' said Mary. 'If you come with Faye or Carol, it'll be a deadly insult to me. So I suggest you try very hard to come in the next five minutes.' She grazed Jack's cock with her sharp fingernails, up and down his shaft, and under the rim of his shiny swollen glans.

Jack thrust his tautly bloated penis at her, striving with all his strength to come, straining towards the painful and fleeting stimulation of her nails. Faye and Carol watched in amazement, fondling one another with mounting excitement as they fully understood the cunning cruelty of Mary's tactics in this uneven battle: she was fencing with Jack's cock, as though it were a sword.

Flick, flick. Mary teased and tormented her victim with the slightest movements of her fingers. Jack moaned through his gag, as though he were being tortured with red hot knives. Mary jabbed at his balls, slashed lightly across his frenum, prodded the slit of his glans, then concentrated on jabs under the rim of Jack's knob, doling out to him exquisite torment in tiny portions, hurting and stimulating the most sensitive flesh of his penis, finding nerves he had hardly known he had, forcing him to experience lustful and delicious pains and pleasures he had never dared to comprehend even in his fantasies and dreams.

'We are aware of nothing, you see,' Mary observed as her nails flicked and jabbed like the claws of a playful kitten practising its future career as a sadistic murderer of birds. 'You, me and Jack. Even David. None of us has even begun to know ourselves. What we are, what we can do and feel. And be. Nobody has begun. The human race is still waiting to be born.' She was masturbating as she spoke, and strange, powerful ideas flooded her mind as she neared the verge of the abyss named orgasm.

Cruelly, she used her hair too, trailing its chestnut strands over Jack's gleaming, rigid glans, flesh so tautly bloated that it seemed as if it could burst. Jack thrust and thrust, all his muscles rigid, straining to come with all his might. Then she used her nails again in all manner of ways. Sweat erupted from every pore of Jack's skin, drool oozed from his gag. All his efforts were to no avail, and he shuddered with frustration.

'Five minutes,' Faye announced.

'So soon? Come on then, Faye, you have a go.'

'He's not going to come in my five minutes, not if I can help it,' Faye announced as she took Mary's place on the chair in front of Jack. Her method of teasing was to use her huge breasts, so attractively packaged in black broad-mesh fishnet. Carefully, she held them in her hands and pressed them to the prisoner's balls and the base of his cock, making brief and repeated contacts while Jack thrust and strained for all he was worth, unable to resist Faye's youthful attractions despite Mary's warning.

Watching Faye aroused Carol and Mary so much that they had to make love on the sofa. Mary came loudly when she was on top and, shortly afterwards, Carol rode Mary and also reached the heights and depths and fires of mindless ecstasy. Jack stared at them with bulging eyes, and strained to come by thrusting the head of his cock against Faye's hard right nipple and the fishnet surrounding it, grunting through his bitter rubber gag like a crazed baboon.

'Oh!' Faye gasped, pulling back sharply. 'Ugh. Yeuk!'

'Did he come?' asked Mary.

'No, but he nearly did. A few drops dribbled out.'

'How disgusting! What a filthy animal! Your five minutes is up, Faye. It's your turn, Carol.'

The remarkably tall girl had an odd expression as she took over from Faye, and Mary suspected that Carol found Jack attractive. That, thought Mary, will be a useful thing to know. It opened up new possibilities. As for Faye, she looked a little anxious as Carol moved the chair away from Jack and stood in front of him. Mary distracted Faye as well as she could by pulling her down onto the sofa and playing with her breasts, though in fact Mary and Faye were both so curious about Carol and Jack that they did not pay much attention to one another for all that they groped and humped.

'You'd like to come, wouldn't you?' said Carol, caressing Jack's balls. She rubbed her breasts lightly on his chest, so that her nipples touched his again and again. 'Even your nipples are hard, so hard,' she crooned, pulling on them. 'You'd like to shoot all over me, wouldn't you? Deluge my face and tits and arse with your filthy sticky smelly mess. Subjugate me. Humiliate me. Fun for you. Nasty for me. But you'd like that. Because you're just bad.'

Tall and slender, supple and strong, Carol looked gorgeous as she took her long pale-gold hair in both hands and caressed every part of Jack's body with its tickly strands before whipping his cock with it, giving him an exquisite, haunting stimulation that seemed to pull his very soul into his penis. His own cock became his own prison.

'I need more than five minutes,' said Carol.

'Take as long as you like,' Mary replied.

Carol rubbed her breasts, belly, thighs and pussy, gazing into Jack's eyes. Then she turned around and bent over, to rub her arse on the prisoner's cock and balls. Sometimes she leaned back, allowing him to thrust with frantic urgency at the cleft between her buttocks, but every time she moved forwards again, leaving his penis to beat hopelessly up and down in the air. For a long time she teased and stimulated him with her hands, hair, breasts and buttocks. She even used her plastic-covered feet, sitting on the chair and holding his penis between them, tormenting his glans. Mary and Faye came at almost the same time, clasping their bodies together. Masturbating with growing fervour, Carol began to pant and grunt.

Suddenly, she pressed her body to Jack's, clasping his waist and rubbing her clitoris up and down on his cock. She gave a strangled cry, and saliva sprayed and dribbled from her open mouth as her tongue stuck far out. Sinking to her knees, she clutched at Jack's cock with one hand, and her pussy with the other. Her mouth suckled hungrily on the taut straining helmet she had tormented so well, and Jack shrieked through his gag as he was torn apart by an orgasm of appalling ferocity.

'No!' cried Faye. She might have pulled Carol away from Jack, but Mary held her back.

Gasping and laughing, Carol leaned back, held her captive cock down, and took jet after jet over her face, hair and breasts. It was an awesome display, and even Mary was impressed. Spattering, splashing and spraying, Jack's penis hosed Carol, submitting her lovely body to a deluge.

'Lick all that mess off her,' Mary ordered, as she began to free Jack's limbs and remove his gag. 'Lick and swallow.'

Once he was free, Jack crouched on the floor to slurp and gulp slavishly, cleaning Carol's long lean body, even sucking the wet spots of her long hair. She clearly enjoyed the attention.

'Carol, you're so bad,' Faye complained.

'I'm sorry. I just couldn't help myself. Please forgive me.'

'Yes, yes, I have to forgive you, you're so beautiful.'

'And now you'll have to be punished,' Mary told Jack when he had completed his task. 'I told you to come while I was playing with you, not Carol or Faye. You deliberately disobeyed me.'

'It was Carol. She made me come.'

'That's disgusting. You blame a woman instead of taking responsibility for your own actions. That earns you a more severe punishment. I'm not even going to make things easy for you by putting you into restraint. No, you'll have to stay still. And afterwards you'll have to show your gratitude by licking my arse.'

Mary had Jack arrange cushions on the floor and ordered him to lie on them face down. He obeyed instantly.

'You may play with your cock while I whip you.'

'Thank you, Mistress, thank you.'

'Don't thank me. I simply want you to associate pain with pleasure even more closely. So I can control and exploit and hurt you. I deserve some pleasure.'

Mary picked up the leather cat-o'-nine and felt a delicious warm surge of anticipation. It was even better than opening a large box of chocolates.

'I'm going to give you twenty blows at unpredictable intervals over the next half-hour,' Mary stated. 'Carol, put this blindfold on him, please; it's better if he can't see when a blow is coming. Jack, you must stick your tongue out a long way and lick Carol and Faye's feet while I whip you. After that we'll tie you up very thoroughly indeed, using as much rope and as many cords, belts and harnesses as we can possibly get around your wretched, puny body. Then I'm sure we'll think of something to do to you.'

Eleven

For the next three days, Mary, Jack, Carol and Faye feverishly dreamed up new combinations and styles of domination, restraint and punishment, which they acted out with the purest pleasure. Jack did not penetrate any of the women, but since he could come in other ways, under peculiarly interesting circumstances, he was not simply happy, but rapturous. He began to agree with Mary that penetration was overrated. Faced with having to decide whether to resume his sales work or stay with three women practising advanced deviations, he actually found it rather a difficult decision to make, being extremely English. Finally, he managed to phone his boss and feign sickness. On the fourth day rather than the seventh they rested, lacking the energy of God.

'I'm going to the shops,' Jack announced after breakfast on the day after that, a day which had dawned with brightness and heat.

'Perhaps you could borrow a few things from David on the way back,' said Mary with a somewhat studied casualness. 'He has so much equipment it'd be fun for the four of us to try. He'll probably lend some to you.'

'Sure,' Jack agreed. 'Anyway, I want to take a look at that bathroom of his. I used to hear so much about it.'

'I wish we could use it,' said Faye. 'Mary, couldn't you sort of pretend to forgive David a little, so we could use his bathroom. OK. A bad idea. I see it in your face.'

'You bet it's a bad idea,' Mary said coldly. 'I hate the bastard. No, I don't even hate him, he's not that important.' She stared at Jack, Faye and Carol with her hazel eyes blazing. Wisely, nobody argued even though nobody believed her. They knew what it meant when her eyes blazed.

When Jack returned nearly two hours later, he had news that gave Mary a shock.

'David is not far behind me,' he told Mary. 'He wants to apologise to you. He's determined to apologise.'

'I don't want to listen to his lies,' Mary snapped.

'Up to you, up to you,' Jack assured her. 'Break his neck if you want to. What do I care? I'll send him in and you can do what you like with him, or to him.'

Mary turned off the Bartok CD she was listening to, and realised that her emotions and thoughts were as jangly and tempestuous as Piano Concerto No. 2. What on earth was she to do or say or feel? She and David had, by now, more history than the Austro-Hungarian Empire.

And then there he was, yet one more time, all of him all at once, joining her in the living room, David himself as real as anything. Yet again she saw him when she had thought, one more time, that they were finished. To start was difficult enough, and then it was even harder to finish. She gave David a chilling look of dangerous hostility, but it suddenly struck her that she had asked Jack to go to David and borrow some equipment because she wanted to annoy David and to find out what he was doing, so she only had herself to blame for David's coming here now. She had prodded a poisonous snake with a stick. Rarely a wise move.

'Hi, Mary. You look great. How are you feeling?'

'Not so bad considering the terrible things you did to me.'

'Yes. You're right. They were terrible.' David sighed heavily and sat on the sofa. He looked grave, upset and guilty, but Mary reminded herself that he had probably decided to look this way.

'I've come to apologise. I did terrible things to you, Mary. You deserve an apology. I'm sorry. Really. I'm a complete bastard. I'm crap. Every bad thing I've done haunts me.'

'Good. You deserve to suffer a little. Well, you deserve to suffer a lot, but a little is at least a start.' Mary stood sternly erect, gazing down at David with her arms folded. She wondered how it would feel to beat him up. Certainly she had the size, strength and skill. He was small and out of shape. Indeed she doubted that he had ever been in shape. To beat him up would be revenge. But would it be enjoyable?

'There isn't any reason for us to talk,' she told him. 'We must have done and said everything possible by now.'

'No, Mary, we haven't said everything. Or at least I certainly haven't. I've always been too cowardly to do one thing. Sexually, I've done just about everything bad that's possible, but that's nothing. In fact I'm a coward, because I've never done the only thing in life that's truly important. With myself and with other people I've never been sincere.'

'That's a great build-up,' Mary sneered. 'I bet you've been planning it for days. So now you're going to be sincere at last, are you, after all this time? How nice!' She was trying hard to be cynical, striving not to be tempted.

'I deserve your disbelief. But anyway. Here goes. The thing is, Mary, I've always been afraid of you.'

'Afraid? That's rich! You afraid of me! For God's sake, David, get a grip. You're the one who dominated me, restrained and punished me, bound and fucked me. You're the one with a weird bathroom and a huge collection of even weirder equipment and garments, and I'm the bloody fool who let you experiment on my

164

helpless body in every perverse, nasty way you could think of, every way physically possible. It's a bit late in the day for you to try to trick me by pretending you're afraid of me. What's the plan this time? You expect me to feel sorry for you?'

'I expect nothing,' David replied quietly. 'There are no plans.'

'No plans. That in itself is a plan.'

'Listen to me for one minute, then I'll leave. Yes. I'm afraid of you. I always have been. Of course I am. How could I not be afraid of you? You're so strong and I'm so weak. You're so strong that you voluntarily, freely, willingly, took everything I could think of. And you demanded more. You were full of ideas for bathroom domination, my own crazy specialised fetish, and all your ideas were good. I had never dreamed any woman could surpass me in my own obsession. I had never even fantasised a woman of such beauty as you. Nor one so strong. You didn't submit to me. You joined me as a partner. And you outdid me. I saw you were willing to go anywhere with me. All extremes. Any depths. I became afraid of you very quickly, but I hid it. Of course I was also having the time of my life, because all my most extreme, bizarre fantasies were becoming everyday reality. But I was afraid. And I became more afraid. Because I'm a coward. I'm weak. So two years ago I drove you away from me because I was so afraid of your strength. Your energy, your lusts, your capacity for punishment, endurance, pleasure, ecstasy. Your joy. Joy is the highest strength. Your trust. I've never been worthy of anyone's trust, especially yours. Your demands, desires. In a way, almost everything about you frightened me, because I knew your strengths and my own weaknesses. And since I forced you to leave me, I've only become weaker. You saw what a mess I am when you turned up again a few weeks ago. That was a huge shock, you turning up again. Seeking me out.

Coming back despite everything after two years, full of hope and courage. You're so brave and good I can hardly stand it. So beautiful. Your beauty and your sexual courage frighten me. So when you returned, my only thought was how to get rid of you again. Stupid.'

Mary tried to force herself to say something nasty, but the words did not even get far enough to stick in her throat. She was sure David was being completely sincere, no matter how much she wanted to believe he was lying.

'Oh God, what a load of crap life is,' she complained with deep bitterness. 'Why can't we just have fun? Everybody is such a mess. I was just getting over you and you have to come and confuse me all over again. Thanks a lot.'

'Sorry. You're right. I shouldn't have come.' David stood up slowly, as though weighed down by his own body. 'I'll leave. I only came to say I'm sorry and to explain.'

'You're not suggesting we start again?' Mary asked, with the strangest mixture of hope, anger and lust that she had ever known. David's answer fell on her like a big stone.

'No. We mustn't. It'd be an even bigger mess.'

'I'm sure you're right.' Mary left the living room with David, intending to see him to the door. Before they could get that far, they were intercepted by Carol, Faye and Jack.

'Could we talk to you for a moment, David?' said Jack.

'Sure,' David agreed. They ushered him back into the living room.

Mary followed. She guessed what they had in mind, and knew fear and hope. How dare they! Yet if only they would.

'This is a little difficult to say,' Jack began. 'The thing is, I've heard so much about that bathroom of yours.'

'Faye and I have seen it,' said Carol, blushing only very slightly. 'When you asked us to catsit. It's fascinating.'

'So we were wondering,' Jack continued, 'if we might be able to work out something for our mutual advantage. Sorry for sounding like a salesman. Force of habit.'

'You can use our pool and we'll use your bathroom,' Faye said brightly. 'Do say yes. It'd be wonderful.'

'A lot depends on whether you and Mary are back together again,' said Carol, adding with a kind of scientific detachment, 'then there'd be five of us, and we could have an interesting time. Sort of a research project.'

'David and I are not back together,' Mary announced firmly. 'We're through once and for all. I'm not getting involved in lunatic group sex with David.'

'Not group sex,' Faye protested mildly. 'We were thinking more of . . . it's hard to say the words.'

'Pleasure without penetration,' David suggested, suddenly becoming more cheerful. 'Perhaps massage, mutual masturbation. Voyeurism. Dressing up. Harmless games. Possibly leading to experiments in mild restraint by mutual, specific agreements.'

'Exactly,' Jack agreed warmly. 'Anything we agree to.'

'Of course, I'd be delighted,' said David.

'Out of the question,' snapped Mary. 'Faye and Carol, you are not going to get involved in any way with David.'

'Sorry, Mary,' said Carol, 'but you're not my or Faye's mother, are you? We're free to do as we please.'

'OK! I wash my hands of you both. You'll regret anything you do with David, but it's none of my business.'

'Oh, come on, Mary, you know you'll have the time of your life if you join in,' Jack insisted. 'Anyway, it's your duty. Carol and Faye are naive, headstrong girls. They need you to guide and protect them.'

'You bloody salesman!' Mary exclaimed. Everybody laughed, and she found herself laughing too.

'You see, Mary?' said Carol. 'You're having fun already.'

'Let's have lunch together,' Jack suggested. 'Then let's go for a swim. It's so hot today! The pool will be great.'

'Mary can go to the library or something,' said Faye, giggling.

'Oh, shut up,' laughed Mary. She had to admit that there was just no way she could resist the temptation to join these four exciting idiots, no matter how determined she had been never to have anything to do with David again. What a group they might make! It made her mind reel to think of the possibilities, and it was obvious the others shared her excitement. Even David seemed to be losing some of his lassitude and depression, and how could he not feel better, thought Mary, faced with the prospect of introducing two such lovely and naive girls as Faye and Carol to his obsessions and perversions. What on earth would David do to them? Not that Mary would allow him to do anything cruel to the girls, of course. Her duties and responsibilities were absolutely clear to her. If David did anything nasty, she would beat him up. It would be easy. No doubt. No worry. And so she thought on, trying hard to tell herself lies about herself, an occupation that consumes half the time and energy of the human race.

To have lunch together was pleasant in itself for all five, as the prospect of pleasure gave them a fresh vitality. Then they changed into swimsuits: Jack and David borrowed from Carol's absent father, Mary put on a scarlet bikini of Carol's, Faye donned a white bikini that showed off her huge breasts, and Carol wore a black one-piece swimsuit with asymmetrical triangular cut-outs at her belly and back. All three women knew

168

that they were ravishing, even before David and Jack saw them and tried not to stare in awe.

To swim on such a hot sunny afternoon was a delight. They splashed and laughed, dived and played, dappled by spots of shade from the fine trees in the large and beautiful garden. The women displayed their bodies with pride, and knew that the men were becoming aroused by their arching shiny wet litheness.

'We have to do something,' Jack announced with a salesman's directness. 'Let's have some fun. We're all dying to. Look, if we keep to this corner the neighbours won't see.'

'I'll sit here and watch,' David said. 'Then we can get used to each other. And I won't annoy Mary.'

'Why don't we do what Jack talked about the other day?' Carol suggested.

Everyone agreed, so they went into the house to get waterproof vibrators, a long-handled plastic scrubbing brush, and swimming masks, plus a scarlet belt with an attached pair of plastic cuffs. On their return to the pool, they fitted the belt to Jack, secured his hands behind his back, and removed his briefs. The women put a swimming mask on Jack and lowered him into the water, then they donned their own facemasks and entered the pool, experiencing a thrilling sense of sensual delight and wickedness.

How amusing and arousing it was to torment Jack! The three women swam around his defenceless nudity, touching and kissing him and each other with impartial delight. His flailing, helplessly erect and useless cock received brief, tantalising contacts from hands, thighs and breasts. Mary used the plastic brush on his butt and cock, making him squeal and thrash, while Carol and Faye caressed her lovely body. Mary felt an irresistible impulse to be naked, so she removed her bikini and flung it at David. Laughing, Faye took off her bikini top, so her huge breasts could float freely in the water,

169

attracting the men's fascinated stares. Mary swam to the bottom of the pool and along its length, then back again, thrilled by the rush of water over her large, hard nipples. Parting her legs as widely as she could, she surfaced with her open vulva uppermost, feeling the caress of the water like a hundred tongues touching her sensitive flesh with their warm tips.

To control Jack even more absolutely, the women tied a long plastic cord to a padded leather strap around the base of his genitals. Such a leash was fun, especially when Jack swam downwards, chasing after a woman at the bottom of the pool, who adopted lewd postures to flaunt arse, pussy or breasts, seeming about to use her lovely body to make his penis explode in ecstasy. Many times they played this game, with Mary especially displaying her great lung capacity and underwater endurance. Jack could not match her abilities, and returned time and again to the surface, trailing silver bubbles while Mary quivered and wriggled around a vibrator.

'You must try much harder to come against any of us,' Mary told Jack. 'Swim with speed and determination. If you thrust your cock hard and fast, you might catch one of us by surprise and even get inside. Try hard, or we'll have to punish you for not trying sincerely.'

'What a great idea!' Carol exclaimed. She put her arms around Faye, and squeezed her lover's huge tits. The ripe flesh bulged between Carol's fingers, and Faye squealed in delightful fear of Jack's penis.

With a strange animal cry of lust and anger, Jack lunged at the gorgeous body of Faye, and actually managed to graze her belly with the tip of his tormented penis before Faye and Carol dodged aside with squeals of excitement. This brief contact maddened Jack, and he went crazy, consumed by the need to relieve the aching internal pressure of his captive and tormented lust.

'That's the spirit, Jack,' Carol cried. 'Maybe you can come after all, if only you can rub your cock against the three of us a few more times.'

'You can do it, Jack,' said Mary, and she turned over to show Jack her magnificent arse, parting her legs to flash her gaping pink pussy.

This game was wonderful for the three women, though for Jack it was an insane nightmare of chasing. Everywhere he looked were sleek female forms so young and lithe, all shiny in the sunlight, so lovely. Carol the long-haired giantess, Faye and her tits like melons, Mary with her perfect body: all three were so insanely desirable, their youthful skins gleaming in the sunlight. Taunting, unobtainable. Maddened, he pursued these visions of wet dreams with all his strength, both on the surface and underwater. Mary, Carol and Faye dodged his lunges and teased him wonderfully, holding their breasts, masturbating, arching, twisting and proffering their lovely young bodies. They flung their long legs far apart, adopted extreme postures, held each other as though to help Jack, and flaunted every detail of their gorgeous bodies. Now and then they rode his back, and often they touched his cock fleetingly with hands, feet and breasts. Most delightfully, they held the long plastic cord attached to the base of his genitals, holding him back just when he thought he might be able to ram his penis home and unleash his trapped semen in lashing spurts. He thrashed around, growing tired and breathless. His efforts were to no avail, but every time his cock achieved a brief contact with breast, belly or buttock, he would be stimulated to fresh, frantic exertions. It was a wonderfully enjoyable game. Sometimes the women embraced him from behind, to tickle his aching penis and testicles with a vibrator. Fun also to redden his arse and thighs by brisk strokes of the plastic scrubbing brush, and to order him to probe between Mary's buttocks with his tongue.

171

Mary could not stop thinking of David even though she told herself not to. She knew he would be massively aroused by the vision of three lovely young female aquanauts tormenting a helpless man so ruthlessly, especially as he had his own fetish for women and water. It was good, she thought, that he should see how sexy and strong she was, so that he would suffer the regret, the agony, of rejecting her former unconditional surrender. It was good too that he should stare in awe and lust at Carol and Faye, a lovely young lesbian couple playing with a man's bloated, burning penis, bursting with a thwarted lust that was, for Jack, an exquisitely agonising pain. No doubt David was consumed by feverish fantasies of binding and punishing the three cruel and wanton women in his insane bathroom, his mind blazing with visions of making them suffer and coming over their captive faces and tormented tits, a fitting punishment for their sexual atrocities. Good. Let him fantasise. Never again would Mary grant him such wet, slippery, shiny delights. Of course she would not help him engulf Faye and Carol in soapy bondage!

And all the time that they tantalised and chastised their twisting, tormented captive, the women masturbated, and caressed each other with mounting ardour, their inhibitions vanishing like frost in the heat of the sunny garden so rich in the scent and colour of flowers, the buzz and whirr of insect busyness, the chatter and fluting trills of birdsong.

An interesting facet of Jack's ordeal was the fact that he was not gagged, so he did not even have the relief of making sounds in his throat that came to nothing meaningful in his rubber-filled mouth. No, he had to exercise self-control, and say nothing, for fear that the neighbours would hear, and make trouble in some way. It would have been much easier for him had he been gagged, and able to try to plead for mercy or scream with all his might.

172

Enthralled and enraptured by Jack's captive, hopeless lust for their loveliness, the women caressed each other, as well as masturbating, with fervent frenzy. Arching and tensing her powerful body, Mary worked a vibrator hard, sliding it in and out of her vagina with long, rapid strokes, throwing her legs wide apart and contorting herself into bizarre poses made possible by the fact that she was in a pool, flaunting her sexuality for Jack and David's arousal and frustration. As she came, Faye and Carol suckled on her nipples, so big and hard, and stroked her belly and buttocks. This orgasm was wonderful for Mary, and it left her fresh, bright and eager for more. She hugged and kissed Carol and Faye as they struck ecstasy, their bodies pressed hard together, dogged and rigid in mutual demand.

After Jack had made further frantic efforts to rub his penis against the gorgeous sirens who lured him into the depths, the women hauled him out of the pool, released his hands and allowed him to pant for a minute or two.

'Lie here, on your back,' Mary ordered him when he had recovered from his exertions in the pool. 'You may handle your cock and come, but only as long as you serve us with your tongue. Laziness will be punished.'

Jack lay on a bench taken from the shed, which was now covered by an old duvet. His face was just at the right height for a woman to stand astride the bench and present her arse and genitals for worship. Just to make it even more interesting, Mary tied Jack's wrists to his thighs in such a way that his right hand could not reach his genitals, while his left hand could just barely, if he tried hard, reach the base of his cock with the tips of his fingers. Jack was so desperate to come that he struggled against this arrangement, but the three women held him down easily. He was now able to masturbate, but he faced a distinctly uphill struggle to achieve orgasm.

'Lick and suck for all you're worth,' Mary told him, 'or we'll simply withdraw your left hand as well.' With that, she stood over him and rested part of her weight on his face, engulfing his features in her powerful buttocks and engorged cunt.

'Oh, this is lovely,' she sighed. 'Great!' She caressed her own breasts and tweaked her nipples, arching her back in delight.

So far, David had not removed his swimming trunks. Now he did so, and began to masturbate with relaxed, simple pleasure.

'Oh God, that really is enormous.' Faye giggled nervously.

'It's huge,' Carol agreed, and shivered.

'It's just a nuisance,' said David. 'Always leading me astray. Yes, it leads me like a farmer leading a pig with a ring through its nose.'

'Pity we can't make it into bacon,' said Mary. She dipped her finger into a jar of menthol ointment and moved it slowly around the rim of Jack's knob before putting some of the ointment inside the mouth of his penis, so like the mouth of a fish. He shuddered.

Carol straddled Jack's thighs, facing Mary, and played with Jack's balls before exchanging kisses and caresses not only with Mary, but also with Faye, who stood beside them, offering her huge udders to their mouths. Mary drank some beer from a can, then poured more over her breasts so that it ran down her body to Jack's face, making him cough and splutter in a way the women found amusing. Quickly, he resumed his fervent sucking and licking, surprising Mary into a swift and deliciously shivery orgasm.

After giving up her place to Carol, Mary could not help but look at David and that cock of his. Or perhaps, she thought, she was looking at a penis and its David. The two of them were the centre of all the problems in her world, a kind of personal Palestine. What a selfish, cruel bastard David was really. Yet she understood him so well, and he understood her, much better than they understood other people. And he had finally apologised and explained. That was very important. Each of them knew what the other was thinking and feeling, and they could make each other laugh – how could you resist such a shock of mutual recognition?

'I'll do it,' she said to David as she knelt down beside him and took his cock in her hand. It felt just right, like a household gadget from Japan. 'Just don't think this means anything, you little rat.'

'I stopped thinking a long time ago.'

'Liar.' At first, Mary had intended to give David a casual, perfunctory handjob, but soon she was using both her hands and all of her skill and care. Carol and Faye meanwhile became massively aroused facing each other astride Jack, taking turns on his face and thighs. As they kissed and caressed one another lovingly, they were both possessed by a sensual madness.

'You know what would be really thrilling?' Carol told Faye. 'If Jack came over us while we made love.'

'Oh, yes, my darling,' Faye gasped. 'I can just imagine it.'

'Go for it,' Mary urged them, eager to see such perversity. Not only would it be exciting to watch, but the more other women did strange things, the better she felt about herself. Carol removed her black swimsuit to reveal her gorgeous nudity.

It was the work of a moment to free Jack and give him his instructions. Faye and Carol lay on an airbed of scarlet plastic against the fence beside the swimming pool, and they kissed and giggled, feeling as though their own audacity had made them completely drunk. Jack knelt beside them and gripped his tormented penis, which quickly began to vomit huge quantities of cream in leaping spurts of shocking length and power, while he arched his body and made strange gurgling sounds, quiet and rapid, his tongue sticking far out, as though he were being tortured. Carol and Faye gasped and writhed as they were lashed by jets of hosing male fluid.

Seeing that David too was going to come, Mary could not resist taking the end of his huge knob into her mouth. Holding his shaft tightly with both hands, she took the stunning blast of his jetting in her mouth. She swallowed none of it. When David was fully spent and subsided, panting for breath, Mary stood up and drooled, making rivulets run down her throat and breasts.

Laughing, the women went indoors for a shower, then returned to the pool where they had insisted the men remain. For another two hours, the five of them had a happy time, alternately swimming in the warm water and resting by the poolside. All became freshly aroused, but decided to save their energy for later. It was only natural that David stay for dinner. And it was inevitable that after dinner the thoughts of everyone turned towards his remarkable bathroom, his bizarre obsession.

'Shall we go to my place and run a bath?' David inquired.

'Just try,' Mary replied, 'to stop us.'

Twelve

To return to that fateful bathroom was so peculiar an experience for Mary that she felt she was dreaming. It was insane to go back. Nothing could be more stupid. It was even impossible to go back. Nobody could. Yet she was doing it. Once more. Yet again. It might as well have been a powerful magnet, and she a tiny fleck of iron. What must David think of her for coming back after all his cruelty? He could only despise her. No doubt he always had. Not that she cared what he thought, of course.

'This is so exciting!' Faye exclaimed as soon as they were all inside David's front door. 'I'm so glad you and David are back together again, Mary.'

'We're not back together,' Mary replied sternly. 'So what if I touched his cock? Big cock, big deal. It means no more than shaking someone's hand.'

'I hope you touch it again,' said Jack. 'I enjoy seeing you do it, it makes me feel utterly worthless and humiliated. It's wonderful.' He was practically babbling, and his excitement was shared by Carol and Faye.

As soon as the five of them entered the bathroom, Mary noticed with a slight shock that David had done a great deal of hard cleaning. Now everything looked as shiny and insanely, nightmarishly beautiful as the first time she had seen it long, long ago, when the universe was young.

David started a foamy bath running. The room was radiant with the golden light of sunset reflected from the leaves of the trees.

'What I suggest is this,' he announced with quiet authority. 'We look at my collection while the bath is running. Then we have fun masturbating and touching. Perhaps, Carol and Faye, you would even allow Jack and I to touch you. No intercourse of any kind, naturally. But if you don't like the idea, that's fine too. No pressure.'

'Oh, I think touching would be OK,' Carol replied at once, and Faye nodded in agreement.

Mary thought that eventually Carol and Faye would find themselves in deeper waters of sexual perversion than they had ever dreamed existed. She felt sure David planned to lure them there by small, easy steps that would seem natural to take, and impossible to refuse. What would these fundamentally innocent girls feel when David revealed his true nature, his overwhelming power? Already she could tell he was freshly alert and active as his old self rose back to the surface from the black depths where he had forced it into hiding. But it was no business of hers what David did with Carol and Faye, if they chose to ignore her frequent warnings. They wanted to experiment. OK. Soon they might find themselves being treated as the subjects of experiments, like laboratory rats.

David opened the huge dark cupboard in the corner, and began taking out costumes, garments, and items for restraint and chastisement. Mary was stunned to realise that many of them were brand new, which meant that David was determined to resume his old ways. All his efforts to give up his peculiar fetish of bathroom domination had been abandoned, and Mary could not help but feel that David was doing the right thing, as his attempts had only led to his being depressed. Jack was seeing these things for the first time, so he was unaware of the deeper meaning revealed by their newness. As for Faye and Carol, they had only seen them once before, and then they had been in something like a state of shock, so Mary was sure that they could not remember them clearly. They too did not understand what these new items meant: the old David was back. Mary looked for a moment into his eyes, and they exchanged a secret smile of complicity. David seemed certain that Mary would not explain to the others that the newness of so many items meant that they were all in danger. The curious thing was that he was right: she would not tell. How well he knew her! Nobody else in her whole life had ever begun to understand her half as well. Mary told herself not to be so pleased by his understanding, by their smile of complicity, but it was no good. She felt a deliciously warm tingle of pleasure spread suddenly through her whole body and soul.

The five of them went into the living room to undress. Faye and Carol were only a little shy and nervous, as they had got used to being naked with Jack and Mary. They returned to the bathroom and took a shower together. The insanely clever design of the room appealed greatly to Jack, Faye and Carol: since the whole floor was tiled, and inclined in gentle planes to four drains, they could be wet and soapy anywhere. Mary broke the ice by soaping the other four, rubbing her body against theirs. At first, Faye and Carol were very nervous when David and Jack touched them, their cocks fully erect. With great excitement, the men caressed the girls' lovely young naked bodies, praising the beauty of Carol's long legs and Faye's breasts. Mary handled their erections with great pleasure, and she rubbed them on her body, filling everybody with almost unbearable excitement. She found the act not simply thrilling, but a profound joy, and shockingly beautiful.

'This is lovely,' Faye whispered, awestruck.

'Why doesn't everybody do this sort of thing?' Carol wondered.

'Because they're trained to settle for less,' Mary replied. 'Much less. Everybody has to be kept dissatisfied to keep capitalism and consumerism going.' She lay on the water bed and masturbated with fine vigour, striking extreme poses to turn on the others even more. They all caressed her and themselves, loving the feel of warm slippery water and bubbling soap. She had Jack lie on the undulating warm plastic of the water bed, and she went on all fours over him, to rub her breasts on his penis. David, Faye and Carol poured warm water over the pair and soaped them both, thoroughly. After a while, Mary lay on Jack facing up, and took his cock between her soapy thighs, masturbating while he played with her breasts. Then she squatted over his head, engulfing Jack's face under the powerful round globes of her arse, using both hands and her mouth on his cock while he gurgled, bubbled, and delightedly gasped for breath, his fingers tweaking her huge rigid teats. Arching and screaming he came, and Mary took his jetting spurts over her face and into her wide-open mouth.

So excited was he that he barely lost his erection for a minute, and he was soon masturbating again as Mary, Faye and Carol slipped and slid around each other on the water bed. Carol and Faye, with a little urging from Mary, began to handle David and Jack's cocks, and it quickly seemed natural and enjoyable for the girls. The men lay on the surging plastic, so soft and warm and slippery, and the three women played games with their cocks, not only handling them but also rubbing their breasts and buttocks on their rigidity. Mary and Carol came like this, and both felt a surge of energy and delight that told them they would keep on coming and coming. There was nothing else in that bathroom except strange ecstasy. The outside world, normal life, everyday routine, had all gone, and it was hard to believe such absurdity had ever existed.

With the greatest delight they entered the bath, and tried all possible combinations of caressing, rubbing and masturbation. They used the bath, the floor, the water bed, the showers, the wooden chair hanging from chains attached to the ceiling and a big inflated blue plastic chair, giving and taking pleasure in extreme doses. For nearly three hours they played in the bathroom. Jack and David both came twice, hosing Mary's superbly athletic body, their cream leaping and splashing on her skin. The women seemed to float effortlessly from one orgasm to another, and by the time they left the bathroom, Faye and Carol trusted David in a way Mary thought misplaced and naive. She was thrilled by their trust, which presented endless possibilities for their shattering disillusionment.

That night, Jack came to Mary's bedroom to make a fervent request: he pleaded with her to dominate him the next day in David's bathroom, and to humiliate him extremely and obscenely with David's bizarre equipment. He spelled out exactly what he so desperately needed.

'I'll enjoy it, so let's do it, if you're sure you can endure such an ordeal,' Mary agreed. 'David will enjoy it too, I'm sure. But we won't have Faye and Carol. It'd be too shocking for them. They might stop joining us altogether.'

'No they won't, they're hooked.' Jack laughed. 'Please, Mary, it'll be wonderful if they're there. I'll enjoy their shock so much. Even if they did refuse to join us again, you'd have done a good thing, saving them from David. I bet he has plans for them, and not nice plans either. Besides, if you and I drove them away, you'd have David all to yourself, wouldn't you?'

'You cunning bastard,' Mary said, laughing. 'I can believe you're a great salesman. All right, let's do it. It'll be bloody exciting. The day after tomorrow, OK? Tomorrow's too soon. Just don't chicken out.'

'I won't, I swear,' Thank you, thank you, thank you.'

On the arranged day, David came for lunch. He not only looked a lot better, but ate a lot more too. There is a man, thought Mary, who has revived himself by getting back in touch with his inner sadist.

'Jack and I have a plan for this afternoon,' she announced as the five of them enjoyed strawberries and ice cream. 'I'm going to dominate him in ways that will be pretty disgusting.'

'Repulsive. Vile,' Jack added cheerfully.

'So I'm sure you'll enjoy it, David. But perhaps, Faye, Carol, you shouldn't come. Watching it will probably make you upset.'

Naturally, the girls insisted on witnessing something repulsive, so they all drove round to David's house.

'You make a great dominatrix, Mary,' he said warmly. 'I can't wait to see what you and Jack do. If it's too much for you two kids, you can always go home, right?'

'We're not kids,' Carol said with a laugh.

They started a foaming bath running. Mary and Jack began their preparations, to Faye and Carol's mystification, by drinking huge amounts of tea and water. Then they all stripped naked together in the living room, an act which by now seemed natural and unexceptional.

Back in the bathroom, Mary dressed up. She donned a black plastic suspender belt with six straps, and translucent black stockings. A corset of scarlet plastic constricted her waist, and her face was adorned with a white domino mask. Beside the huge scarlet bath she placed a pair of strappy black leather shoes with high heels. The next step was for Mary to lubricate and put into place a flexible tube of transparent plastic which encased Jack's cock. It grew wider to accomodate the base of his glans, and above that it narrowed.

182

'It feels wonderful.' Jack sighed with delight. The startling rigidity of his erection showed he did not lie.

From the tip of his penis, some five inches of tube projected. At the end of the tube was a shiny metal screw fitting. The next item that Mary fitted was a short, flexible rubber plug through which passed a rubber tube. Lubricated, the plug slid between his buttocks and Jack gasped with pleasure. Mary fastened the rubber straps, which were attached to the tube, around his waist and upper thighs. These would help hold the plug in place, and also gave him a pleasing sense of restriction. This second tube, projecting two feet from his body, also had a screw fitting at its end. Faye and Carol stared in awe and thrilling anxiety, their arms around one another's waists for comfort.

'You understand that this will be a truly terrible and prolonged ordeal,' Mary said to Jack. 'You can still back out. I promise I won't hold it against you. There is such a thing as going too far.' She spoke in all sincerity. Now that they had reached this point, she felt nervous about doing something so strange, a forbidden act that put on her many responsibilities. And how would Jack feel afterwards? She did not want to make him even more crazy.

'It'll be fine, Mary,' he assured her gravely. 'Don't worry.'

'You can do it, Mary,' David said with equal gravity. 'It'll be wonderful. I can always give advice if the need arises. Jack, I just want to say that I respect and admire you for doing this.'

'Thanks, David,' said Jack, and the two men exchanged a handshake. Mary could see they were now firm friends.

'Male bonding time,' she punned, and everyone laughed.

Jack donned, with Mary's help, a black rubber helmet that encased his head and throat. He could see through

183

plastic eyepieces, but the only openings in the helmet were at his nostrils and his mouth. From his mouth protruded a rubber tube some nine inches long, again with a screw fitting at the end. The tube was firmly and seamlessly secured to the helmet, which clung tightly to his head.

Now Jack sat down in the foaming waters of the bath, which were still shallow, though deepening with every passing moment. Mary set about binding him with extreme thoroughness. David assisted. Black leather belts were fitted around Jack's ankles, above his knees and around his thighs. Leather straps with O-rings were fitted to his wrists and below his elbows, and these were connected so that his left wrist was held to his right arm strap, and his right wrist to his left arm strap, behind his back. A black leather belt was fitted around his waist, and another around his upper chest. Jack lay down. Mary tied a long red cotton cord to a ring fitted to the rear of his helmet, and took it down his back to tie it around his ankles and feet, so he could not sit up. He was now absolutely trussed, his whole body constricted. With the three tubes projecting from his body, he was shockingly helpless and totally vulnerable. His penis was so hugely turgid and rigid that it pulsed visibly with the rapid beats of his heart.

Mary was breathing hard, as though she had just taken violent exercise. Drizzle veiled the double-glazed window at the far end of the room. Out there was a bizarre world of great strangeness and sadness. Mary suddenly realised how glad, how very glad, she was to be here in David's wonderful bathroom. She looked into his eyes, and her heart leapt with joy to see his warm approval and fascination.

Now Mary could admit to herself that she was putting Jack through this ordeal partly, even mainly, to impress David. To capture his imagination. To make

184

herself a necessity for him. David the addict, she his beautiful heroin.

'Now for the final pieces,' said David. He went to the cupboard and took out six things, which he laid beside the bath. Three of these were black plastic objects like large cups, with protruding screw fittings. The other three were transparent, flexible pieces of plastic tubing with screw fittings at both ends. Two of these were about a foot long, straight and undivided. The third was Y-shaped, with screw fittings at all three ends. Carol and Faye gasped as they understood what was about to happen.'

'This is what Jack wants,' Mary told them with a slight shrug of her strong shoulders.

'I'm going to give you something to drink,' Mary told Jack. 'And you'll have to drink all of it, you worthless slave. I shall torment and humiliate you more badly than you could conceive of in your worst nightmares. Or perhaps in your case I should say your best dreams. This is your opportunity to worship me absolutely, to show your devotion by embracing your degradation. Your complete surrender will give me pleasure, so let that be your consolation.' She took one of the large plastic cups and connected its bottom screw fitting to the tube leading from Jack's helmet. Then she dipped it in the foaming water of the bath and half filled it before raising it high. Jack did not drink. 'What! You dare to imagine the possibility of defying me?' Mary exclaimed. She got into the bath, knelt beside Jack, and lightly squeezed his balls. Still he did not drink, so she took a plastic brush and flicked it under the rim of his knob. Jack convulsed, then gulped down his enforced drink.

'In future, just drink whatever I tell you to drink,' said Mary. 'Or your punishment will be far more severe. In fact, you still have far too much freedom of movement. You can roll and thrash around, it's very irritating.' David fetched two lengths of white cotton

185

cord from the cupboard, and handed them to Mary with a sudden flash of his warm and happy smile, that wholehearted, somehow childlike smile that had once gone straight to Mary's heart. And now? It went straight to her heart. Carefully, she used the cords to fasten Jack's ankles and the metal ring at the top of his black rubber helmet to two of the metal rings set so firmly into the bottom of the huge scarlet bath.

'Don't be worried,' David reassured Carol and Faye. 'What Jack and Mary are doing is beautiful and courageous. They're acting out the kind of fantasy that other people have but are too cowardly to act out. I admire them both for this.'

David's complete sincerity had a real effect on the girls.

'Let's sit on the edge of the bath and tease Jack,' Carol said to Faye.

'You're right. It's silly to just stand about watching.'

'That's good,' Mary assured them. 'Jack will love it. You could use your feet on him. Just fool around. Do what you like.'

Faye and Carol sat on plastic-covered cushions next to the bath, their feet in the water, sitting in the bath, facing Jack. Mary was on the other side, so now he was surrounded by a trio of lovely young women as he entered into his prolonged, superbly extreme ordeal. Carol and Faye laughed as they poured bathwater over each other with a plastic bowl. The sensual magic of the hot foaming waters quickly had its way with the excited girls, so they kissed and caressed each other, loving the feel of skin made wet and slippery. David turned on bright red lights to make the women shine. Mary caressed her breasts and began to masturbate.

David happily gave the women vibrators, and one of the shower hoses so they could enjoy its spray. Now Carol and Faye fully appreciated just why the showers had such long lengths of flexible plastic tubing: they could be used anywhere in the room. They loved the feel of pulsing water so vivid and tingling against their sensitive flesh and, as their arousal and pleasure mounted, they lost their feelings of shock and nervousness at the way Mary treated her thoroughly bound and tubed victim.

Jack's ordeal lasted two hours from the moment Mary gave him his first drink, the time he and Mary had agreed on beforehand. It was a remarkable experience for the three women and two men in that astonishing bathroom, one that transformed their relationship and even the way they thought. At the deepest level, it seemed to be a dividing line in their lives, so that afterwards they would look back and feel they had become different men and women during Jack's ordeal, people for whom the realm of dreams and nightmares had penetrated decisively and irrevocably into the world of everyday reality.

After this, there was no possibility of going back.

There were three tubes through which fluids could be poured into Jack by Mary, and two tubes out of which fluids could be expelled by Jack. There were three ways in which the three tubes could be connected together by means of the screw fittings, which were designed so well that it was a matter of a few seconds to fasten and unfasten them. Since there were also the three black rubber cups with the same screw fittings, and as each of the cups could be used at the same time as one of the connections, the number of permutations grew to nine. This was the core of Jack's ordeal, but it was very far from being the whole story, as there were so many things that Mary, Carol and Faye could do to Jack's helpless, floating body, a huge variety of ways in which he could be aroused, stimulated, threatened, tormented and punished, as well as all kinds of acts by which the women could pleasure themselves and each other while Jack stared longingly and hopelessly.

Fluids surged, gurgled and bubbled through the tubes. In and in, in and out, out and in. With growing fascination, Carol and Faye stroked Jack's slippery body with their feet, while Mary used not only her hands and mouth but also her breasts and crotch, as well as jetting water from the shower, hot and cold in invigorating alternation. It seemed that Jack's aching penis must burst of lust as Mary sucked his balls and slid her fingernails slowly up and down his thighs and belly. The variety of cruel and amusing games she could play with her defenceless and vulnerable male bath toy was without limit.

Since Jack was not gagged he was able to talk, or rather babble, since his lust and bizarre stimulation left him so aroused that he sounded like a man in a malarial fever. The tube emerging from his helmet made his ravings pleasingly muffled. At David's suggestion, Faye and Carol donned red plastic stockings and stroked Jack's body with their feet. Mary sat on the side of the bath opposite the two girls, and put on the high-heeled black leather shoes she had placed there ready for the intriguing game of bringing Jack to heel. David poured bowls of bathwater over Mary and caressed her with tender passion, and she felt herself melt, and start to forgive him, no matter how much she told herself that what he had done was unforgivable.

After using her heels with confident cruelty for several minutes, Mary removed her shoes and got back into the bath to fit a genital harness to Jack, a superbly made interlocking network of narrow padded black leather straps with hard round lumps on the inside that pressed in complex harmonies on his cock and balls. She did the straps up tightly, then stood up, holding a rubber cup attached to one of the tubes, and gave of herself for Jack to worship.

'Thank you,' he moaned. 'Thank you, my goddess.'

Mary realised with some surprise that she no longer despised Jack or even found him foolish and annoying. No, they were beyond such petty feelings. Herself, Jack,

David, Faye, Carol: they were all five becoming partners in a great enterprise of exploration. They had to burn bridges behind and press on towards unknown and unknowable goals. They truly were aquanauts.

'Now I admire Jack,' she announced.

'Me too,' David said huskily. 'Though not as much as I admire you. I don't want to, but I can't help it.'

Mary could not help but feel pleased even though she knew that if David admired a woman, it was certainly not David who was in trouble.

Lithe and pantherish, she got off Jack's face and allowed him to gaze up at her loveliness. She caressed his body for a minute, gazing into his eyes, before teasing his cock and balls for another full minute with her fingernails. Her cunt commanded her to make a momentous decision. A mistake, she thought, but she had no resistance.

'Come on then,' she said to David. 'We might just as well fuck, to torture Jack. But don't think it means anything, about you and me, I mean, because it doesn't.'

'Thank you, Mary,' David said with warmth and eagerness. It struck Mary that he really was getting more and more like his old self. He had said that she wanted to be Baron Frankenstein, and bring the monster back to life, and now it began to look like she might have succeeded. Nothing, she thought, is as dangerous as success.

Yet there was always lust and pleasure. Mary went on all fours in the foamy warm water, limbs holding Jack in a cage of flesh and bone, and presented to David her wet shiny arse. He knelt behind her and pushed his huge penis into her yielding, succulent flesh. They both gasped. Mary was shocked, because it felt so good, so simply and purely good. Her internal muscles went into involuntary rhythmic spasms, strong and rapid, and David sighed with delight as he leaned forwards, holding her on both sides of her back, gripping the wet scarlet plastic of the corset that constricted her waist, putting a lot of his weight on her, a weight she was strong enough to bear, and proud to endure. Deeper and deeper thrust his huge cock, stretching her flesh. Jack's cock thrashed and jerked as he gazed helplessly at David and Mary's united genitals just above his face.

Faye and Carol quickly moved onto the water bed, overcome by need, and lay on their sides, rubbing their bodies together with frantic urgency. Soon they both came with thrilling gasps and moans.

So near to orgasm was David that he did not move at all, in order to prolong his delight. He slapped Mary's buttocks and squeezed her breasts. Her cunt clutched tightly at his penis, so long and broad. As he slowly, so slowly, began to come, David rubbed Mary's clitoris with his hand, and she came in an explosion of insanity, which seemed completely unlike any orgasm she had ever known. Pure force. David gave a terrible groan and jetted endlessly.

David and Mary stared into one another's eyes. They said nothing, because it seemed they knew everything. So powerful and absolute had their climax been that it felt as though nothing else could truly exist. She basked in David's approval as she used various instruments on Jack's cock and balls.

And then the two hours were up. Mary removed the tubes from her enraptured captive, held Jack's cock and mounted him, sucking him helplessly up her cunt. With a terrible cry, as though he had been stabbed simultaneously by a trio of assassins, he came in the longest and most violent male orgasm Mary had ever witnessed, a stunning affair of sharp angry cries, a raven on fire screaming, every muscle in his body jerking in a spasming ecstatic epilepsy.

'Christ!' David exclaimed when it was over. 'Another

190

day, you must put me through an ordeal like that Mary. Only longer. Harsher.'

'But I thought,' said Carol, 'you were, you know . . .'

'A sadist? Mainly, perhaps I am. But now I realise more than ever that the whole sadist/masochist business is just silly. An artificial construct of words. A typical example of how we embrace definitions and limitations out of fear. Fear of freedom, fear of being. From now on, no more compromises.'

'Oh God,' Mary said, laughing. 'Until now the monster has been compromising. Or he imagines he has. Now we're all in real trouble.'

She slid off Jack and sat in the inflated plastic armchair. David, Carol and Faye freed Jack, and he instantly crawled to Mary to suck and lick her, giving her an intimate cleansing.

Then he rushed to the toilet cubicle in one corner of the room, and made a lot of noise.

'That was incredible,' said Carol. 'Frightening. Yet some kind of liberation. Embrace the forbidden and know freedom.'

'I was disgusted,' Faye said thoughtfully. 'Yet it's an exciting kind of disgust. It's frightening and horrible, but it'd be hypocritical to deny it's thrilling.'

'I enjoyed it,' said Mary. 'A lot.' She smiled such a bright and totally happy smile that it would have made anybody feel much better about their own lives, and the world itself, as a world that could produce such joy could only be seen as a joy.

Thirteen

As the next afternoon was sunny and hot, all five of them took a swim at Carol's home, playing happily in the water's brightness. Often they swam underwater, out of sight of any observers in nearby houses, to kiss and caress each other through their swimsuits, and also touch themselves, building desire. Later, they moved to David's bathroom, where they played an amusing and delightful game: each of the five took a turn in the bath, masturbating, while the other four sat around the edge of the bath, stroking the masturbator with their feet, or stood and posed to arouse the others. Everyone talked of their sexual pleasures and fantasies.

Next day, the five of them took the train to London, and enjoyed shopping, eating at a French restaurant, and seeing a movie. This rest set them up for the next day, when they spent hours in the bathroom. First, they massaged each other with ice cream and hot custard, enjoying the contrast of heat and cold, both slippery. Mary slowly brought off David and Jack by her hands, thighs and breasts. After a meal they returned to the bathroom where they all tried on strange and beautiful garments and harnesses, and played with sex toys. David and Jack sucked Carol and Faye, while Mary handled their cocks.

Restraint was demonstrated by Jack and David the following afternoon, in both senses of the phrase, as

192

they put Mary into all kinds and positions of bondage in the living room, yet refrained from any form of abuse. Instead, they pleasured her with their hands and mouths, and only came after they released her, when the three of them stood together with Mary giving each man a hand. So they gave Carol and Faye the idea that to be in restraint could be harmless. The girls could not resist making love while Mary, Jack and David watched.

All five of them were addicted to having fun together by then, and they were fresh and eager to carry on the next day. The three women dressed up in plastic, and put Jack into several forms of elaborate bondage. Instead of teasing or punishing him, they made him come three times by constant stimulation, all four together in the big red bath, with Faye and Carol using their hands and breasts on Jack, while Mary also gave him her mouth, and pleasured her pussy on his cock. Then they had David in the bath, without putting him into restraint, and handled him to two orgasms.

After a day spent avoiding David's bathroom, they returned with happy inevitability the day after that, and spent happy hours naked and warm together, giving and taking massages with oil, soap and jetting water, in and out of the bath. Their bodies seemed to glow and hum with pure physical pleasure. All three women tried on various costumes, and used vibrators. Oiled, Mary made David and Jack come together over her nude body, hosing her with powerful jets, after which she lay on the water bed and massaged the cream into her skin before masturbating to a startling orgasm. Her own wickedness, taken to a new extreme, filled her with a warm, tingly delight and pride.

On the following day they drove to the Berkshire Downs and walked a great way in weather so fine it was hard to believe they were not dreaming.

Messy fun combined with the humiliation of Mary and Jack was David's plan for the next afternoon.

'It's logical,' he told Carol and Faye as they all had lunch together in his house. 'Jack and Mary both like to be dominated, so we should see what happens if they submit together. It'll be marvellous.'

The five of them were thrilled by the many possibilities opened up by such a situation. Even the weather seemed to be on their side: with thunderstorms chasing each other recklessly across the shuddering sky, it felt good to stay in a warm, soundproofed bathroom. Naked, they eagerly entered that peculiarly logical room, the result of David's obsession taken to its limits – who else but David, Mary thought, had ever been brave enough to do as much? For Carol and Faye it now seemed somehow safe and normal to be naked with Mary and two aroused men. It amused Mary to wonder when their illusions would be shattered.

On the floor of the bathroom lay an inflated blue plastic paddling pool, of circular shape and a little over two metres in diameter. Around it were three bright-red plastic inflated armchairs. Carol and Faye joined David in an extremely thorough and ruthless binding of Jack and Mary, which left the two prisoners enmeshed and compressed by interconnected, tightly fitted ropes and straps. They lay on their sides in the paddling pool, with cords tautly tied from their bodies to metal rings in the floor, so that it seemed they could touch one another if only they could make a supreme effort, so short was the distance separating male from female flesh. This impression, however, was an illusion of David's contriving. In reality, their utmost efforts would never quite enable Jack's cock to touch Mary's shiny wet lips and swollen clitoris, though they could just barely, by supreme and somewhat painful effort, bring their nipples into teasing contact. It was a situation of some interest.

Messy, sticky, slippery substances had already been prepared by David. With great enjoyment, he and the girls started to use these to deluge their captives. First was a gallon of wallpaper paste, a brand without fungicide. Laughing, Faye and Carol donned long gloves of black plastic and rubbed the shiny fluid over every part of Jack and Mary's bodies as David slowly poured it out of a red bucket, which he held high to make the paste splatter. This massage aroused the captives greatly, and they strove fruitlessly to press their flesh together and achieve orgasm. David then made an announcement that upset Mary.

'You see the beauty of this arrangement? Mary will be trained to see Jack as more desirable, so finally she'll be satisfied by him. At last she'll stop chasing and annoying me.'

'I've already stopped annoying you, you little rat,' Mary protested, and she would have said much more had David not calmly fitted her with a gag of black rubber, which reduced her to animal grunts and moans. Outrage burned in Mary. How could David say she was chasing and annoying him? Even if she had once or twice acted in a way that could be misunderstood to mean that she wanted David, that was all over and done with. Obviously, they were now in a new phase of experimentation and adventure. But perhaps David had spoken insincerely, just to tease and mock her as part of the game.

'Sorry, Mary, but I mean it,' David said coolly, when he met her gaze and read her mind as he did so often. 'You're still chasing me, and I'm going to have to make you stop, no matter how it hurts. You'll hurt. Not me.' Smiling slightly, he slowly poured two pints of warm custard over her perfect breasts, while she wriggled and writhed in helpless, futile, anger and frustration.

Mess oozed upon squelching mess. Tins of soup and beans, instant mashed potato, chopped tomatoes and squashy, overripe bananas were all mashed into Jack and Mary's skins. Between periods of caressing and arousing their captives, David, Faye and Carol masturbated as well as touched each other. The two young lesbians thoughtlessly handled David's cock as though the act had no risk, a provoking attitude Mary suspected they would soon come to regret.

'If I remove your gag,' David said to her, 'will you be quiet and obedient? If you complain or even just talk, I'll have to gag you again. You really do talk too much, Mary.'

Mary nodded her agreement to David's terms, and he removed her gag, then untied the cord that fastened her to the floor and had her kneel in the mess. He fitted a leather collar with an attached dog chain, which he held firmly, using it to pull her head towards the solid mass of his penis. Mary took his huge knob into her mouth and used tongue, saliva, lips and suction to serve it with all her heart and soul, finding the servitude a strangely sweet delight that sent frissons of pleasure from her nipples to her clitoris as Faye and Carol innundated her with handfuls of ooze scooped from the pool, which ran down her skin in a prolonged, slow-motion caress.

'Could you soap and stroke me?' David politely asked the girls, as if he were asking them to hold something for a moment while he changed a light bulb.

Carol and Faye complied at once, first showering David with warm water and then caressing his whole body with liquid soap. He gasped and moaned with pleasure so great that it sounded almost as though he were being tortured. For a long time David enjoyed himself in this extremely pleasant way, while Jack writhed in terrible frustration, and Mary grew very uncomfortable kneeling in the harsh confines of her bonds. Despite this, she was able to observe that Carol, unlike Faye, took a real pleasure in stroking David with her gloved hands, and in rubbing her breasts and crotch against his flesh, though she tried to hide her great interest in David so as not to upset Faye, who gave Mary the impression of mimicking Carol's actions so they might not be so obvious. Mary had no doubt that

David had made the same observations, and concluded that Carol was a ripe target for cruel exploitation.

Years seemed to pass while Mary slavishly suckled on David's twitchingly rigid penis, so long and thick. Now and then, he gathered ooze and gunk from the pool using a small plastic bucket, and poured it over Mary's head. She could only gasp and shudder, her every muscle on fire with the grip of her intricate and cruel restraints.

'If I release you, will you put on a show for us?' David asked Mary at last. 'Masturbate? Torment Jack?'

'Of course, sir,' Mary spluttered through her mask of slime.

David used the shower to remove most of the mess from Mary, while the girls unfastened her bonds. Freed, she donned, with desperate haste, the swimming mask that David gave her, and then she took from him a pair of long, slender, flexible and waterproof vibrators, and plunged into the deep, warm, foaming waters of the bath, which had been filling while she was humiliated with sticky slimy messes. What a fantastic exhibition she made of her lovely young body, so shapely and lithe! Rarely in her life had she known such terrible lust. So sharp and extreme was the sudden contrast between restraint in the paddling pool, with abject slimy degradation, and the freedom and cleanliness of the huge scarlet bath, that it combined with her appalling need for multiple orgasms to drive her half insane.

Splashing, spluttering, swearing and bubbling, Mary launched into an orgy of extreme masturbation. Using the two slender vibrators to the best possible effect, she rolled and arched, thrust and flailed, attacking her own flesh with the ruthless savagery of a do-or-die assault on the enemy's stronghold. After her first ferocious orgasm, when she yelled her soul out to the foaming slippery waters, she simply had to carry on, she had no choice, though she was able to think a little more of her audience, and adopt extreme and provocative postures while ploughing the buzzing vibrators in and out of her stretched and succulent flesh. Thrusting out her arse and tits, arching her back like a snake, parting her legs impossibly wide, she showed how remarkably lithe and supple her body was, and forced David to know that her beauty and fearlessness had no match. Only she could be the insane mermaid of his dreams.

Resisted by David, she carried on, heaving and splashing, all lithe energy and shiny curvaceous perfection like a dolphin. She was sure of David's resistance. His mind was open to her alone. If he jumped on her now it would be her decision, her seduction of him, his admission that he needed her loveliness boiling around his bloated penis. His mind worked in peculiar ways, but she could wallow in even weirder thoughts, and so take from him the victory.

Carol and Faye had put two of the inflated red plastic armchairs together, facing, and they sat on them and intertwined their legs so they could rub their pussies together, but they looked at Mary more than each other, as she thrashed, arched and bubbled like a fish dropped into boiling waters. Jack strained to watch her from his pool of slime, cock twitching. Suddenly, David could not hold himself back any longer, and he threw himself on Mary, plunging his huge penis into his mermaid, this all too vividly real incarnation of his dark fantasies. He held her as she writhed and shuddered, and she surrendered absolutely to him, holding one vibrator to her breasts, and pushing the other into her vagina. Ripped apart by an orgasm that was pure ferocity, stretched and filled to the utmost, she submitted her body and soul to the stinging jets of his explosive climax, which made him whimper and beg for mercy.

For his satisfaction, for her seduction of him, Mary lay flat and still as he came and came in viciously powerful spurts, and she allowed him to ride her strong back just as though he were her master. After they had slowly disengaged they sat for a while in the bath, too satisfied to move or speak or to think of moving or speaking. Faye and Carol meanwhile made love on the water bed, and shuddered in simultaneous ecstasy.

Knowing suddenly that she needed to come again a thousand times, Mary released the cord that connected Jack's cunningly bound body to a ring in the floor, sat in the third red plastic seat, and accepted a fervent sucking from the captive. She repaid this favour, after she had come, by mashing him into the slime with her feet, and soon Faye and Carol joined her, the three of them comfortably seated, all playing with themselves while using their feet on Jack, and enjoying his sobbing pleas.

At last they decided to let Jack come. After showering the gunk off him, they stood him against a wall and secured him to metal rings. Mary, Carol and Faye entered the bath briefly to wet their flesh, then squatted on the floor in front of Jack, soaped each other, and played with their prisoner's swollen, tormented cock and balls, teasing and pleasing him for a long time.

'This is such fun!' Mary exclaimed.

'It is,' David agreed. 'But why can't I quite forget the idea that you're still trying to take control of my life?'

'Because you're insane!' Mary replied. David joined in her laughter.

When Jack finally came, it was like the train shooting off the broken bridge over the River Tay and smashing into stormy deep waters with an explosion of steam and a hundred falling screams. Faye was rubbing her soapy breasts, so round and huge and soft, against his penis, while Carol and Mary stroked his thighs and belly. He gave a terrible cry, and all three women took a grip on his cock and balls as he spurted impossibly high, hard and long jets, his tongue protruding, saliva spraying mindlessly from his mouth along with sounds that it seemed could never have been made by a human. Mary,

Carol and Faye were showered again and again as they gasped in awe at such a display of male ecstatic power.

'Oh my God,' Carol murmured. It was almost a prayer.

Quickly, they released Jack, and then they put him in the bath to stroke and cuddle him, as though his orgasm had been a kind of catastrophic accident that demanded sympathy.

'Now,' Mary told Jack, 'it's time to obey me willingly and prove your devotion.'

'Thank you, thank you,' he replied fervently.

Nervously he watched while David, Carol and Faye helped adorn Mary's beauty with strange garments: a bra of black rubber with holes through which her large nipples and part of her breasts emerged tautly, a helmet of the same colour and material, with holes for her eyes, mouth and nostrils, plus long gloves of black plastic. Last came a frightening and ominous object that made Jack shudder: a black rubber strap-on dildo. It had a flexible, ridged stalk that fitted inside Mary's vagina, and soft ridges to stimulate her labia and clitoris. Straps of black rubber fitted to its base went around Mary's upper thighs and waist, with four straps joining the waist strap to the base of the dildo, arranged in such a way that the valley between her superb buttocks was left clear. The dildo had realistic, big balls and a valved inlet, so that when Mary squeezed the fake testicles, fluid could be shot from the tip of the lifelike rubber penis.

'Come and massage me, slave,' Mary ordered Jack as she got into the bath and lay down in its supportive, luxurious, warmth and slipperiness, which made her aware of every nerve in her skin.

Worshipping her beauty and strength, Jack stroked and kissed her reverently for many minutes while she touched her own belly and thighs, then the dildo that pleasured her own genitals. She played with it as a man masturbates. Now and then she gave Jack's cock and balls a squeeze.

'Now suck my cock, you pig,' she commanded.

Hesitant and disgusted, Jack nevertheless obeyed. She sat in the foaming water and felt a strangely delightful frisson of power and pleasure as he sucked and licked. She squeezed the rubber balls, so foamy water shot into Jack's mouth, which he swallowed at her command. Carol and Faye sat in the red plastic armchairs and watched in fascination while David massaged them with baby oil. They both handled his huge cock in return, exclaiming artlessly at its size and hardness. Then he went down on them and masturbated. Mary could not help but grudgingly admire how David was so cunningly training the lovely, innocent young women to trust and believe in his harmlessness. To trust in a lie. What skill! Sweet danger.

'I want to hear you beg for mercy,' Mary told Jack.

'Please, Mistress, don't punish me. I know I deserve only punishment, but please, have mercy, have mercy, I'm frightened.'

'If you were truly frightened your nasty little worm of a penis would be soft,' Mary sneered. 'As eventually it will be. You may masturbate. But I warn you, if you choose to come, I'll continue to use you for my own amusement. And you'll suffer more when your dick is limp.'

'If I come I'll soon get hard again. You're my Goddess. You're so gorgeous. I'll stay hard forever. But have mercy on me. Please, don't hurt me. Allow me to worship you, and I'll come and come and come if only you have mercy, please.'

'Come and come and come,' Mary scoffed, and gave Jack's cock a slap. 'This dirty worm will vomit up its life once and then die. If you come and don't get hard again quickly, very quickly, you'll suffer like a soul in hell.'

'You can do it, Jack,' David said. 'Spray the bitch, hose her down, innundate her. Then do it again and again.'

'Oh, so you encourage him?' Mary scoffed. She stood up in the bath, grabbed Jack's head, and squeezed the rubber balls at the base of the dildo she wore so that jets of water shot up Jack's nose and into his mouth, making him splutter. 'You two get on very well together. If you were real men you'd be competing for me, fighting and hating one another, but instead you're friendly. Too friendly. Why don't you leave us women alone and just play with one another?'

'That's very good, Mary,' David said without sarcasm.

Trying to ignore him, Mary went to the cupboard and took a folded clear plastic sheet from a drawer.

'Lie down on the water bed, face up,' she ordered Jack. When he had done so, she poured liquid soap over his body. 'Open your mouth wide and close your eyes. Properly.' She squeezed a large amount of toothpaste into his mouth, startling him. 'Keep it in your mouth. Don't swallow it or try to spit it out.' Then she unfolded the plastic sheet and lay it over Jack, covering him completely. 'Come on, girls, try my cock,' she said to Carol and Faye, who came to join her, both giggling.

Rubber cock thrusting out, a strange threat and promise, Mary arranged Carol on all fours, with her hands and knees on either side of Jack's body, and then she crouched behind Carol and slowly slid the dildo home into her slippery cunt, above Jack's face. Both women gasped. Mary rocked back and forth, feeling a delicious sense of pleasure and power. No wonder men were so obsessed with their cocks! It was really something to fuck a woman. After a series of sharp thrusts, Mary withdrew and tried Faye in the same way. After that, the three women tried several positions and combinations, with David staring in dangerous fascination. Then Jack emitted a series of loud, choking gasps, spraying toothpaste from his mouth as his penis erupted.

'Oh, the dirty beast has come!' Faye exclaimed in disgust.

'You'll have to be punished for that,' Mary told Jack. 'Help me get him into the bath, girls.'

Red-faced and gasping, Jack was hauled into the bath and dumped into the water with his arse uppermost. Faye, Carol and David watched closely as Mary pounced on her weak male victim, her lovely curvaceous body all shiny muscular litheness and strength. She soaped her rubber dildo while Jack babbled, pleading for mercy. He tried to resist, but Mary squeezed his balls and moved over him with pantherish grace. He gave a loud series of girlish, high-pitched cries as Mary gripped him with her long, strong arms and legs, her gorgeous big round buttocks rising and falling, muscles taut. Jack burbled and bubbled as she rode his back in the deep, warm, foamy waters, her right hand jerking his cock back and forth. Soon it was hard, and his writhings and protests, his futile resistance, all evaporated into absolute surrender.

'Take that! And that!' Mary hissed between clenched teeth. Finally, she came from the delicious rhythmic pressure of the soft, juicy lips at the base of the dildo, and the force of it was a shock that made her rear up on her outstretched arms, pushing Jack down as she thrust endlessly.

Panting for breath, dazed, she finally pulled away from the coughing man she had punished so deliciously, and David helped her unstrap the dildo. He kissed and cuddled her as he never had before, and she was dismayed at how everything inside her seemed to melt.

'That was wonderful!' he exclaimed. 'Mary, I need you, I need you so badly. Come onto the water bed.'

'Not so fast,' Mary snapped. 'For ages you've been trying to drive me away, to get rid of me like I was a piece of rubbish. Two or three times you've forced me to leave you. Four even. Oh God, I can't even keep count any more. This time it's not going to work. You want to come, you can always jerk off.'

'OK,' David agreed. It made Mary even angrier to see him give a little shrug, and to feel he truly was not very bothered by her refusal.

'Oh, Mary!' Faye exclaimed.

'You two bring him off if you want to. But don't complain to me when he ends up treating you like white rats in his wet laboratory of weird sex.'

'It can't be so bad, Mary,' Faye pointed out. 'Because you keep coming back, don't you?'

Mary opened her mouth wide to yell at Faye, but then she was overcome by the simple truth of Faye's statement.

'Yeah, well. But that's because I'm a fucking idiot.'

'No you're not,' Jack said fervently. He got out of the bath and gave Mary a comforting hug.

'Be nice to her,' Carol whispered to David.

'I don't do nice. I've told her many times.'

'Be nice to her or you'll lose her to Jack.'

'That's the plan. My latest plan.'

'Don't you ever get bored making nasty plans?'

'No.'

'What I would like,' said Mary, 'is for you to ask me nicely, David. And to acknowledge that soon you'll be trying to get rid of me again. And you could even try to explain why. Because sincerity and honesty are good things, that's all.'

David hesitated, then took a deep breath.

'Let's make love, Mary, please. I know I'm a complete bastard who doesn't deserve to even touch you, and I admit I'll probably try to drive you away again. Why? I like being alone. And I have nothing to give except crap. And I'm afraid of intimacy, I suppose. And of being understood.'

'That'll do,' sighed Mary. 'Your sincerity is pretty scary, David. I'm going to be on top this time. You lie on the water bed.'

David agreed with alacrity, and then Carol and Faye helped Mary massage him using baby oil for twenty minutes. By then he was gasping and writhing with lust. Mary mounted him, sitting on his cock, and the girls took turns presenting their breasts and open vulvas to his mouth, as Mary asked them to do, while she stayed still and used her powerful vaginal muscles, developed by daily exercises, to squeeze David's huge penis. He did not move either, but simply lay and tried to relax his every muscle so as to prolong his pleasure. Jack caressed and kissed Mary, his erect cock pressing against her strong thighs. Mary and David breathed more and more rapidly, then reached orgasm at the same time precisely, with loud groans, cries and sobbing gasps.

'You came together,' Faye said a minute later. 'Like a perfect couple. It's romantic even if you both say it isn't. Which you will say.'

'It's not romantic,' Mary protested. 'It was just coincidence.'

'Simultaneous orgasm,' David insisted, 'doesn't mean anything.'

'Isn't it sweet how they agree?' said Carol.

'And they get all flustered denying the truth.' Faye giggled.

'What I'm going to do now is to punish you, Jack,' Mary stated, resolutely ignoring Carol and Faye's teasing. 'You deserve it for annoying me so much.'

With pleasure, she bound Jack's ankles to rings in the floor using white cotton cords, so that he stood with feet parted and immobilised. Secondly, she tightly fastened a black leather corset around his waist, and strapped his wrists into the long leather cuffs, beautifully and strongly stitched to the back of the corset. Thirdly, she linked a metal ring at the back of the corset to a ceiling ring with a long white cord which forced Jack to remain standing. Her final act was to fasten a leather harness around his cock and balls, and to secure this to a ring in the floor, so that his penis, already becoming erect, was held down at an intriguing angle which would cause

Jack greater and greater discomfort as his cock grew rigid. Mary then caressed Jack and herself, teased the head of his penis with her fingernails, and smiled as its downward-pointing erection did indeed make Jack whimper and plead.

David, Faye and Carol stared in wonder at Jack's superb confinement. Mary could not help feeling proud of her inventiveness, skill and cunning.

'What a predicament you've got yourself into, Jack,' she commented cheerfully. 'You look wonderful. Good enough to punish. If you're foolish enough to surrender your body for my strange experiments, something very bad is bound to happen to you.'

'That's amazing,' Faye murmured in awe.

'Well done, Mary,' said David. 'I can see you and Jack are perfectly suited for one another.'

'Oh, shut up. Let's tease him.'

Spraying Jack with water was fun, as he spluttered and wriggled so. Hot, cold, warm and cold. The three women showered each other with hot water then soaped Jack and themselves, teasing him with great delight, rubbing their breasts and crotches on his chest and thighs.

'Oh, please, fuck me, Jack, I need your cock so badly,' said Mary as she straddled his harnessed penis, kissing its helmet with her warm, wet, slippery lips. It shuddered to full erection, held down at an angle, and she laughed gaily as he groaned.

For some minutes the women had fun caressing each other and their helplessly aroused prisoner.

'How dare you display your disgusting penis in this way!' Mary suddenly snapped. 'I didn't give you permission for you to have an erection. Stop it at once!'

'I can't stop it,' Jack moaned.

'So you disobey me? Now you'll have to be chastised, and severely. My young acolytes will do it for me. They need the practice.' Mary took two black leather tawses

206

from the cupboard and offered them to Carol and Faye.
'Hit him. It's fun.'

'I don't know,' Carol murmured nervously.

'Go on,' said David. 'You both look so beautiful.'

'No, no, please, don't,' Jack pleaded.

'Ignore Jack,' laughed Mary. 'He's just pretending.'

'Come on, Carol, it'd be a new experience,' said Faye.
'It's no big deal. You try it, then I'll try it.'

Mary was momentarily surprised to see that Faye was
truly eager for Carol to strike Jack. Then she guessed
the reason: Mary had sensed that Carol had a real
sexual interest in David and Jack, that she was far from
being a complete lesbian as Faye seemed to be. Doubtless Faye knew of Carol's feelings towards men, and
would like to see her lover treat Jack ruthlessly.

'Oh, I'll go first,' Faye said impatiently, snatching the
tawse from Carol, who was undecided and hesitant.
With no delay, so as not to give herself time for moral
qualms, the big-breasted young lesbian struck Jack
seven times on his outer thighs. The first blow was very
hard and loud, and startled her almost as much as it did
Jack. The next three were light. Then she regained her
nerve, and hit Jack three more times very hard indeed,
with long pauses between the blows, during which Mary
caressed her huge udders and murmured words of
encouragement. She and David were profoundly thrilled
to see her punishing Jack with such determination.

'That's wonderful,' Mary told her warmly. 'He de-
serves much worse, and I'm sure you'll torment him more
and more from now on. Really, he'd like to stick his penis
into you and Carol and inject you with his mess.'

'I know,' Faye hissed. 'He does deserve worse. And
we'll give it to him, won't we, Carol? Come on, you hit
him. We can't leave all the work to David and Mary
while we just fool around and watch like a pair of
voyeurs. That's not fair. We have to be more active.'
She pressed the leather tawse into Carol's fingers,

practically having to push them into position. 'If you love me like I love you, Carol, you'll hit him hard.'

'Of course I love you,' Carol protested.

Mary and David exchanged looks. As if by telepathy, she knew what he was thinking: if Faye and Carol both punished Jack, they made themselves fair game. They would deserve punishment for their sex crimes – it would be David's duty to teach them that cruelty had consequences. And so they would become bondage toys in a fantasy bathroom, twats in torment, nasty lesbian sluts in cruel restraint. Yes, Mary knew how David's mind worked: nastily. As bad as hers.

Suddenly, Carol swung her arm and hit Jack hard on his left thigh. She whimpered and mouthed the fingers of her left hand. Jack moaned and quivered, his cock huge and rigid. Faye kissed and stroked Carol, and the blonde Valkyrie, so tall and slender, gritted her teeth and hit the helpless male captive eight more times, very hard, as if trying to persuade herself of something, striving to achieve a certainty.

'That's wonderful,' Mary said brightly.

'Beautiful,' said David. 'Just beautiful.'

'Jack, thank these lovely girls and ask for more pain,' Mary commanded.

'Thank you, Carol and Faye, thank you. Please hurt me more, give me more pain. I need –'

Jack's babbling was cut off by Mary's slipping a rubber gag into his mouth and strapping it in place. Realising how he had been tricked, Jack struggled in his bonds and made animal noises in his throat and through his nose, but it was too late.

'Let's play with each other for a while,' David suggested. 'Then you can really punish Jack.'

Delightedly, they stroked and kissed in front of the captive, and all became massively aroused. Their orgasms so far only seemed a prelude to what was to come now that Faye and Carol were dominating Jack with mounting lust and cruelty. Cunningly, David and Mary caressed and praised the girls, stimulating them further with teasing caresses from vibrators and their tongues. Then David and Mary got into the bath. She lay down, proffering her lovely arse, and he mounted her with a sigh of pleasure. She held the rail at the side of the big red bath so they could watch Faye and Carol get to work on their helpless prisoner.

What a wonderful sight it was! Mary and David shivered and groaned in almost unbearable excitement as they watched and fucked. Carol and Faye, so lovely, and so fundamentally innocent, egged each other on, and inflicted more and more severe pain on Jack with their lashing leather tawses. Innocence actually helped them inflict more suffering, as they lacked both experience of physical pain and empathy, and were more easily swept away by the excitement of landing blows on a helpless male. Domination was to these lovely girls a fresh and amusing novelty.

'Remember it was my idea to involve them,' Mary murmured to David.

'You nasty bitch,' he muttered. 'I'll punish you with my cock.'

Truly it was delicious, thought Mary, to lure such charming, nice girls into the ways of absolute sexual corruption. It had been done to her, so they deserved it too. And if it felt so marvellous, how could it even be wrong?

Now she understood David better than ever. He had enjoyed corrupting her as she now relished corrupting Faye and Carol, two fresh-faced girls becoming addicted to sexual deviation. Suddenly, she felt she might be able, could even be forced, to forgive David for all he had done to her, for she was imitating him with such success and pleasure.

From now on, Carol and Faye were themselves deserving of punishment.

Fourteen

'I want to thank you, Mary,' said David.

'You know what's coming next?' Mary said to Jack. 'He'll thank me for absolutely the wrong thing. He always does, on the very rare occasions that he thanks me for anything at all.'

'Do I really do that?' David asked in surprise. 'Oh, well. Every human being is allowed one bad habit.'

'He only has one bad habit, Jack. What a paragon.'

'Anyway,' David continued. 'I want to thank you for helping me get out of Thailand.'

'You're hallucinating! I'd remember if I'd ever done such a thing. What, you think I smuggled you out in my private jet?'

'Stock exchange?' Jack inquired through a mouthful of fish and chips.

'Stock exchange,' David replied, shaking his head at Mary's babbling of aircraft. 'The SET, Stock Exchange of Thailand, was the world's best-performing stock market last year, and this year it may well manage second. But who knows? A few hundred-quid bombs and the whole economy could go down the drain. Very cost-effective, terrorism. So I sold out the other day. Better to take a profit than wait for a loss.'

'So where do I come in?' Mary inquired.

'I have to thank you because you made me wake up. You turned up uninvited, out of the blue, a few weeks ago, and you annoyed me and tried to take over my life, and that shook me out of my lethargy, so I was able to think properly about my investments again and decide to get out of Thailand with a profit.' David raised his glass of orange juice to Mary and drank it with an air of victory.

'You see how disappointing and bloody irritating it is when David thanks me for the wrong thing?' Mary said to Jack.

'Certainly,' he agreed warmly. 'So I praise your beauty, goodness, intelligence and sense of humour. What a contrast I am with David! And does it do me any good? Does it fuck. You wouldn't notice if I set myself on fire.' Jack laughed sharply, and put vinegar on his fish with some vehemence.

'Don't worry, Jack,' David said. 'I've been thinking, and I'm sure I've thought of a way to solve your problem. And mine. And Mary's. We'll start on it today. It's a good opportunity, with Carol and Faye working on their summer projects. Now the three of us can get down to the real stuff, the core of our problems.'

'What problems?' Mary asked in surprise.

'First, Jack's problem. He loves you, and he also wants you to dominate him, to allow him to worship you as a goddess. This wouldn't be a problem except that you're too stubborn to accept his devotion, Mary. Which brings us to your problem: you love me and you want to stay here and prove your devotion to me by giving yourself to me and encouraging me to be cruel.'

'You're dreaming,' Mary sneered. 'You fancy yourself. You assume too much. If I ever loved you, I stopped a long time ago. I'm cured of my adolescent infatuation.'

'Ha!' Jack exclaimed. 'Liar.'

'For God's sake!' Mary exclaimed. 'What are you two bloody fools analysing me for? Look at all the exciting games we're playing, all the great sex we're having.

211

That's what's important, the excitement. I'm here now just for the physical pleasure.'

'There are some people in the world who can play domination games without serious emotions,' David said slowly, staring down into his cup of Chinese tea. 'But none of them happen to be in this house right now.'

'I refuse to waste my time arguing,' Mary stated.

'Lastly,' said David, 'we come to my problem, which is that I want to be alone. I love being alone. I think clearly when I'm alone and I feel much better. But I can't be alone if you keep pushing your way in here, Mary.'

'What an arsehole you are!'

'Yes, as I keep telling you. So there we have the three problems. But I've hit on a way to solve all three at the same time. And we'll also have an exciting time.'

'In your bathroom of course,' Mary sneered.

'Of course,' David agreed without embarrassment. 'It's a simple idea, but it'll be great. Jack and I will dominate you together, Mary. I'll teach him how to dominate you in ways that will satisfy you both. Then you might just end up together. I'm sure the two of you could be happy together, really. Don't reject the idea out of hand, Mary.'

'It's rubbish,' Mary protested. 'You think you can palm me off with Jack and then throw us away, into the bin, so you can go back to being by yourself and rotting in loneliness and depression because you're too cowardly to be with anybody and admit who you really are. You're too weak to love, too weak to be yourself. Pathetic! If you want me to go away I will, but by myself, not with Jack. And anyway I won't go until I'm good and ready, which is not right now, before you ask.'

'Fine, fine,' said David, raising the palms of his hands to Mary as though trying to fend off a dangerous physical attack. 'So it's an interesting challenge, right? Jack and I will try to make you attached – or whatever word you like, Mary – to Jack instead of me, so –'

212

'Attached like a limpet,' Mary complained. 'So you dream.'

'So we need you, Mary, to surrender your body to us unconditionally for twelve hours. Come on, you know you want to try it. Two men. Twelve hours.'

'I'd have to be crazy to agree to that,' Mary sneered, pouring herself another cup of tea. When she looked up from the cup, she saw the two men looking at her in amused silence. 'All right, so I am crazy,' she admitted. 'But not half as crazy as you two. All right, let's try this challenge. Can you make me love Jack by dominating me? But there's one thing you have to do first, David.'

'Something really annoying, I bet.'

'I suppose so. You have to ask me nicely. And not only nicely, but sincerely.'

'Oh God,' David groaned. 'Deep down, very deep down, you're far stronger and more sadistic than I am, Mary.'

'You just realised? Pretty slow on the uptake.'

'Women are absolutely ruthless at heart because for millions of years they had to do terrible things so their children would survive,' David mused. 'And the worst thing, the cruellest trick, that women ever did is this: they pretend to submit to men. And men are stupid enough to fall for it.'

'Which gains women a further advantage for their children,' said Jack. 'At last I start to understand women.'

'But for you,' Mary stated, 'it's far too late.'

'Cheeky, perky, provocative,' David noted, frowning slightly with distaste.

'You still haven't asked me politely and sincerely,' Mary said very quietly, leaning towards David and staring into his eyes.

'Such a simple thing. It's nothing. So why do I feel that if I do it, something terrible will happen?'

'You'll only know the answer to that after you've asked me. Nicely. Bad luck. For you. Not me.'

David visibly hesitated, pulled himself together, had second thoughts and several kinds of doubt before saying: 'Please, Mary, submit to Jack and I. We need you.'

'Yes, for twelve hours I'll obey your every command,' Mary replied, certain of David's sincerity and truthfulness. He had said he needed her, which was a great step forwards.

'I'll run a bath,' she said at last.

'It's running,' David replied. 'It's been running a long time.' His voice had its flat tone of subdued anger, the anger which was in David, even more than in other men, an integral part of lust, perhaps indeed not just a part but the core. To inspire such dangerous and strong emotions was, Mary thought, really something. Her greatest achievement. David had got rid of other women, but she had stayed the course. She was like a horse, bridled and saddled, a slave, yet a slave carrying its rider, David, further and further into black, airless, realms where all her strange and frightening fantasies became reality. The more she submitted to David, the further she dragged him into dangerous waters. No wonder he felt such lust and anger.

Lunch was soon finished, and Mary insisted as usual on their doing the washing-up and tidying the kitchen. Then the three of them undressed in David's bedroom with the curtains drawn against a drizzly day of dullness and mundanity. How much better to be in what Mary thought of as her house. With her man. Dreams, she thought. So what. Dream harder.

Naked. Vulnerable. David and Jack stared at Mary in all her strength and loveliness. She was going to submit for twelve hours. Unconditionally. It was insane. Her whole body seemed to twitch and tingle and hum with vitality. She dressed herself up for a bath and, as she did so, both men's cocks shuddered erect. So huge, so threatening. Slowly she put on a black plastic corset, and black stockings that each had three straps attached to rings at the base of the corset. She encased her long white throat in a red plastic collar, high and padded, and her long fingers were sheathed in soft gloves of black leather.

'Come along, my poor silly mermaid,' said David. 'It is time for some truly serious bathing.'

In silence the three of them entered the bathroom, where many items were laid out, strange and compelling, but there was more, for David had bought three female shop window dummies with adjustable limbs. He and Jack had dressed them in plastic and rubber, and bound them severely in extreme postures of inventive cruelty. Mary shivered with fear.

'Masturbate,' David ordered her quietly. 'Put on your best show ever. Or we'll whip you so you daren't show your striped skin to Carol and Faye for a month.'

Shivering with strange lusts and bizarre fantasies that seemed to crawl over and into every part of her body like a river of starving ants, Mary went down on all fours and crawled to the huge red bath full of foaming hot water, slipping into its heat and divine weightlessness, its infinitely seductive lubrication and its absolute insanity, to masturbate with real fury and frenzy, her black-gloved hands squeezing and stroking her shining wet flesh as she struck more and more extreme and outrageous poses.

In the huge mirror fitted to the wall, heated from behind to prevent condensation, she saw her hard ripe curves and long legs, her tits and arse flashing wet and shiny, the open and inviting lips of her powerful young cunt.

Sliding slowly like a snake she crawled out of the bath, removed her swimming mask, and moved to the mirror on the wall, staring into it with her bright hazel eyes locked on their own reflections. Slowly, she put out her tongue and licked the glass, then rose up with languid, unhurried grace to rub the tips of her nipples against the mirror, then her belly and thighs, sliding slowly up and down, making love to her own reflection so perfect and lovely. Jack and David were sweating as they stared at her, sitting in red plastic chairs, their cocks shivering and hard as though freezing cold and turning to rigid ice.

Smiling slightly, Mary made love to herself in the mirror, her clit tickling and teasing the image of itself as she pulled back its hood and thrust its sensitive head against the glass, holding her breasts as she stood there, before sliding slowly down to go on all fours, presenting her buttocks to the men and reaching behind herself to probe every crevice. Then she crawled over to David and licked his thighs, tasting his tangy fresh sweat and enjoying every drop. Revelling in her sexiness, she sucked David's balls, then Jack's. Both men shuddered. With a harsh grin of triumph, she opened the mouth of David's penis and flicked the tip of her tongue around the red flesh inside, and then suddenly she darted away from him and lay on the water bed, eagerly seizing the items she needed to probe and restrain her own body in a deliciously perverse act of bondage.

First, she removed her gloves so she could use her fingers properly. Then she took a two-metre length of black plastic strap with O-rings at either end and several metal rings set along its entire length at regular intervals. This she placed over her shoulders and under her crotch, crossing between her breasts and in the middle of her back. She fastened it tightly, then wound a second identical strap around her waist and thighs, and around her chest above her breasts. After fastening this too, she lay down and wound the third strap around her feet, ankles, calves, below and above her knees, around her thighs, then her waist. She gagged herself with a red rubber bulb attached to a set of black plastic straps that she fastened around her head. Lastly, she wound a red cotton cord around her wrists, twisting it tight, fastening her hands behind her back. Now she was caught in a constrictive, ruthless trap of her own contriving. Arching and writhing, gasping and straining, she began to struggle desperately, striving with all her might to reach the orgasm she so desperately craved.

A minute passed. Another. Sweating and straining, shaking up and down on the undulating water bed, she began to feel she could do it. Not yet. Soon. Cruelly confined and constricted as she was, she felt more as though she were flying, using all her muscles to achieve the freedom of orgasm. She felt sure she had impressed David despite all his efforts to remain calm. Cold. He always tried to be cold and uninvolved, but really he was hot with volcano heat.

'Let's take control,' David snapped, jumping from his seat. He jumped to Mary's side and fitted wrist straps with O-rings which he attached to rings at the back of her black plastic corset. He removed her gag.

'Mary, only Jack can make you come. But you must pleasure and worship him first. You must beg for his cock.'

Mary decided to do just that. Sure that David expected her to resist out of her habitual stubbornness and contrariness, she wanted to annoy and confuse him by obeying him at once.

'Master Jack, please, sir, make me come with your huge cock. I need to come so badly,' she pleaded. 'Grant me orgasm, my beloved master. Please don't let David touch me, he's just a weasel, a rat.'

'Very clever, Mary,' said David, staring at her sternly. 'You see what an annoying bitch she is, Jack? She's obeying, but in an insincere way, with sarcasm. But it doesn't matter. No Mary, you won't put us off our stride. We have all the time in the world. We'll break your spirit, and in the end you'll be begging Jack in all sincerity, worshipping him with all your heart.'

Ruthlessly, the two men hauled Mary into the bath and made her kneel. David squatted behind her and teased her with his clever, knowing hands, stroking and squeezing her in every way except for the way that would make her come. Tweaking her big hard nipples between his fingers, he thrust his huge penis against her slippery warm wet back. Firmly bound as she was, Mary could only squirm. Jack stood in front of Mary, held the shaft of his cock in his right hand, and worked the glans in and out of Mary's mouth, then beat it against her tongue when she stuck it out, before having her suck him for a long time. Determined to make him come so that David would see how sexy she was, and how lacking in self-control Jack was, Mary put all her heart and soul into her mouth, sucking and licking Jack with superb expertise. Finally, she held the rim of his knob lightly with her teeth and pulled on it, though not too hard, while swirling her tongue round and round his sensitive flesh at high speed. Gasping and groaning like a woman giving birth, Jack filled her mouth with jetting cream, and Mary gulped it down noisily, making a production of it to annoy or arouse David. Hopefully both.

'Thank you, master,' she told Jack.

'You can be as insincere as you like now,' David said to her. 'By the time we get to the third or fourth hour you'll be pleading with Jack and worshipping him sincerely. And then we'll still have eight or nine hours to break your spirit absolutely, once and for all. Plenty of time, lots of equipment and two men.'

Confidence was so strong in David's voice that Mary felt an unexpected frisson of fear. What if he did break her spirit? Who would she be then, and what would she do? Would she become all normal and boring? The prospect was chilling.

'I'll show you an amusing thing to do with Mary,' David told Jack. 'Then later on you can try it.'

Jack got out of the bath and squatted beside it, watching his teacher like a good student. David lay back in the bath, then pulled Mary to lie on top of him, facing up, as was he. Sighing with pleasure, he insinuated his penis between her bound thighs, then stroked and squeezed her lovely body, enjoying the vigorous workings of her thigh muscles as she struggled to come like a fish struggling to escape a net. Later he pushed his cock into her hot, wet, vagina, which seemed to suck him in with the greed of a growing cuckoo's mouth, but he did not thrust. Rather, he stayed still, and began to tease her breasts with the stiff bristles of a long-handled plastic backscrubber. He smiled at her writhings, and grunted in pleasure.

'It's very interesting,' he told Jack, 'to be inside a woman as you torment her. Usually, women are so lazy they do very little with their cunt muscles. They need encouragement. Do you want her to suck you? Practise giving her orders.'

'Suck my cock, slave,' Jack said as convincingly as he was able, which to Mary did not seem very.

Jack quickly regained his erection, and soon he took David's place under Mary, while David teased and punished Mary with quiet competence and deep pleasure: he used a vibrator on her nipples, then poured water over her face and body, holding a plastic bowl high so that the water struck her with some force. He took a tawse and gave her a score of blows, mostly light, on her thighs, before sucking her nipples, making them even bigger. Next, he arranged Mary as though she were a sex doll, turning her over so she lay face-down on Jack. He masturbated casually as he gave Mary ten blows to her arse while she wriggled and strained with all her strength, striving with all her heart and soul to come, and finally she came, she came as a bomb falls from the sky, screams tearing the air apart, to kill the innocent in all their useless amazement, and she swore

219

with all the filthy words and insults that she could think of in her fury at David tricking her into coming like that, whipped and helplessly bound, riding Jack's cock.

'We're making progress,' David commented. 'Not so calm now, are you, Mary? Soon you'll be worshipping the ground Jack walks on.'

David then removed all of Mary's bonds and garments. She toyed briefly with the idea of leaving, as she could see that this was going to become a terrible ordeal, but quickly realised that to run away now would only be an admission of defeat. Having promised to surrender her body unconditionally for twelve hours, to do anything less than that would be the foolish, irritating act of a weakling. To submit absolutely was to embrace David in her crushing coils, and achieve victory by her power to endure, her beauty in distress, and by her compelling, overwhelmingly seductive helplessness.

Due to this obsessive, stubbornly held idea of Mary's, David and Jack were able to move her from one form of restraint to another over the hours they shared in that strange bathroom, that perfect external realisation of David's inner visions and lusts, a true mirror to his mind. And the hours passed with pleasure and pain that mounted incredibly. Soon all three of them knew that this twelve-hour period would be a turning point. The two men and one woman who eventually left this luxurious wet torture chamber would not be the same people who had entered it so long ago.

By the third hour, Mary's entire body was singing with dangerous rapture. Caresses and punishments, the pressure of two men's bodies, the suction of their mouths and the gripping of their hands, combined with the use of special instruments to probe, suck, sting and clasp her body, made Mary aware of every piece of her flesh, inside and out, and her every nerve hummed with news.

Every perverse act was a thrilling song of lubrication: water and soap, oil, saliva, cunt juice. How Mary loved David to stroke her slippery thighs, belly and breasts! What use was sex without lubricated skin? David had taught her, and had seduced her, until finally she shared his peculiar addiction to bathroom sex, all slipperiness, heat, weightlessness and freedom.

Restraint took second place with Mary seated on an inflated red plastic armchair with its back touching the wall opposite the huge mirror. To see herself there, submitting to perversity and bondage, filled her with astonishment. Red cords attached to leather straps around her wrists were tied to metal rings set in the wall at her back, and straps around her ankles and above her knees were tied to two more rings higher up. Mary was utterly immobilised, with her legs held high and wide open, displaying her genitals and anus which protruded forwards over the edge of the seat in startlingly provocative vulnerability. A broad white plastic belt tight around her waist eliminated any possibility of vertical movement, as its O-rings were connected to metal rings set into the floor by red cords, while the angle at which her arms were held, stretched right out behind and to either side of her, also served to immobilise her torso, leaving her stunningly defenceless. She stared at herself in the mirror. Could that crazy whore over there really be her? What a sick slut!

Greatly pleased, David and Jack massaged her with baby oil, and teased her for a long time, rubbing the heads of their cocks on her breasts and thighs. Then each took a tiny leather whip, almost like a bootlace, but thicker and heavier, and gave her hundreds of blows to her sensitive spots. Each blow was nothing by itself, yet the cumulative effect became alarmingly irritating, like a whole series of bad mosquito bites. The men alternated groups of blows with periods of penetration, using Mary's gorgeous body as they chose. Then they stimulated and tormented the flesh between her legs with various devices, making Mary plead until she was gagged, after which David pushed his large and rigid penis, lubricated with oil, into the secret depths of her body, enjoyed her for minutes, then groaned loudly as he hosed her palpitating hot internal flesh, so exquisitely tight that it prolonged his orgasm longer than Mary had ever thought possible. Then the men made her come by directly stimulating the head of her clit in every way they could think of, an overstimulation that was cruel in its intensity.

After her release, Mary exercised her limbs to relieve their aches. Then she was instructed on the next perversion: she would be fitted with all kinds of tubing, in the bath, and would not be restrained. David had a bizarre collection of tubing gear, plastic and rubber, including valves, doubled tubes and tubed body harnesses, helmets and dildos. The two men used every item on her. Mary felt neither shame nor humiliation, for she had reached a state of sexual inebriation in which every strange and shocking stimulation was felt as pleasure, even joy.

And there was David, of course. Mary reluctantly realised that so long as that bloody rat, that lunatic, paid any kind of attention at all to her, she knew an imbecilic happiness.

Nearly two hours passed in a flash as they played with the elaborate equipment. Accepting everything, Mary knew the dazzlingly real freedom of unconditional obedience, and the eager welcoming of every fresh stimulation.

David and Jack thrust their stiff cocks wherever they liked, and both came. Mary was rocked by a whole series of orgasms that seemed to be bubbling up from unsuspected depths.

When they left the bath, they were all getting hungry, so after a shower the men fetched food and drink from the kitchen, and they all ate in the bathroom, as none of them wanted to leave, not even to eat. Mary took her food from bowls placed on the floor, on all fours like an animal.

David drained the bath, and ordered Mary to clean it, which she did thoroughly. Then he began to refill it with hot water, without any bath salts or foam liquids. Mary knelt to suck both men, and they regained their erections with ease. She felt the same as they did: the perverse excitement of going all-out in a twelve-hour session meant that each orgasm only seemed the gateway to an even deeper ecstasy.

'Doubtless you think you're unshockable now, Mary,' said David. 'Fortunately for both of us, I think I still have plenty of ideas in mind that will shock you, and help you to leave me alone and go with Jack, who loves you as I never can. Now we'll put you into restraint so you'll be ready for a nasty surprise.'

Full of foreboding, Mary submitted to being bound, standing with her arms stretched out so she could lean forwards against the wall opposite the big mirror. Her long legs, slightly parted, were straight and at an angle to her torso, which was held down by a cord attached to a strong corset of black plastic. Firmly attached to rings set in the wall and floor, she was immobilised leaning forwards, presenting her strong round arse.

David left the bathroom briefly, returning with a plastic box from which he took a white plastic ice-cube maker. There was not much ice in the moulds, and it was irregularly shaped. Mary was puzzled.

'I've been saving my semen when I masturbated,' David said calmly. 'I've had a feeling for months that you'd return, so I kept it in the freezer. And now you're going to know the meaning of absolute humiliation.'

Mary was so shocked she could not say a word. David flexed the tray carefully to loosen the ice.

Numbly, Mary accepted when he put several small pieces of ice in her mouth. Then he fitted a white, soft rubber gag, over which he placed a helmet of thin white latex with a large hole for her nose. To her astonishment, she found he had put a lot of ice inside the helmet, which quickly started melting all over her face.

Never had Mary known such humiliation. It was astonishing that despite all that she and David had done, he could still catch her unawares and take her to new depths of degradation. For a few minutes, David let Mary stew in his own juices, and then he pressed pieces of his frozen ejaculate between her buttocks and into her vagina. She tried to resist, but when David gave her a few hard slaps on her arse with the flat of his hand, she relaxed her muscles and submitted to the icy and humiliating violation.

Smearing Mary's breasts, buttocks, thighs and belly was David's next step, after which he and Jack amused themselves greatly by rubbing vibrators over her slimy skin. Finally, her gag was removed, and she drank the remaining liquid with its unpleasant taste when Jack held the ice-cube tray to her lips. She even put out her tongue to lick up every drop, feeling that to resist would only be an exercise in pain and futility.

Coated with semen, Mary donned a suit of stretchy red latex, with a hole at her crotch. Over this went twenty black plastic straps with numerous shiny O-rings, and David demonstrated to Jack all the ways in which Mary could be bound by joining different rings together. In countless strange positions, she simultaneously served two demanding cocks.

Briefly they rested, then Mary was stripped naked.

And then she was put into severe restraint at the centre of the room and subjected to a harsh and prolonged whipping. With teasing, long pauses, blows in unexpected places as well as unpredictable force, and periods of stimulation and copulation, all interspersed so she never knew what would come next, it was one of the most painful ordeals of Mary's real life or fantasies.

Finally, Jack and David released Mary and massaged her with baby oil. She did the same for them, and then they entered the warm water of the bath. David ordered her to pretend to resist them, and they pounced, holding her together and pressing their cocks against her oily flesh while she struggled, and pleaded for mercy. Mary's feigned resistance and apparent fear aroused the men greatly, and their cocks were hugely rigid as they grappled with the lovely young woman, splashing and sliding in supremely sensual struggles, until Mary submitted, and was used in every way. Massively aroused, the men fucked her superb, shiny and slippery body ruthlessly.

After a long session of wet wrestling and screwing, all three of them came mightily, and they subsided, panting for breath.

'Time's up,' David said at last. 'So, Mary, no matter how stubborn you are, I hope you begin to see that Jack will soon be able to dominate you better than I ever could. Because he loves you.' For twelve hours, David had been teaching and encouraging Jack.

'You love me more than he does, but you're too cowardly to admit it even to yourself,' Mary sneered. She stood tall and proud beside the bath, nude and shiny, and the men stared in awe at her beauty. Never had she seemed more stunningly desirable. Every part of her body felt exquisitely sore, tender and excessively aroused. Her buttocks stung, while her breasts and genitals felt hugely engorged by stimulation and torment. She had never felt so alive. 'All Jack wants is to be dominated, don't you, Jack? You didn't like dominating me, did you?'

'No, I didn't,' Jack admitted. 'It's no good, David. I can never enjoy it like you can. You're so good at it.'

'You two are as annoying as each other,' David complained. 'You reject the easy and natural solution to your problems.'

'Of course,' Mary said, laughing. 'Doesn't everyone?' She felt a deep joy that made her body and soul sing and thrill, as she sensed that this day had been a turning point: David had done so much to her, under the cover story of teaching Jack, that he surely could never stand it if she left him. What they had done was so extreme that David must once again be in the grip of his addiction. She must win.

Fifteen

In a spirit of pure generosity – his own words – David continued with his plan of making Mary and Jack share a mutual love, or at least a common interest in difficult orgasms. The next day, Jack was bound for three hours to be tormented by Mary. She found the session so intensely exciting that she began to wonder if David's plan could succeed. Was it possible that she could walk away from David and be satisfied with Jack? One problem: it was the presence of David that made it fascinating to play with Jack, a man whose faults could be summed up perfectly by saying that he lacked Davidness.

Difficult orgasms. What power! Ease eroded everything's worth, availability led to emptiness. The value and strength, the satisfaction and joy, of an orgasm, needed to be fed and grown, pushed and forced, by profound difficulties. Since everything has become too cheap and easy, there is nothing left to do but to recreate suffering, to build new hells on the ruins of the old. Thus, Jack was cruelly bound in the bath, and fitted with saddle and complex bridle, so that Mary could sit astride his back, hold the reins, and punish his arse and thighs with a riding crop, while allowing Jack to see her so gorgeous in the heated wall mirror. Difficult indeed was his orgasm: at the end of the three hours Mary tormented his tautly bulging helmet with brushes, elastic bands, probes and straps, vibrators and clips, her fingernails, and the very tip of her tongue slowly drooling saliva, until Jack came with screams of ecstasy indistinguishable from horror.

Showing remarkable willpower, David refrained from orgasm while Mary dominated Jack, though he did have sex with her. Mary found it aggravating and silly that he refused to come, and knew he did it to annoy her, and as a kind of boasting. Impressive it was not, she told herself firmly, and, of course, she was impressed anyway.

After a light meal, the three of them returned to the bathroom, where Mary agreed with David's idea that they should display all that could be done in the bath, for Jack's further instruction. In deep, foaming, warm waters, David and Mary demonstrated the use of specialised equipment and advanced aquatic techniques. With tubing devices, complex helmets, harnesses and probes, they copulated strangely and magnificently, their bodies arched in passion and ecstasy. Fluids surged and gurgled, in, out and over shining flesh, and they shared the rapture of the deep. Mary displayed all her skills, courage and trust, and both man and woman inflicted orgasms on one another like the hammer blows of cruel fate. Happily, they did everything they could conceive.

Next day they abstained from sex and did a lot of shopping instead. How can I ever leave David, Mary asked herself, if he follows up strange sex with great shopping?

Carol, Faye, Mary, David and Jack were reunited the following afternoon, which was wet and windy, as Carol and Faye felt they had made enough progress on their summer projects to salve their consciences. It was remarkable how natural, and how exciting, it felt for all five to find themselves naked and aroused once more in David's bathroom, with that huge red bath filling with foamy hot water, a tempting and thrilling centre for slippery pleasures.

'It's great to be here again!' Carol exclaimed.

'Yes, it's like real life, somehow,' said Faye, 'more real than anything else.'

Smiling vivid smiles of joy, both girls seemed to glow and hum with youthful vigour and lust. Their beauty was a form of radiance that made David and Jack extremely aroused. Mary sensed that all of them had gone too far, and now must come some kind of price to pay, a settling of accounts.

'Let's have Mary and Jack bound together,' David announced. 'If we thoroughly tease the two of them at once, and punish them together, they'll be bound to love one another. To suffer together is so romantic.'

Carol and Faye were deeply thrilled by this idea, and they chattered excitedly as they helped David put Jack and Mary into severe restraint, immobilising them in positions of extreme provocation and tantalisation. Mary protested so much that David gagged her with a rubber ball fixed to a black leather head harness. The highly aroused man and woman were bound standing, facing one another, with their wrist and ankle straps bound to rings set into the floor behind them. Cords from their wrist straps were tied to rings in the ceiling, and passed through rings in their head harnesses to keep them in a standing position. With all their strength, Mary and Jack strained to unite their bodies in an explosion of orgasmic ecstasy.

There was just one problem: no matter how they strove, the best they could achieve was contact between their nipples, but so aroused were they that even this seemed infinitely precious, and they stretched and arched and suffered to enjoy the electric contact of male and female. By flexing his muscles and swinging his hips, Jack could very nearly, but not quite – horrifyingly not quite, from his point of view – touch Mary's belly with the tip of his flailing, bloated penis. He felt that if only he could make a brief contact, he could come. Mary too felt, or hoped, that she might eventually be able to climax if only she could rub the tips of her hugely turgid teats for long enough against Jack's nipples. And so they strained and struggled and made funny noises through their gags, and their gleaming nude bodies striving to unite created a gorgeous and hypnotic spectacle that made David, Carol and Faye stare in awe.

'It's so beautiful!' Faye exclaimed. 'And romantic.'

'And too sexy for this universe,' murmured Carol.

Eagerly, the girls began to caress the pair of tantalised and desperately aroused captives, stroking and squeezing every part of their skins, kissing and licking to build their lust to heights that were a source of fear. To want something so much, and not be able to get it: this was now revealed as the heart and soul of being human. What else was there to life? To witness and to know such truth and lust was to be swallowed up in warm wet mindless sensuality, to be eaten alive by exquisite terror.

Silent and trembling with awe, Carol and Faye sprayed Mary and Jack with liquid soap, then rubbed their breasts, thighs and bellies on the prisoners and each other, their hands sliding over slippery flesh. David stroked and squeezed Mary's beautiful and helpless body, holding his penis and rubbing its huge helmet on and between the lubricated bodies of the three young women as if they only existed for his delight.

Literally panting with lust, Faye and Carol were overcome, and rubbed their genitals with increasing blatancy and urgency against Jack and Mary's thighs, hips and buttocks, using the helpless captives to pleasure their clits without granting in return the relief they longed for. Noisily squelching, panting and moaning, Carol and Faye came almost at the same time, tensing and arching their lovely gleaming bodies, so curvaceous and radiant with lithe strength. Appalling frustration burned in Mary, and she screamed through her gag.

Even David could no longer restrain himself, so insanely arousing was the bizarre explosion of lust he had created with such skill. As Carol and Faye sank trembling to the floor, dazed by the power of their ecstasy, David casually arranged them as if they were a pair of sex dolls he owned, having Faye lie face down on the water bed and Carol lie on her back facing upwards, so that the girls' buttocks were pressed together, wet and slippery for his convenience. Groaning with pleasure, David mounted Carol without penetrating her or putting his weight on her and Faye. Rather, he moved above Carol on all fours and kissed her as his long thick penis slid into the delicious new orifice made by four female buttocks, and then he shivered and grimaced in burning pleasure as he thrust repeatedly. Finally, he gave a series of sharp, yelping cries as he stood up to spurt over Mary's lovely body.

For Jack and Mary the frustration was excruciating. It was even worse for Mary, as, shortly after David came, Carol moaned in the throes of her own climax, so turned on was she by David's belly and pubes rubbing on hers. Mary shuddered with the agony of jealousy. Carol liked men all right, and if David had his way, she might soon be stretched around his cock.

'Let's spank them,' David suggested, and immediately gave Mary a resounding blow on the arse that made her squeal through her gag. Her buttocks burned as further smacks followed, usually with long pauses in-between during which the three tormentors had a wonderful time caressing each other and the two captives, as well as masturbating. What amazed Mary was the way in which Carol and Faye spanked Jack and herself without any urging from David, as though to spank a bound man and woman was an act as natural as breathing. Mary had a premonition that by accepting everything in this dangerous bathroom of David's, these two innocent girls were heading for a catastrophe.

'Let their bums cool down a bit,' David told Faye and Carol. 'They're trying to climax by spanking.'

Mary and Jack could only moan and writhe in the agony of frustration as their tormentors stroked them all over, save for the areas that might grant them orgasm.

The teasing of the two prisoners continued for what seemed to them like eternity. At last, however, Carol and Faye felt sorry for them, and also grew a little afraid of their frustrated lust. David swiftly modified Jack's restraints, so that he was able to move forwards another inch or so, and then Faye and Carol took control of his penis, rubbing its big shiny helmet on and around Mary's clitoris. Jack struggled madly to come as the girls' cool fingers handled his shaft and squeezed his balls, and Mary strained too, while David rubbed his cock against her strong arse, sliding it up and down the valley of her buttocks.

'Bring Jack off,' he told Carol and Faye. 'Make him spray Mary's clit.'

Grunts of animal desperation burst from Jack's throat as the girls gripped his penis firmly and moved their hands, and then he snorted and squealed like an injured pig as he shot powerful spurts that spattered against the swollen head of Mary's clitoris, filling her with strange sensations that were a kind of exquisite agony. Calmly, David landed five heavy blows on her arse with his hand, then gripped her breasts from behind as she came, to be torn apart by an orgasm that was all blackness, an ecstatic pain in which her every nerve seemed to be on fire. It was not at all pleasurable or satisfying, but rather a kind of torture.

Humming a happy tune, David released Mary and Jack, who sank to the floor clutching at themselves. What Mary had just experienced, indeed endured, hardly seemed to her an orgasm at all. She felt as though she were being forced towards a desolate plateau up in the clouds, a chilling realm of ecstatic agony. Her fresh understanding of her own body and soul fed her fear.

'That was so sexy,' Carol moaned. 'Jack and Mary were too beautiful. I can't stand it.' With a look of real suffering and desperation on her face, she grabbed David's cock with one hand, while the other went behind his back to pull him to her. He thrust into her and pushed her against a tiled wall, then held onto metal rings set into the wall as they fucked mightily. Both moaned with mindless passion as David's huge penis serviced the strong, fit young woman who was much taller than him, a gorgeous blonde Valkyrie.

It had all happened so quickly and spontaneously that Jack, Mary and Faye were caught unawares, and then they were momentarily awed by the sheer power and frenzy of the couple's screwing.

'Oops,' Jack said thoughtfully.

Mary felt under a barrage of conflicting urges: she wanted to hit David, or Carol, or both of them, and she also wanted to cheer them on, to applaud or caress, or to worship in an extreme of masochism. Faye was not as confused as Mary, but she was more amazed.

'Stop it,' she croaked, almost inaudibly, after long seconds of stunned silence. She coughed and cleared her throat. 'Stop it,' she yelled. Reaching out to grab David, she recoiled from his flesh, unable to touch him while he was deep inside her lover, and then she ran to the cupboard, grabbed a cat-o'-nine-tails of black leather, and swung her arm as she ran at David with a despairing cry of pain, for Carol was already coming noisily, writhing like a wounded snake impaled on David's big cock.

Instinctively, Mary pressed her body to David's, to protect him from Faye, and also from the need to thrust her breasts against his back, her pubes against his buttocks. Hearing the cat whistle through the air, she just had time to decide that what she was doing was really bloody silly.

The blow never landed. Mary looked over her shoulder and saw Jack holding Faye. She stopped struggling and dropped the cat. David came strongly, and it seemed a long time before he and Carol finished their panting and moaning. Everybody except Mary began talking at once. Mary would have talked too, but she knew that nobody would listen. Carol and Faye had a hysterical argument, David said a lot about freedom and how nothing was his fault, and Jack babbled about how magnificent Mary had been, rushing to protect David. Nobody paid any attention to anybody else, and they all four repeated themselves a great deal. Mary always got bored when people other than herself said more than a few words, so she took a cold shower, then wrapped herself in a towel, went into the kitchen, and made a pot of tea. What else was there to do at this late stage in the game?

By the time the others joined her in the kitchen, she had worked her way through a sandwich, seven biscuits and two doughnuts, and was feeling better even if she preferred to stand rather than sit on her fiery buttocks.

'You're the one to blame, Mary,' announced Faye. David, Jack and Carol all showed their agreement.

'I knew you'd decide that,' Mary replied, and poured four more cups of tea. 'Let me guess whose idea it was. Oh, it's so difficult! I'll never get it right! A desperate shot in the dark before the time limit expires – it was David's idea.'

'Yes, I suppose so,' he admitted sheepishly. 'But it's true even if it is bad of me – according to you – to put the blame on you.'

'I'm the only one here strong enough to take the blame.'

'Yes. That's the right way to see it. Oh come on, Mary. You wouldn't leave me alone, you dominated Jack and made him your slave, and you suggested getting Faye and Carol involved. It actually is all your fault that these nice girls are upset and in danger of ending their happy relationship.'

'I admit it,' Mary proclaimed. 'I am the Svengali behind poor little David. Doctor Mabuse, Satan and the four horsemen of the Apocalypse: they're all me. And I bet David has a nasty plan already worked out for my punishment.'

'How well you know me!' David exclaimed, shaking his head. 'No wonder I'm afraid of you when you know me so well. Yes, of course, I have something nasty in mind.'

'Good,' Mary told him, smiling a warm and happy smile. 'I told you you'd feel better if you resumed your real life as a sadist, and look at you, you're flying. I've succeeded in recreating the monster, how very clever of me! Sit down all of you, have a cup of tea, and then we'll go back to David's bloody bathroom.'

Feeling a little deflated and puzzled by Mary's attitude, the others calmed down and accepted tea from her. She felt a calm, strong sense of joy and clarity, as though she had climbed through the clouds and could see every star. When they returned to the bathroom, the wind and rain had stopped and, as the sun began to set somewhere behind thick grey clouds, Mary saw a blackbird singing on the high white fence, though she could not hear it through the double glazing. So what, she thought, if birds only sing as part of an endless fight about their territory? It still makes me feel good.

Quickly all five of them were naked once more.

'With your permission,' said David, 'Jack and I will help you three ladies dress up for an interesting new game. You'll need to go down on all fours.'

'We won't let you tie us up,' Carol insisted.

'Of course, you and Faye won't be tied up,' David replied with what Mary thought was suspicious warmth.

'This will be a terrible experience,' she told Faye and Carol. 'For all three of us. I know that gleeful look of David's. But so what?'

'Faye and I have to do this,' said Carol.

'David promised,' Faye added, 'that punishing you in this way will make us feel like a real couple again, a gang of two, united and strong.'

'David doesn't lie,' Mary told the girls, 'but you do have to think about the exact wording. Like making a pact with the Devil.'

'I'm not much of a fallen angel,' David said, laughing. 'Except in your dreams. Put these on, please.'

Step by step, the trio of lovely young women were transformed into gleaming, hard-curved sex objects, as they willingly submitted to another experiment in calculated perversity. Tense with expectation, Carol and Faye donned broad belts, elastic-topped stockings and long gloves, all of shiny black plastic, while Mary adorned herself with identical items of scarlet. Then strap-on dildos of flexible black plastic were fitted to the girls, but not to Mary, by a cheerful David and Jack, who fastened the shiny black plastic straps around thighs and hips, with their own cocks growing erect in anticipation. Carol and Faye gnawed their lips and looked wide-eyed at the artificial cocks and balls that jutted from their bodies, making them look so very strange. The broad and curving bases of these dildos had soft, lubricated flanges, knobs and cavities, which engaged the nervous girls' labia, clitoris and vagina in a prolonged, warm, and succulent embrace.

The next stage was to fit shiny leather head bridles, which included padded bits that pressed down on the tongues of Mary, Carol and Faye, making intelligible speech an impossibility. Faye and Carol had been gagged before they realised what was happening, but they were nervous rather than alarmed.

'We don't want you to hurt your hands or knees on the floor,' said David. He and Jack strapped large pads of soft rubber to the women's calves, and then engulfed their hands in big fingerless gloves of the same material. Mary realised that this covering of their hands made it impossible for them to manipulate straps. Nevertheless, she submitted to the gloves which effectively rendered herself and the girls absolutely helpless, though Carol and Faye did not yet understand their predicament. She could not help but admire David's cunning.

Mary offered no resistance whatsoever as David fitted a red plastic legspreader to her ankles that kept her legs well apart, so that she seemed to proffer her arse and cunt. Then he strapped her wrists together, and attached the rings in these straps to a ring at the front of her bridle with a red silk cord, so that she could not move her wrists more than about one foot from her throat. A wave of excitement swept through her as she submitted absolutely.

'This is a simple game, with simple rules, aims and prizes,' David announced, literally rubbing his hands together in glee. Mary had only seen him do that once before, a long time ago. 'Carol and Faye, you have to try to punish Mary by screwing her with your dildos. Mary, you have to try and avoid this. If you succeed, I'll invite you to stay here with me for three months. Who knows? In three months you might make yourself so useful that I'll marry you. Stranger things have happened. Carol and Faye, if you succeed in penetrating Mary, I'll give you a set of video tapes of which you are the stars. You see those mirrors in the ceiling? Behind two of those, I can set up cameras in my bedroom and make a souvenir of what goes on in here. Today I'm not taping, so you needn't be self-conscious. But you'd feel better, I'm sure, if you had the tapes I've already made of you. Otherwise, who knows? Images from them and even your addresses, could end up on the internet one day if I were to feel you hadn't made a real effort to catch Mary.'

Carol and Faye were stunned. Before they could gather their wits, David and Jack placed elasticated black plastic hoods over their heads. These hoods had holes for the mouth and nose, but not for the eyes. The two girls were rendered sightless before they could even think of offering resistance. At once they stood up, raised their hands and tried to remove the helmets and the bits in their mouths, only to find that owing to the thick fingerless rubber mittens strapped in place on their hands, they could not get a grip on anything whatso-ever. They could not remove the helmets, or the bits in their mouths. David had kept his promise to Carol and Faye: the girls were not tied up. And yet they were utterly helpless. As Mary had warned, David's prom-ises, like the Devil's, depended on a misleadingly precise use of words.

Mary could not but feel pleased to see Carol and Faye brought down to her own level at long last. It had surely been inevitable from the start, once they had been naive and foolish enough to get involved with David. Suddenly, Mary had a sense of a full circle: she had crawled around on the bathroom floor masturbating, all alone, when she had returned to David's house weeks ago, and now she was going to crawl again, but with four other people joining in, so she was no longer lonely. What progress!

'Now then, Carol and Faye, get down on all fours and play the game you agreed to play,' David said with some sternness. 'This is a fine chance for you to take revenge on Mary, and to get the tapes of yourselves. Besides, it's such a good game.' He took a black leather tawse from the cupboard, and Jack followed suit. 'Go down on all fours, you disobedient bitches, or you'll have to be punished. Co-operate and we'll have a lovely time.'

Carol and Faye were close to panic, but they realised it was hopeless to defy David in these circumstances, so they went down on all fours, making noises through the bits in their mouths by way of mutual reassurance. Mary felt certain they were angry with her for getting them into such a mess. Silently, she moved away from where the girls had last seen her, in anticipation of the game starting. She was utterly determined to resist Carol and Faye, and to resist successfully. Never would such silly girls violate her with their repulsive dildos for David's amusement. Not only was she resolved to prove to David how strong and superior she was, but also she knew he would use his tawse on her if she made anything less than a wholehearted effort. She refused to believe that she hoped to win the game so he would invite her to stay for three months: that, she told herself sternly, was meaningless. She did not care what bloody David did or said, he was just vomit.

'Carol and Faye, you are now hunting dogs,' he announced with real smugness. 'Mary, you are the prey. A rabbit? No, you're not innocent enough. A fox. A vixen, rather. Before we start, we'll wash you.'

How David and Jack enjoyed washing three lovely, helpless young women, submissive on all fours! They poured bowls of water from the bath over them and soaped them, and also rubbed their cocks all over their lovely bodies. Every item that adorned Mary's body was scarlet, while Faye and Carol were decorated by items of black, now all as shiny as their skins with water and foam, as Jack and David caressed them in this fetishistic cleansing ritual.

Looking at the two captive girls, and in the mirror at herself, Mary knew they were all three a stunning sight of almost startling beauty, helplessness and perverse allure. She could not help feeling a sense of pride to be participating in such an insane sexual deviation.

'Get ready,' said David. 'Get set. Go!'

Sixteen

Instantly, Mary began sliding over the tiled floor, propelling her restrained, soapy body as well as she could with limited movements of her hands and feet. David pushed and pulled Carol and Faye round and round on all fours to disorientate them, then gave each of them a light blow to their arses with his tawse.

'Go on!' he cried. 'Get Mary quickly, or you'll get much worse than that.'

'What a great game!' Jack gasped in pure amazement.

'Mary's over here!' cried David, and he hit her hard on her right buttock, making a sound like a pistol shot.

'Go on, get her!' Jack urged Carol and Faye.

'Left a little, Faye,' said David. 'Perfect! Go straight ahead as fast as you can.'

Aroused beyond measure, David and Jack gazed in awe at the fantastic sight of three young females, their bodies shiny with lather and fetish garments, trapped inside a game of sublime cruelty. Mary slithered on her hands and knees, frantically pushing herself along: an absurdly vulnerable female with limbs bound, head helmeted and ripe arse defenceless.

Laughing excitedly, David and Jack played with their living sex toys: they grabbed the slippery women and rubbed their cocks against them; they squeezed their tits and slapped their buttocks; they poured bowls of water from the bath over them to make them gleam and splutter, and they soaped them again, caressing and squeezing the lush, strong and curvaceous bodies of three superb young women.

The men found it hugely amusing to tease and arouse Faye and Carol especially, and the sightless girls squealed in distress.

What really shocked Mary was to see that David looked truly happy for the first time in ages, and she was further shocked by the depth of her own warm delight in his happiness. How good it was to see him smile and laugh and lust with such simple and wholehearted pleasure. Surely, even if he was a cruel master, he could only look so happy if he possessed some basic and sublime goodness, long in retreat and hiding, yet never truly defeated.

Here and now, that was the only place to be. In creating this insane, grotesque, and disturbingly beautiful scene of two young women hunting a third in a bathroom, David had broken all barriers, opened the gates and won free. With his imagination and determination, he had forced these five human beings into the rare triumph of absolute nowness.

No more compromises, never again despair. End the waste of time. Mary saw this in David's face as he rubbed his cock on Carol's buttocks, enjoying her big body so stunningly captive and captivating on all fours, her long pale-gold hair hanging down in shiny tendrils, dripping water like boiling silver. Everything was so beautiful and so terrible in its reality that Mary wanted to weep.

'Come on you lazy sluts!' David exclaimed, slapping Carol with his palm, raising a fine sound from her bum. 'Fuck Mary, you silly bitches.'

Carol lunged forwards, and her hands rested a moment on Mary's back. Desperately, Mary rolled sideways, teetering for an instant on the edge of the bath. Somehow she recovered, and slithered away from the water while Carol, misled by false advice from Jack, sightlessly went in the wrong direction. Faye came near Mary, listening carefully. Mary froze and tried to stay silent. David turned on a wall shower, soaking Faye and making her cough and splutter, so Mary was able to crawl away unheard. All this soapy, slippery writhing made her breasts and pussy sing with fresh lust, greatly heightened by her anxiety.

Sighing with pleasure, David poured another bowl of hot water over Mary, soaped her lavishly, and then screwed her for a few minutes while Jack held Carol and Faye together on their sides, face to face, ordering them to stay in that position or be severely tawsed. He masturbated over them with cheerful delight. Then the men changed places, and Jack enjoyed Mary while David used a wall shower on the girls, soaped their gorgeous gleaming flesh and rubbed his penis on and between their hot foaming bodies, so soft and slippery.

'This is great,' he gasped. 'Oh, you lovely bitches, you soapy slits! Now you're just starting to learn about serious bathing. I'll train you, you bimbos. You'll be my captive aquanauts.'

'Queens of water sports,' cried Jack.

'Mermaids in restraint, wet sluts, pet fish!'

Delirious with excitement, the men released the three women and savoured the hallucinogenic vision of the gagged young beauties, lathered and restrained, crawling around the bathroom, under the threat of the tawse.

'Here, here she is,' yelled David, giving Mary a brief foamy fuck. Squelch, squelch, splat, splat. He pulled out just as Faye and Carol lurched on all fours to the scene, shiny round butts swaying. Now Mary was in trouble! The girls laid their bound hands on her and made 'mmms' of encouragement to each other through their gags. Mary wriggled and squirmed desperately, undulating like a snake, her spread, defenceless arse flashing in the golden sunlight. Carol strove to mount her, to ram home her long thick rubber dildo. But even as she flung her weight on top of her prey, Mary twisted aside and slipped out from under Carol, aided by the soap's lubrication. Faye then grappled with Mary, and savagely jabbed her with the dildo she wore. For an instant it seemed certain to penetrate Mary, and she squealed through her gag, but again the lather helped, and the dildo slid off. Mary raised her feet sharply and shoved Faye aside, then squirmed away. She struggled to get onto the water bed, feeling she might be safer there, and watched the men tease Faye and Carol. The bizarre scene filled her with such lust and anxiety that she thrust her pussy repeatedly against the undulating water bed, and achieved an orgasm that left her momentarily stunned.

Carol and Faye were in no position, however, to take advantage of Mary's lustful distraction. David and Jack had seized them, and given them several cracking, foam-splashing blows with their wet leather tawses. How the girls squealed, sounding, through their gags, like distressed sows.

'Ridiculous!' David exclaimed. 'You should have had her then, you lazy dykes.'

'Try harder!' Jack admonished. 'Take that!'

For nearly an hour, David and Jack had a wonderful time, playing excitedly with their three sex toys like children on Christmas morning. Happily, they rubbed their cocks on and between the women's breasts and thighs, and penetrated Mary whenever they desired. How easy it was, and how much fun, to play all kinds of games! They clipped heavy dog chains to the women's bridles and led them around, they held Mary still and gave Carol and Faye verbal directions so the girls almost caught her, stabbing angrily with their dildos, then they let Mary go so she could crawl away like a damaged insect. Cheerfully, the men flicked their tawses at the vixen and two hunting bitches alike, accusing them of not trying hard enough, and they masturbated with pure and simple pleasure as they drank in the sight of three gagged young women crawling around in their shiny fetish garments, trapped in utter humiliation.

David and Jack got more and more aroused, but they were also struck by the humour of the situation, so they had to laugh, or rather giggle. To think that three young women could be reduced to such a state – no, it was too funny. They guided Carol around and tricked her into trying to mount Faye, and they ordered Mary to climb on Carol and try to hold her and bring herself off by rubbing her pubes on Carol's wriggling arse. Really, thought Mary, if they cannot take our degradation seriously, they are just bad children. Yet she was pleased to see David happy again after all this time, and she wanted to spoil him more and more. He had come fully alive again, and it was all her doing.

Delighted by their ingenuity, the men told their animals, as they called them, to take a rest. They showered them with water, rubbed them dry with warm soft towels, then covered them in baby oil. Mary was freshly amazed at the insane beauty of the girls, the men, herself in the mirror, the whole bathroom. Yes, it was so beautiful, too beautiful to bear, like a hallucination born of fever, and, yes, it was clearly insane. David had broken every barrier, he had accepted himself as he truly was, so now the past and the normal world were dead, and there was nothing left for the five of them in that bathroom but the present, which was a terrible wonder. All my doing, Mary thought again, with shame and pride, and she was ashamed of her pride and proud of her shame.

With the smug air of a magician pulling a rabbit out of a hat, David took three small silver bells from a box and clipped them to Mary's belt and bridle.

'Mary is belled,' he announced. 'Come on Carol, Faye, you must be able to get her now. Sorry, Mary. I really don't want to invite you to stay. Bad luck.' Then he took a grip on Mary's bridle, knelt down with one knee on the calf of her left leg, and gave her five heavy slaps to her magnificent oily and shiny arse.

As he released her, Jack flicked his tawse under Carol and Faye's torsos, promising them much worse if they did not catch the vixen very quickly. Mary, her buttocks burning, moved away as quickly as she could, only to hear her bells tinkling. The sound filled her with a tingling, strangely erotic desperation. David thought of everything, even infuriating little bells. What could she do against such a monster except yield? If he was so cunning and bad, she had every excuse to give in. And joy was there, she could smell it, joy was in surrender.

The bells, the bells! She was Quasimodo, that was what David had brought her to, because she had forced him. Desperately, she crawled up onto the water bed and tried to slip down between the little gap between it and the wall. She wriggled there like a worm, making David and Jack laugh uncontrollably, in some kind of hysteria. David pulled on Carol's chain, guiding the big strong girl he had fucked.

'Come on, Carol,' he cried. 'Get the vixen. You can do it. You're my favourite bitch now.'

And Carol was on her, but Mary struggled, and slid out from under her hot and heavy flesh. Then Faye too was on her, jabbing furiously with the dildo. How angry Carol and Faye were by now! Mary knew real fear. She was trapped between the girls and the wall. The three women struggled and writhed, oiled buttocks and breasts and plastic flashing. Mary was breathless and her limbs trembled with exhaustion. Two stabbing dildos. Expertly, the men flicked their tawses at the writhing female trio, and the sweaty shiny women grunted through their leather bits. They drooled.

Animals. They were purely animals – but what else had they ever been, what else could they ever be? Faye

245

was between Mary and the wall now, and she used her legs as well as her arms to hold the struggling prey. She held Mary from behind, and they were lying on their sides as Carol pressed on Mary's front, holding her helpless, sandwiched between two angry girls. Mary could not close her legs because of the legspreader David had strapped to her, so Carol was finally able to thrust her dildo home with a savage grunt of animal triumph.

And Mary was fucked ruthlessly. Jack moaned as he masturbated, and he soon came, standing over the oily, sweaty, crazed young females, showering them, as he cried out again and again, a sound of anguish. Mary, his queen, had been captured and violated. He could, should, have helped her, but he was only a worthless coward.

Grunting and drooling, arching her long, long body, Carol came, thrusting with all her strength in lustful revenge. All the while, Mary gazed at David, drinking in the sight of his helpless cruelty, his vicious arousal. She ignored Carol and Faye, and she adored and despised David now and forever as she presented him with her defeat.

'It's disgusting!' David exclaimed. 'Disgusting, dirty, stupid bitches. How can the three of you behave like this? What have you come to? Why do women always follow the wrong kind of man, and lead him further astray? What hope is there? It's over, all over, there is no hope.'

You say that, thought Mary, but your cock is huge and solid. She shuddered as Carol recovered her wits after her climax and resumed her cruel and vengeful ploughing. Mary felt sure that Carol had been utterly corrupted. Having sex with David, and now, as his hunting dog, joining in his strange games with total abandonment, meant that she had left normality behind, and would never be able to find it again even if she wanted to. Later would come the really hard part, harder than any mere sexual perversion: Carol would have to decide whether to feel regret or hope, sorrow or gladness. There, right there, was the real weight of living.

'Enough, you greedy bitch,' said David. 'Leave Mary alone, now,' he snapped, pulling at Carol's chain. With a kind of snarl she resisted, twisting her long, powerful body to thrust her dildo into Mary, taking a savage delight in stretching her victim's flesh. 'You nasty cruel slut!' David exclaimed, and gave Carol's hard muscular buttocks four strong blows with his tawse, snapping and cracking the leather on her reddening, heaving arse.

Still Carol resisted, but Jack helped David, and together they were able to haul the big girl away from Mary and attach her chain to a wall ring. Mary wondered if David felt sorry for her. That would be something, she told herself, though in her heart of hearts it seemed a disconcerting sign of a new weakness. His next words proved that he was in fact badder than ever.

'Get in the bath, Mary,' he snapped. 'What a lucky bitch you are! I'm going to give you a chance to show us all what you can do.' He fastened Faye to another wall ring, then removed the girls' plastic helmets so they could see again. Then he helped Mary into the water with his right foot against her arse. She went on all fours in the deep warm water, and he took off her legspreader, rubber mitts, head bridle, and wrist straps, restoring her complete freedom of movement. She still had on her gloves, stockings and belt of scarlet plastic. When David entered her it felt so right, so warm and filling and good that she knew she was lost, lost now and forever.

Despite everything, all she wanted was to please this man, this nasty little creep. So Mary gave him her all. She gave him everything. Every part of her body had only been created to give him pleasure; her heart, soul and mind were his even though he did not want them, had no idea what to do with them, and was not worthy of receiving from her a single one of her farts. None of that mattered, because in fact she was his, that was all she could do and all she could be. Let him use her as he pleased, let him take delight from her body and soul so slavish and dazed with submission.

Accepting all his cruelty, Mary made an exhibition of herself in one position after another, pleasing his penis in every way possible with all the beauty, skill and strength of her flesh, the invention of her mind, and her complete knowledge of David in all his perversity. All her wonderful abilities, firm and succulent body parts, and powers of endurance she gave to him without reservation, performing for his pleasure in the deep foamy water so warm and slippery. For him she became a performing seal.

Never had she felt such joy, such a surge of lust. Exhibitionism became a simple, childlike pleasure, and she delighted in amazing her audience. Jack caressed Faye and Carol, and the three of them stared at Mary. She knew that what she was doing now with David was not only sex, but the breaking of the last barriers, a revelation.

Orgasm's submerged powers and love's deep secrets, the power of the body all breathless in ecstasy and the currents of the soul's ocean floor so dark and secret: all now surfaced. David came shrieking like a rat in a trap. Mary passed down from depth to depth, the rapture of the deep and deeper, until she achieved annihilation.

Jack helped David and Mary out of the bath, pulling the dazed man and woman from the waters like the last survivors from a shipwreck.

'My dear friend, my brave girl,' David muttered, moving strands of Mary's chestnut hair from her face. 'My bad mermaid, my brave aquanaut.'

'I love you, David,' Mary announced.

He looked frightened, and drew back.

'It's the last thing you want and the last thing I want, but so what, it's there. You're a nasty, selfish, perverted little rat, but I can't help it, I love you anyway. I wouldn't choose you, never in a million years, and here we are anyway. You're a nasty little rat and you're my nasty little rat. Lucky me. A small rodent. You don't even want me here, all you want is for me to go away, and me too, I'd love to go away and never see you again, but I can't. I can't. That's all. I've tried so hard not to love you. Ever since I met you. You know, the first time I met you, I told myself, "Don't fall in love with this creep, you idiot." I thought I'd got over it, I really believed I had. And I wouldn't admit to myself that I still loved you.'

'I knew it all along,' David said gloomily. 'Bugger.' He turned away from Mary as though determined to try to ignore her, she who could not be ignored. 'I suppose we'd better release poor Carol and Faye. Or should we keep them prisoner for a week and play games?'

The girls exclaimed in horror through the leather in their mouths and began to struggle.

'Just kidding, just kidding.' David laughed. 'Calm down. Stay still. We'll set you free, don't worry. Just try not to have any ill feeling, OK? I was only teasing when I said I might put you on the internet. Have you got that? Be calm. We didn't do anything really bad.'

With some apprehension, David and Jack removed the girls' strap-on dildos, bridles and rubber mittens, then unfastened their chains. Carol and Faye were silent and subdued until complete freedom gave them reassurance.

'That was terrible!' Carol exclaimed, rubbing her reddened arse. 'How could you treat us like that?'

'Very easily,' Mary had to say.

'I was frightened,' said Faye. 'It was horrible.'

'You're not really angry are you?' Jack said to Carol and Faye. 'Think of all the things we can do!'

249

'You'll have to do them without us,' Carol told him.

'That's right,' Faye agreed. She and Carol quickly removed their black plastic garments, and angrily pushed Jack away when he tried to help.

'It's entirely up to you,' David said with a smile. 'But if you want to come here again, we'd be delighted.'

'Even we're not that crazy,' Carol insisted. Mary noticed that Faye did not look so determined.

'Anyway, whatever you decide, I want to thank you all,' David said with warm sincerity. 'Yes, even you, Mary.'

'Even me. Wow.'

'You woke me up and we've all had a great time.'

'Faye and I just had a horrible time,' Carol protested.

'Oh, I don't know,' Faye said hesitantly. 'It was exciting, wasn't it? Being a hunting dog. I was frightened, but you have to admit it was exciting.' She looked at Carol defiantly.

'Well, yes, I suppose it was,' Carol admitted.

'You can't quit!' Jack exclaimed. 'Think of what fun you'll have taking revenge on me for treating you so badly.'

'There is that,' said Carol.

'It would be good to have revenge,' Faye said with a sigh.

'Maybe we should torment Jack one more time,' said Carol.

A strange thrill passed through Mary's body as she heard these words, and all her nerves tingled in anticipation. Carol and Faye were clearly unable to make a clean break from herself, David and Jack, and from David's insanely thrilling bathroom with all its strange eroticism. They were fascinated, and they were trapped. They would be drawn into deeper and deeper waters of perverse sex, just as she had been, and their lovely young bodies and charming characters would be corrupted as they became the playthings of David's rich imagination. The thought filled her with glee: they would become as bad as her, so she would not be alone in her badness.

'Now you'll have to ask me nicely to stay,' she told David firmly. 'Or else I'll leave you with Jack, Carol and Faye, and that wouldn't work. You need me so you can take out your worst impulses on me, you see. You know it as well as I do.' She gazed confidently into David's eyes, and he read her determination.

'Of course I want you to stay, Mary,' he blurted out. 'Yes, I need you. We all need you.'

'Fine. I'll be glad to stay. You only had to ask.'

Deep delight sung through Mary's body and soul: she had won. At last. David was hooked again, and could not face the break-up of this group, his willing and eager aquanauts.

'You're so clever,' she told him, and gave him such a strong hug that he squealed.

She could not resist David, she thought happily. In the end she had seduced and forced him to accept both her absolute surrender, and his own nature. So they would go on from strength to strength, together. She could do nothing except love the little rat. No one else but David was strong enough not only to have a fantasy of a strange, magical bathroom where mermaids in restraint gave their all, but also to build it, to make it a reality and then bring others to share in his vision, to join him in these bathroom games that were his dreams and his nightmares. What strength he had! And in the end a woman admired nothing in a man save strength, and the honesty that comes from strength.

Yes, he also had that essential honesty. He said he was a sadist with a bathroom fetish, and that was the truth. How rare and admirable was such truthfulness. How strong he was to dare to speak the truth, and be true to himself. Others were so weak that they lied. Mary could only follow his strength and truth. What

251

else was there to do? What else in the world was worth anything?

'I love you,' she told him.

'This is great,' Jack laughed.

'It's all right for you,' said David. 'You've escaped.'

'What we've done today . . . it was all so much.' Mary sighed. 'Too much. It made me see the truth.'

'Bugger.'

'Now we're getting somewhere,' said Carol. 'It's romantic.' She and Faye smiled warmly, touched deeply by Mary's powerful love.

'Why are you so happy?' asked Mary. 'You and Faye should be angry. You've just been badly treated.'

'Who can be angry with you and David?' Faye replied. 'Look at all the fun and games we've had. And will have. All the fun and excitement. Besides, you're both so nice.'

'I am not nice,' David insisted.

'I am,' said Mary. 'I'm nice, definitely. And it always gets me into trouble. Just the other day –'

'You talk too much,' snapped David. 'All right, listen. Since I can't drive you away, because you're too stubborn and stupid to leave me alone, and you hold onto the frame of my front door, not letting me prise your fingers from the death grip, so I can't close the bloody door and shut you out of my bloody life forever, because you won't go, you can stay. But leave me alone a lot of the time for God's sake.'

'Thank you, thank you, thank you,' Mary gasped. She began to sob as she hugged him tight.

'Not so tight, I can't breathe. You're so bloody strong. You exercise too much as well as talk too much. Everything about you is just too much, I can't stand it. You obey me too much and love me too much. I'm already suffocating.'

'It's so romantic,' Carol said.

'It's lovely,' said Faye.

'I know you're all waiting for me to say I love Mary,' David snapped. 'It's a cheap word, an easy word, a word devalued by overuse, the favourite word of fools and liars. You all want me to say it, but I won't.'

'That's why I left him the first time, two years ago,' said Mary. 'Silly of me.'

'You left David because he wouldn't say he loved you?' Jack said in wonder. 'You never would explain it to me, so, of course, I thought it was something to do with this bathroom. Some strange secret sex shocker. I thought about it a lot.'

'So did we!' laughed Faye. 'We wondered and wondered.'

'Mary wouldn't tell us,' said Carol.

'I didn't want to tell anybody,' said Mary, 'I felt ashamed. Now I just don't care about anything. It's a lovely feeling.'

Then David said the words that set the seal on Mary's happiness. 'Two years ago, Mary tried to force me to say I loved her,' David said grudgingly. 'You know how stubborn and crazy and talkative she is. So, of course, I had to tell her I didn't love her and never would. What else could I do?' He paused, patted Mary on the back, then continued with reluctance as palpable as treacle mixed with soot, as though making a confession that must seal his fate.

'Unfortunately, I was lying.'

nexus

The leading publisher of fetish and adult fiction

TELL US WHAT YOU THINK!

Readers' ideas and opinions matter to us. Take a few minutes to fill in the questionnaire below and you'll be entered into a prize draw to win a year's worth of Nexus books (36 titles)

Terms and conditions apply – see end of questionnaire.

1. **Sex:** Are you male ☐   female ☐   a couple ☐?

2. **Age:** Under 21 ☐   21–30 ☐   31–40 ☐   41–50 ☐   51–60 ☐   over 60 ☐

3. **Where do you buy your Nexus books from?**
☐ A chain book shop. If so, which one(s)?
_____

☐ An independent book shop. If so, which one(s)?
_____

☐ A used book shop/charity shop
☐ Online book store. If so, which one(s)?
_____

4. **How did you find out about Nexus Books?**
☐ Browsing in a book shop
☐ A review in a magazine
☐ Online
☐ Recommendation
☐ Other _____

5. **In terms of settings which do you prefer? (Tick as many as you like)**
☐ Down to earth and as realistic as possible
☐ Historical settings. If so, which period do you prefer?
_____

☐ Fantasy settings – barbarian worlds

- ☐ Completely escapist/surreal fantasy
- ☐ Institutional or secret academy
- ☐ Futuristic/sci fi
- ☐ Escapist but still believable
- ☐ Any settings you dislike?

_____

- ☐ Where would you like to see an adult novel set?

_____

6. In terms of storylines, would you prefer:

- ☐ Simple stories that concentrate on adult interests?
- ☐ More plot and character-driven stories with less explicit adult activity?
- ☐ We value your ideas, so give us your opinion of this book:

_____

_____

_____

7. In terms of your adult interests, what do you like to read about? (Tick as many as you like)

- ☐ Traditional corporal punishment (CP)
- ☐ Modern corporal punishment
- ☐ Spanking
- ☐ Restraint/bondage
- ☐ Rope bondage
- ☐ Latex/rubber
- ☐ Leather
- ☐ Female domination and male submission
- ☐ Female domination and female submission
- ☐ Male domination and female submission
- ☐ Willing captivity
- ☐ Uniforms
- ☐ Lingerie/underwear/hosiery/footwear (boots and high heels)
- ☐ Sex rituals
- ☐ Vanilla sex
- ☐ Swinging

☐ Cross-dressing/TV
☐ Enforced feminisation
☐ Others – tell us what you don't see enough of in adult fiction:

_____

_____

_____

8. Would you prefer books with a more specialised approach to your interests, i.e. a novel specifically about uniforms? If so, which subject(s) would you like to read a Nexus novel about?

_____

_____

_____

9. Would you like to read true stories in Nexus books? For instance, the true story of a submissive woman, or a male slave? Tell us which true revelations you would most like to read about:

_____

_____

_____

10. What do you like best about Nexus books?

_____

_____

11. What do you like least about Nexus books?

_____

_____

12. Which are your favourite titles?

_____

_____

13. Who are your favourite authors?

_____

_____

14. Which covers do you prefer? Those featuring:
(tick as many as you like)

☐ Fetish outfits
☐ More nudity
☐ Two models
☐ Unusual models or settings
☐ Classic erotic photography
☐ More contemporary images and poses
☐ A blank/non-erotic cover
☐ What would your ideal cover look like?

_____

15. Describe your ideal Nexus novel in the space provided:

_____

_____

_____

_____

16. Which celebrity would feature in one of your Nexus-style fantasies? We'll post the best suggestions on our website – anonymously!

_____

THANKS FOR YOUR TIME

Now simply write the title of this book in the space below and cut out the questionnaire pages. Post to: Nexus, Marketing Dept., Thames Wharf Studios, Rainville Rd, London W6 9HA

Book title: _____

TERMS AND CONDITIONS

1. The competition is open to UK residents only, excluding employees of Nexus and Virgin, their families, agents and anyone connected with the promotion of the competition. 2. Entrants must be aged 18 years or over. 3. Closing date for receipt of entries is 31 December 2006. 4. The first entry drawn on 7 January 2007 will be declared the winner and notified by Nexus. 5. The decision of the judges is final. No correspondence will be entered into. 6. No purchase necessary. Entries restricted to one per household. 7. The prize is non-transferable and non-refundable and no alternatives can be substituted. 8. Nexus reserves the right to amend or terminate any part of the promotion without prior notice. 9. No responsibility is accepted for fraudulent, damaged, illegible or incomplete entries. Proof of sending is not proof of receipt. 10. The winner's name will be available from the above address from 9 January 2007.

Promoter: Nexus, Thames Wharf Studios, Rainville Road, London, W6 9HA

NEXUS NEW BOOKS

To be published in March 2006

FORBIDDEN READING
Lisette Ashton

Librarian Justine is given a chance to acquire La Coste: an unpublished story that is supposedly the most disturbing work written by the Marquis de Sade. Alleged to contain details of his most twisted indulgences, La Coste is being put up for sale to anyone who can prove themselves worthy of owning this long lost catalogue of excess and depravity. Justine's quest will bring her face to face with extremes of punishment and pleasure. Certain to face sacrilege, sadism and subversion she knows there are no limits in the pursuit of forbidden reading.

£6.99   ISBN 0 352 34022 3

DICE WITH DOMINATION
P S Brett

Having taken up the reins of river-side casino The Paddle-Boat, the dazzlingly sexy and wickedly imaginative Valerie McKnight is determined to bring a new service to her thrill-seeking gambling public. Her beautiful and libidinous croupiers are retrained to provide a profitable sideline in Domination and Fantasy in the newly appointed cellar of the grand casino building. Rumours of the activities in that subterranean den of iniquity soon attract the attention of many curious local gents.

£6.99   ISBN 0 352 34023 1

DERRIERE
Julius Culdrose

Julius Culdrose has spent over four decades delighting in every aspect of the female bottom – the different shapes and sizes, the possibilities for presentation, the aesthetics, the uses – and now reveals his explicit experiences and frank thoughts.

This is not only an epic journey to the extremities of bottom adoration, but the second book in the new Nexus Enthusiast imprint: an original series that will explore, reveal and tantalise the reader with the most highly detailed fetish literature actually written by genuine enthusiasts for genuine enthusiasts. As kinky as fiction can get!

£6.99   ISBN 0 352 34024 X

If you would like more information about Nexus titles, please visit our website at www.nexus-books.co.uk, or send a stamped addressed envelope to:

Nexus, Thames Wharf Studios,
Rainville Road, London W6 9HA

NEXUS BACKLIST

This information is correct at time of printing. For up-to-date information, please visit our website at www.nexus-books.co.uk

All books are priced at £6.99 unless another price is given.

ABANDONED ALICE	Adriana Arden 0 352 33969 1	☐
ALICE IN CHAINS	Adriana Arden 0 352 33908 X	☐
AMAZON SLAVE	Lisette Ashton 0 352 33916 0	☐
ANGEL	Lindsay Gordon 0 352 34009 6	☐
THE ANIMAL HOUSE	Cat Scarlett 0 352 33877 6	☐
THE ART OF CORRECTION	Tara Black 0 352 33895 4	☐
AT THE END OF HER TETHER	G.C. Scott 0 352 33857 1	☐
BARE BEHIND	Penny Birch 0 352 33721 4	☐
BELINDA BARES UP	Yolanda Celbridge 0 352 33926 8	☐
BENCH MARKS	Tara Black 0 352 33797 4	☐
THE BLACK GARTER	Lisette Ashton 0 352 33919 5	☐
THE BLACK MASQUE	Lisette Ashton 0 352 33977 2	☐
THE BLACK ROOM	Lisette Ashton 0 352 33914 4	☐
THE BLACK WIDOW	Lisette Ashton 0 352 33973 X	☐
THE BOOK OF PUNISHMENT	Cat Scarlett 0 352 33975 6	☐

THE BOND	Lindsay Gordon 0 352 33996 9	☐
CAGED [£5.99]	Yolanda Celbridge 0 352 33650 1	☐
CHERRI CHASTISED	Yolanda Celbridge 0 352 33707 9	☐
COLLEGE GIRLS	Cat Scarlett 0 352 33942 X	☐
COMPANY OF SLAVES	Christina Shelly 0 352 33887 3	☐
CONCEIT AND CONSEQUENCE	Aishling Morgan 0 352 33965 9	☐
CONFESSIONS OF AN ENGLISH SLAVE	Yolanda Celbridge 0 352 33861 X	☐
CORRECTIVE THERAPY	Jacqueline Masterson 0 352 33917 9	☐
CRUEL SHADOW	Aishling Morgan 0 352 33886 5	☐
DARK MISCHIEF	Lady Alice McCloud 0 352 33998 5	☐
DEMONIC CONGRESS	Aishling Morgan 0 352 33762 1	☐
DEPTHS OF DEPRAVATION	Ray Gordon 0 352 33995 0	☐
DISCIPLINE OF THE PRIVATE HOUSE	Esme Ombreux 0 352 33709 5	☐
DISCIPLINED SKIN [£5.99]	Wendy Swanscombe 0 352 33541 6	☐
DOMINATION DOLLS	Lindsay Gordon 0 352 33891 1	☐
EMMA ENSLAVED	Hilary James 0 352 33883 0	☐
EMMA'S HUMILIATION	Hilary James 0 352 33910 1	☐
EMMA'S SECRET DOMINATION	Hilary James 0 352 34000 2	☐
EMMA'S SECRET WORLD	Hilary James 0 352 33879 2	☐
EMMA'S SUBMISSION	Hilary James 0 352 33906 3	☐

EROTICON 1 [£5.99]	Various 0 352 33593 9	☐
FAIRGROUND ATTRACTION	Lisette Ashton 0 352 33927 6	☐
THE GOVERNESS ABROAD	Yolanda Celbridge 0 352 33735 4	☐
HOT PURSUIT	Lisette Ashton 0 352 33878 4	☐
IN DISGRACE	Penny Birch 0 352 33922 5	☐
IN HER SERVICE	Lindsay Gordon 0 352 33968 3	☐
THE INDECENCIES OF ISABELLE	Penny Birch (writing as Cruella) 0 352 33989 6	☐
THE INDIGNITIES OF ISABELLE	Penny Birch (writing as Cruella) 0 352 33696 X	☐
THE INDISCRETIONS OF ISABELLE	Penny Birch (writing as Cruella) 0 352 33882 2	☐
INNOCENT	Aishling Morgan 0 352 33699 4	☐
THE INSTITUTE	Maria Del Rey 0 352 33352 9	☐
JULIA C	Laura Bowen 0 352 33852 0	☐
KNICKERS AND BOOTS	Penny Birch 0 352 33853 9	☐
LACING LISBETH	Yolanda Celbridge 0 352 33912 8	☐
LICKED CLEAN	Yolanda Celbridge 0 352 33999 3	☐
NON FICTION: LESBIAN SEX SECRETS FOR MEN	Jamie Goddard and Kurt Brungard 0 352 33724 9	☐
LESSONS IN OBEDIENCE	Lucy Golden 0 352 33892 X	☐
LETTERS TO CHLOE [£5.99]	Stephan Gerrard 0 352 33632 3	☐

LOVE JUICE	Donna Exeter 0 352 33913 6	☐
THE MASTER OF CASTLELEIGH [£5.99]	Jacqueline Bellevois 0 352 33644 7	☐
MISS RATAN'S LESSON	Yolanda Celbridge 0 352 33791 5	☐
NAUGHTY NAUGHTY	Penny Birch 0 352 33974 4	☐
NEW EROTICA 6	Various 0 352 33751 6	☐
NIGHTS IN WHITE COTTON	Penny Birch 0 352 34008 8	☐
NO PAIN, NO GAIN	James Baron 0 352 33966 7	☐
NURSE'S ORDERS	Penny Birch 0 352 33739 7	☐
THE OLD PERVERSITY SHOP	Aishling Morgan 0 352 34007 X	☐
ONE WEEK IN THE PRIVATE HOUSE	Esme Ombreux 0 352 33706 0	☐
ORIGINAL SINS	Lisette Ashton 0 352 33804 0	☐
THE PALACE OF PLEASURES	Christobel Coleridge 0 352 33801 6	☐
PALE PLEASURES	Wendy Swanscombe 0 352 33702 8	☐
PARADISE BAY [£5.99]	Maria Del Rey 0 352 33645 5	☐
PLAYTHING	Penny Birch 0 352 33967 5	☐
PUNISHED IN PINK	Yolanda Celbridge 0 352 34003 7	☐
THE PUNISHMENT CAMP	Jacqueline Masterton 0 352 33940 3	☐
PENNY PIECES [£5.99]	Penny Birch 0 352 33631 5	☐
PET TRAINING IN THE PRIVATE HOUSE [£5.99]	Esme Ombreux 0 352 33655 2	☐
PETTING GIRLS	Penny Birch 0 352 33957 8	☐

THE PLAYER	Cat Scarlett 0 352 33894 6	☐
PRINCESS	Aishling Morgan 0 352 33871 7	☐
PRIVATE MEMOIRS OF A KENTISH HEADMISTRESS	Yolanda Celbridge 0 352 33763 X	☐
PRIZE OF PAIN	Wendy Swanscombe 0 352 33890 3	☐
THE PRIESTESS	Jacqueline Bellevois 0 352 33905 5	☐
THE PUNISHMENT CLUB	Jacqueline Masterson 0 352 33862 8	☐
RITES OF OBEDIENCE	Lindsay Gordon 0 352 34005 3	☐
SCARLET VICE	Aishling Morgan 0 352 33988 8	☐
SCHOOLED FOR SERVICE	Lady Alice McCloud 0 352 33918 7	☐
SCHOOL FOR STINGERS	Yolanda Celbridge 0 352 33994 2	☐
THE SCHOOLING OF STELLA	Yolanda Celbridge 0 352 33803 2	☐
SERVING TIME	Sarah Veitch 0 352 33509 2	☐
SEXUAL HEELING	Wendy Swanscombe 0 352 33921 7	☐
SILKEN SERVITUDE	Christina Shelly 0 352 34004 5	☐
SILKEN SLAVERY	Christina Shelly 0 352 33708 7	☐
SINS APPRENTICE	Aishling Morgan 0 352 33909 8	☐
SLAVE ACTS	Jennifer Jane Pope 0 352 33665 X	☐
SLAVE GENESIS [£5.99]	Jennifer Jane Pope 0 352 33503 3	☐
SLAVE REVELATIONS [£5.99]	Jennifer Jane Pope 0 352 33627 7	☐
THE SMARTING OF SELINA	Yolanda Celbridge 0 352 33872 5	☐

STRIPING KAYLA	Yvonne Marshall 0 352 33881 4	☐
STRIPPED BARE	Angel Blake 0 352 33971 3	☐
THE SUBMISSION GALLERY [£5.99]	Lindsay Gordon 0 352 33370 7	☐
THE SUBMISSION OF STELLA	Yolanda Celbridge 0 352 33854 7	☐
THE TAMING OF TRUDI	Yolanda Celbridge 0 352 33673 0	☐
TASTING CANDY	Ray Gordon 0 352 33925 X	☐
TEASING CHARLOTTE	Yvonne Marshall 0 352 33681 1	☐
TEMPTING THE GODDESS	Aishling Morgan 0 352 33972 1	☐
TICKLE TORTURE	Penny Birch 0 352 33904 7	☐
TIE AND TEASE	Penny Birch 0 352 33987 X	☐
TORMENT INCORPORATED	Murilee Martin 0 352 33943 8	☐
THE TRAINING GROUNDS	Sarah Veitch 0 352 33526 2	☐
UNIFORM DOLL	Penny Birch 0 352 33698 6	☐
VELVET SKIN [£5.99]	Aishling Morgan 0 352 33660 9	☐
WENCHES WITCHES AND STRUMPETS	Aishling Morgan 0 352 33733 8	☐
WHEN SHE WAS BAD	Penny Birch 0 352 33859 8	☐
WHIP HAND	G.C. Scott 0 352 33694 3	☐
WHIPPING GIRL	Aishling Morgan 0 352 33789 3	☐

- - - - - - ✂ -

Please send me the books I have ticked above.

Name ....

Address ....

....

....

.... Post code ....

Send to: **Virgin Books Cash Sales, Thames Wharf Studios, Rainville Road, London W6 9HA**

US customers: for prices and details of how to order books for delivery by mail, call 1-800-343-4499.

Please enclose a cheque or postal order, made payable to **Nexus Books Ltd**, to the value of the books you have ordered plus postage and packing costs as follows:

UK and BFPO – £1.00 for the first book, 50p for each subsequent book.

Overseas (including Republic of Ireland) – £2.00 for the first book, £1.00 for each subsequent book.

If you would prefer to pay by VISA, ACCESS/MASTERCARD, AMEX, DINERS CLUB or SWITCH, please write your card number and expiry date here:

....

Please allow up to 28 days for delivery.

Signature ....

Our privacy policy

We will not disclose information you supply us to any other parties. We will not disclose any information which identifies you personally to any person without your express consent.

From time to time we may send out information about Nexus books and special offers. Please tick here if you do *not* wish to receive Nexus information.   ☐

- - - - - - ✂ -